GOING
ONCE

SHARON SALA

GOING ONCE

HARLEQUIN® MIRA®

ISBN-13: 978-1-62490-834-7

GOING ONCE

Printed in U.S.A.

Grief is as much a part of life as breathing
and comes to all of us, no matter our station in life.
It must be felt to pass from us. We have to weep for
what was lost before we are able to laugh again.

And laugh we must, for there is nothing worse than
quitting on life when there is still breath in our bodies.

I dedicate this book to those who have learned
the hardest lesson of all—how to go on alone.

One

Queens Crossing, Louisiana

Nola Landry was out-of-her-head sick with a three-day fever and had lost all track of time.

It had begun raining the day before she got sick, and it was still raining the next morning when the aches and fever began. She'd gone to sleep with the sound of rain on the roof and dreamed crazy, fever-ridden dreams about alligators in the front yard and her daddy shooting at them from the porch. Then she woke up remembering Daddy had died when she was twelve.

She fell back asleep to the sound of rain blowing against the windows and dreamed Mama was calling her to breakfast and she was going to be late for school, and when she woke up, it was dark and she remembered Mama had died just before Christmas last year.

She crawled out of bed long enough to go to the bathroom and get a drink, then fell back into bed. Her long dark hair had lost the band keeping it in a ponytail, and was damp and in tangles from the fever that came and went. After soaking her last clean nightgown from a fever-drenched sweat, she'd crawled back into bed nude.

The last thing she remembered as she was falling asleep was wondering how long it would take someone to find her body if she died.

Sometime later, another dream began, and in it Mama was running through the house, going from window to window and wringing her hands when all of a sudden, she began calling Nola's name.

Nola! Nola! Wake up this instant! Put on your clothes! Get some food and water and get out! Hurry, hurry! You have to run!

Nola woke with a gasp, looking around her darkened bedroom in feverish confusion. She knew her mother was dead, but the urge to obey was so strong that she threw back the covers, turned on the lamp beside her bed and began to dress. She grabbed a pair of jeans and a T-shirt, then pulled a hooded sweatshirt on over that. Her hands were trembling, her legs shaking as she sat down to tie her tennis shoes. The urgency to obey was increasing as she dropped her cell phone in a pocket.

She went through her house, stumbling on shaky legs, then into the kitchen, muttering to herself.

"Get food and water…food and water."

She grabbed a bottle of water, a few sticks of string cheese and a package of peanut butter crackers, and put them in the front pouch of the sweatshirt and started toward the door.

"Car keys…gotta get my car keys."

She found the keys on the coffee table and was still moving on instinct when she opened the front door. Even though it was dark, she sensed something was wrong. She was all the way out onto the porch before she realized she was walking in water. Her heart skipped a beat as she backtracked to the kitchen for a flashlight.

Her hands were still shaking as she went back to the porch and swung the flashlight out into the night. It took a few seconds to recognize what she was seeing, and then, when she did, she was struck by pure, unadulterated fear.

There was nothing but black water as far as she could see.

The flashlight beam was weak, but the horror was real as she stepped off the porch into the rain to test the depth. When it went up past her ankles, she had to face the fact that her car keys would do her no good. The only road out would already be underwater.

While she had slept, the Mississippi River, which was nearly a half mile from her house, had gone out of its banks. She didn't question what she'd been dreaming because her mama had just saved her life. Her reality now was the need to get to high ground.

She looked back once at her beloved home, thinking of all she was about to lose: her studio, the half-finished paintings she was working on and the ones ready to ship, all of her brushes and paints, and the contacts she'd spent years accumulating.

When she thought of the family keepsakes and the pictures of her loved ones since passed on that would be washed away, she had to accept that none of it mattered if she lost her life with it.

The thought popped into her head that she could climb on top of the house and wait to be rescued, but the moment she thought it, she dismissed it. Mama had said run. So she ran through the rain toward the highest point of ground within striking distance: a stand of trees nearly a hundred yards away.

Slogging through the steadily moving water was exhausting, but fear gave her strength. When something live suddenly bumped against her leg she screamed, remembering that the gators would be flooded out, as well, but whatever it was moved past her.

In a moment of gratitude for the danger that had passed, Nola leaned forward, bracing her hands against her knees to steady her racing heart.

"God, help me do this," she said softly, her heart pounding as she made herself take that next step.

She was halfway between the house and the trees

when she stepped into a hole and fell forward, catching herself on her hands and knees, and splashing water all over her face. Again she thought of the gators, snakes and snapping turtles that would be in there with her, and she scrambled to her feet and, in a panic, began running.

The next time she fell she lost the flashlight in the water and spent precious seconds feeling for it in the murky depths. When her fingers finally curled around the metal shaft, she grabbed it. By the grace of God the light was still shining, but she had no idea how long it would last. She swept the beam across the darkness, caught a flash of contrast in the distance when the light swept past the trees, and kept on moving.

The water was getting deeper now, almost up to her knees. The sweeping force of the flow made it difficult to stay upright. The urgency to get out of the water was paramount as she finally reached the grove. Sheltered somewhat from the downpour, she began trying to find the tallest, strongest tree she could physically climb, and just as she settled on one, the flashlight began to dim.

Without waiting, she swung herself up on the lowest limb just as the flashlight went out. Groaning with dismay, she had no choice but to drop it into the flood, grab the limb with both hands and begin climbing, feeling her way in the dark with the rain hammering against her face and the roar of the rushing water loud in her ears. She reached for the next limb, and then the next, climbing until she found a branch strong enough to hold her weight and managed to pull herself up, then straddle it. Exhausted, she wrapped her arms around the trunk, laid her cheek against the bark and screamed through the downpour just to hear the sound of her own voice. Just to remind herself she was still breathing.

When dawn broke in the east, Nola's clothes were soaked and she was exhausted. But daylight brought hope. It was no longer raining, and her fever had broken. She was weak, but what the hell. Things could be worse.

Twice during the night she'd had to climb higher to stay out of the water, and she was again straddling a limb and hugging the trunk. Her skin was raw from the abrasion of the bark, and the palms of her hands were bleeding from holding on so tight.

New horror came with daylight when she looked back at where her house once stood and realized it was gone. Either it was underwater or had washed off the foundation and moved past her in the night. Her vision blurred as she quickly looked away. No need dwelling on what she'd lost. Unless she got rescued, the issue was moot.

She looked down into the dark churning water below her, then out through the branches to the vast expanse of flooded land, and gasped. The water was rife with the remnants of people's lives, like the boiling stew in a witch's cauldron with its eye of newt, a goblin's ear and the scale from a fire-breathing dragon. This cauldron had pieces of houses swept from their foundations, bloated animal carcasses and uprooted trees, all caught up in the floating debris, all rushing downriver at a breakneck pace.

Her heart was pounding so hard she couldn't think, her hands shaking so badly it was difficult to hold on. It finally occurred to her that part of this was her body's cry for sustenance, and she remembered the food and water.

She found the phone as she was digging in her pocket for the food and felt a few moments of relief, thinking she would soon be rescued. She'd completely forgotten she had it. Her hands were shaking as she took it out, and as she did, water ran out of the case and down her arm.

The sight sent her into a new wave of despair. She was sobbing as she tried desperately to get a signal, moving it in every direction, but it was obvious the phone was dead, water-soaked and beyond repair. She dropped it in the water and leaned her forehead against the tree. Her face felt hot. Her eyes were burning, which meant her fever was back up. Scared and shaky, she dissolved into tears as the runaway river rolled on beneath her feet. When she managed to get herself together, she finally ate some cheese and drank some of the water, wishing time would move as fast as the water rushing past her. But the law of physics was impervious to the Mississippi flood, and so she closed her eyes, held on to the tree and focused her thoughts on happier days.

She was sitting in Granny's lap on a hot summer night, listening to the bullfrogs croak and the night birds calling while Granny was putting her to sleep. The soft, low-country drawl of the old woman's voice was soothing to a little girl's heart.

"The Lord is my shepherd, I shall not want..."

Creak, creak, creak, went the rocker as it rocked against the loose boards in the porch.

"He maketh me to lie down in green pastures. He leadeth me beside still waters."

Nola sobbed. Where, God? Where are those still waters now?

Creak, creak, creak. Still rocking. Still listening as the verses spilled out of Granny's mouth as easy as honey in a spoon. Still feeling the strength and the love in Granny's work-worn hands.

"Thou preparest a table before me in the presence of mine enemies..."

"Granny?"

"What baby?"

"Why are we feeding the enemy?"

Granny's laugh rolled through Nola like wind through the trees.

"Close your eyes, baby girl, and just listen."

Creak, creak, creak, went the rocker on the same loose board. The last thing Nola heard before the Sandman took her under was Granny's voice.

"Surely goodness and mercy shall follow me..."

It was the loud crack, and then the sound of a big tree dying as the roots gave way that woke Nola up with a start. She looked down just as a tree from the grove fell into the flood with a tremendous splash. She watched in horror as it hit and bounced, making waves large enough to reach up within feet of where she was sitting. Then it was pulled into the current and became part of the debris floating downriver.

She threw back her head and screamed, both in fright and in rage, wondering how long it would be before her tree went down and took *her* under, too.

As the river continued to rise, she was forced yet again, to climb to a higher limb. But once she'd reached that height, it became apparent she was not the only one stranded in this location.

The Lewis family were her nearest neighbors. Their house was across the road and about a hundred yards upriver, normally hidden from view by trees. Only now the trees were gone and Nola had a clear view of the house, which was nearly submerged. Only the very top part of the roof was visible, and the occupants—Whit and Candy Lewis, and Candy's mother, Ruth Andrews—were on it and clinging to each other, just feet away from being washed off and into the flood.

Horrified by the sight, Nola started to call out to them, but then decided it would serve no purpose. She was just as stranded as they were, and just as likely to drown. She hugged the trunk a little tighter and once again, let her thoughts drift to the past.

Out of nowhere, Tate Benton's face popped into her mind. She used to love to look at him. From an artist's perspective he had a most interesting face: a broad forehead, high cheekbones that angled down toward a very stubborn chin, with a nose that was in perfect proportion to his other features—perfect except for that bump from breaking it in the eleventh grade. He'd grown to well over six feet before his sixteenth birthday. It had taken him until his second year in college to grow muscles to fit that height. By then he was a man, both in physical strength and attitude. He'd known from a young age that he wanted to be in law enforcement, and they had planned all the way through college to go back to Queens Crossing to begin their life together.

Then, one night just after they had graduated college, he came to her house in a panic and told her he was leaving. He begged her to go with him but wouldn't tell her what was wrong. She kept begging him to stay, to explain what had happened, but he wouldn't. They fought. He walked out, and she never heard from him again. Without an understanding of what was wrong there was nothing to hold them together, and he disappeared from her life.

She wondered if he was married, and if he would feel bad when he heard they'd pulled her body out of the river. Then she told herself it was the fever making her think crazy. Screw Tate Benton. She didn't want to think about him anymore, but when she closed her eyes, the first thing she saw was his face and the way his eyes crinkled up at the corners when he was laughing. Because he'd lived in town, he'd always loved to come out to her place to go fishing. He had a fishing pole, and she had her sketch pad. He fished while she drew him over and over and over. She still had those sketch pads somewhere.

And then she looked out across the water and remembered she didn't have anything anymore. The river had taken it away, just like it was trying to take her. She climbed a branch higher, struggling to stay awake by drinking more of the water and eating. She ate another piece of cheese and one of the peanut butter crackers, then had to move because her legs were so numb from hanging down she could no longer feel her feet.

As she was shifting her perch, she began hearing what sounded like a helicopter. She looked up, craning her neck, praying it would fly over this way, but when she finally spotted it, it was so far away she knew they would never see her or the Lewises. After that her fever came back, raging through her body until she was half out of her head.

She began looking at the sight before her with the eyes of an artist, thinking how she would make it come to life on canvas, planning what colors she would mix to get it right.

On the surface, the water just looked black, but it really wasn't. It made her think of dark brown chocolate with varying shades of umbers and reds. And the sky was streaky—a mixture of pewter-gray, a tinge of marine-blue and just the least bit of titanium-white to muddy the sharpness of the hues. The sharp greens of the treetops seemed out of place in the dismal landscape, as did the incongruity of seeing a bright red pickup being pushed past her location by a pile of debris.

She drank another sip of water and then burst into tears when she caught a glimpse of a dog out in the stream, paddling frantically to stay afloat. This was a nightmare without end.

She closed her eyes and tried to concentrate on something positive.

Favorite food: shrimp and grits.

Favorite color: aquamarine blue.

Favorite holiday: Christmas.

Favorite memory: making love to Tate.

Thinking of Tate again made her sad and, at the same time, angry. Enough of favorite things.

She looked across the way at the Lewis house and thought she could hear singing, or maybe praying. She couldn't tell what they were saying, but their presence was comforting.

A short while later a big alligator swam into her line of vision, obviously flooded out from its normal habitat. The mere sight of it made her draw her feet up onto the limb, even though she was in the thick of the tree and safely out of reach from a snap from its massive jaws.

The sun was directly overhead when she began hearing an outboard motor, and once again the sound gave her hope. She craned her neck to get a better view upriver, and when a motorboat suddenly came into view, she gasped.

Praise the lord, they were about to be saved!

When Whit Lewis suddenly stood up on the roof and began waving frantically and laughing, she knew he'd seen the boat, as well. When the man in the boat turned in their direction, she felt like cheering.

Even from this distance she could tell he was in uniform but couldn't tell what kind. She was debating with herself about when to climb lower to get his attention when she saw him suddenly raise his arm, then switch something he was holding from his right hand to his left. She didn't know it was a gun until she heard the shot.

* * *

Fifty-year-old Whit Lewis and his wife, Candy, had watched daylight break over what looked like a scene from a horror movie, while Candy's mother, Ruth Andrews, continued to pray aloud for mercy. Bloated carcasses of animals floated past on rushing waters, reminders of what could happen to them if they faltered. Whit knew his neighbor, Nola Landry, had been home the day before because he'd seen her car in the carport. Now her house was completely gone, and he had no idea if she'd gotten out or had already drowned.

One hour passed into another and then another as the water continued to rise and their hopes for rescue grew dimmer. Once they saw a helicopter in the distance, and although Whit stood up and waved and waved, the copter soon disappeared from view.

There was less than two feet of roof left between them and the floodwaters when he heard the sound of an outboard engine. Candy and her mother were praying so loudly he wasn't sure if he'd imagined it, and then he heard it again.

"Candy! Ruth! Listen! I hear a motor."

They froze, clutching each other in desperation. "I hear it, too!" Candy cried.

"Praise God," Ruth added, as they looked upriver.

When they saw the motorboat coming toward them, they began screaming and shouting, waving at the parish policeman manning the motor. When he turned in their direction, they began crying with relief. The policeman angled the boat up close to the roof.

"Praise the Lord. We thought it was over," Whit said.

"And you were right," the officer said.

He pulled out a pistol, then switched it to his left hand and put a bullet between Whit's eyes. Before the women could react to what had happened, he'd shot both of them dead. He watched their bodies roll off the roof into the floodwaters, and waited until they sank before moving away from the site.

When Nola saw Whit fall, she thought for a few seconds she must be hallucinating. But then she heard the same pop she'd heard before, when Whit dropped and fell into the water, and now she was seeing the women falling one by one into the flood, as well. The horror was real.

When the officer revved the motor and made a half circle away from the house before moving back into the flow of the current, she realized he was going to pass right by her. Her heart was hammering so hard in her chest that it felt like thunder. Surely he would hear it. Surely he would see her, and if he did, she didn't have a chance. She would die after all, just not like she'd expected.

In a last-ditch moment of desperation, she climbed higher into the tree, as far up into the thickness of the foliage as she could get, and then clung to the backside of the trunk, praying he would pass her by.

She could hear the sound of the outboard as he came closer and closer. She was almost afraid to look for fear any movement would alert him she was there, yet at the same time, she had to see him. But when he finally moved past her, from this height, the cap he was wearing concealed most of his face. All she could see was a white, middle-aged man with salt-and-pepper hair and a big mustache. As the boat moved past the tree and then downriver, she went limp with relief.

"Thank you, God," she muttered, and tried not to think of her neighbors' bodies now part of the morass that was the flood.

She clung to the tree through the late afternoon as her fever returned. She drank more water, trying to fend off the delirium, but it was no use. The longer she clung, the weaker she became. When she felt herself on the verge of passing out, she took the string out of her hoodie, tied one end around her wrist, put her arms around the tree and tied the free end to her other wrist. The last thing she remembered was feeling the tree trunk vibrating against her cheek from the water's rush.

Shug Wilson had been a chopper pilot for the Louisiana National Guard most of his adult life. His first military mission had been flying choppers in Desert Storm, then, after 9/11, his military missions had been in Afghanistan. His last tour had been sixteen months in Iraq, and he had been home less than four months when the Mississippi flooded.

When the governor called out the National Guard, he was the first one at the armory, and he'd been flying rescue for days. They'd been sent down to this area yesterday and had been on the job since just before daylight this morning. This was their first trip into a new quadrant after a refueling stop.

The two soldiers with him were PFCs Wilson and Carver, who were on the lookout for live bodies as Shug flew over the flood zone. They'd been in the air less than thirty minutes when Carver suddenly pointed.

"Hey, Colonel, circle back over that stand of trees and take it down."

Shug nodded as Carver's voice came in loud and clear on the headset.

"Roger that," he said as he made the loop and went low.

"There! Look there!" Carver said. "There's someone in that tree."

"I see him," Shug said, and settled into hover mode as Wilson quickly hooked up his body harness. He gave Carver a thumbs-up, okaying him to activate the winch to lower Wilson down.

The backwash from the chopper blades was whipping the tree limbs with hurricane force, battering the victim to the point that he apparently lost hold.

"He's going into the water!" Carver yelled.

Wilson heard the voice in his headset and gritted his teeth.

"Not if I can help it," he muttered, and went feet first into the treetop, grabbing at the body just as it lurched off the limb.

Wilson's reaction to the situation was immediate as he assessed the situation.

"Okay, boys. It's a woman, and she's tied herself to the tree. Damn smart, because she's unconscious. Hang on while I cut her loose."

"Ten-four," Shug said.

Nola came to just in time to realize a strange man had a grip around her waist. She couldn't see his face for the helmet he was wearing, but she saw the knife and began fighting for her life.

"Easy, lady, I'm trying to help you," Carver said.

He wasted no time cutting her free and then pulled her up into his arms.

Nola was conscious just long enough to register the National Guard insignia on his jumpsuit, and then she passed out again.

"She's out again. Take us up," Wilson said.

She woke up in the chopper, flat on her back. She saw soldiers, heard the rotors and knew they were in the air. Someone was talking to her, but she couldn't hear what they were saying and turned loose of conscious thought.

The next time she came to she was in a hospital bed. There was an IV in her arm, and a nurse was standing at the foot writing on her chart.

"Where am I?" Nola asked.

The woman looked up and smiled. "Well, hello there. You're in Tidewater Municipal Hospital. Can you tell me your name?"

Nola's head was pounding. Tidewater? That was forty miles south of Queens Crossing.

"Nola Landry."

The nurse smiled again. "Finally a name to go with that pretty face. You came in as an unidentified rescue. Do you have any family we need to notify?"

It hurt to answer. "No."

The nurse's smile slipped a little, but she didn't waver.

"How do you feel?"

"Sore, confused." Then she put a hand to her forehead. "But no fever!"

"No fever is right. That broke about noon yesterday," the nurse said.

And just like that, Nola remembered the killer. "Yesterday? How long have I been here?"

"This is your second day, honey."

"I need to talk to the police. I witnessed a murder."

"A murder?"

"Yes, of a whole family."

The nurse eyed her curiously. "Are you sure? You were out of your head. You don't think it might have been a hallucination?"

The question made Nola angry. "No! Oh, my God, no! They were my neighbors. Never mind. I'll call them myself."

She began pushing back the covers and trying to sit up, but the room was spinning.

"I'm going to be sick," Nola muttered.

The nurse grabbed a wet washcloth and immediately put it on the back of Nola's neck, then gently wiped it across her face and forehead, and just like that, the wave of nausea passed.

"I need the police," Nola mumbled.

The nurse gave her hand a quick pat.

"I'll call them for you."

Nola fell back against the pillows, shaking.

"Call now. Promise?"

"I promise," the nurse said, and hurried out of the room.

Two

The minute the nurse left, exhaustion took over again and Nola drifted off to sleep. The next time she came to, her heart was pounding because she thought she was falling out of the tree. It took a few moments to reconcile her reality with the dream, and she was still shaking as the door swung inward. It was a nurse with a food tray.

"Lunchtime, honey. Are you hungry?"

"I guess," Nola said. "Did anyone call the police? I need to talk to the police."

The nurse elevated the head of the bed to sit her up, then swung the tray table across the bed and took the cover off the plate.

"Yes, they called. I'm sure they'll come soon. Can you manage this?" she said, eyeing the abrasions on the palms of Nola's hands.

"I think so, and thanks."

"If you need help, press the call button. I'll be back later to get the tray."

Nola eyed the square of meat loaf, the spoonful of scalloped potatoes next to the green peas, and reached for her fork. After a quick taste, she reached for the salt.

It was the first solid food she'd had in days, and it didn't take long for her to get full. When she quit eating, she kept the cup of iced tea and shoved the tray table aside. Moments later the door opened. She thought it was the nurse coming back for her tray, but it was the R.N. with a policeman.

Nola saw the badge clipped to his belt and caught a glimpse of a shoulder holster under his suit coat. The nurse looked none too happy that there was an armed man on her floor and gave Nola a steady look as she introduced them.

"Miss Landry, this is Lieutenant Carroll with the Tidewater Police. He's been apprised of your claim and is ready to take your statement."

Nola tensed, her fingers curling around the cup of iced tea as she eyed the tall, bald-headed man.

"Thank you, ma'am. I'll take it from here," he said to the nurse, who glanced at Nola, then nodded and left.

The officer smiled at Nola, revealing perfect white teeth. His tan jacket was only a couple of shades lighter than his skin, and his dark eyes sparkled in a friendly manner.

She watched him pull a chair up next to her bed and then take out a notebook.

"For the record, would you please state your name, age, occupation and where you're from?"

"Nola Landry, twenty-nine years old. I'm a professional artist from Queens Crossing, Louisiana."

"Thank you. I understand you've been through quite an ordeal," he said, eyeing the raw marks on her wrists and the obvious wounds on her face and hands. "You are one very lucky woman."

When his face suddenly blurred, she took a quick sip of her iced tea to gather her emotions.

"Luckier than my neighbors by far," she said, and then wiped her eyes with the corner of the sheet.

"About your neighbors...are those the people you claim were murdered?"

She frowned. "It's not a claim, it's a fact. They were on the roof of their house. I could see them clearly from the tree I was in."

"How many, and what were their names?" he asked.

"There were three. Whitman Lewis, his wife, Candy, and her mother, Ruth Andrews. She lived with them."

He was writing. "Okay, now tell me about the murderer. Where did he come from?"

"He was in a motorboat, coming downriver. I heard the outboard engine before I saw him, and they did, too. They stood up on the roof and began laughing and waving. They were so happy." Her voice broke. "For a few moments we were all happy, thinking we had been saved."

She took another sip of the tea and swallowed tears along with it.

Carroll gave her a few moments to regain her composure and then continued questioning.

"Were they upriver from you, or did the man have to pass you to get to them?"

"They were upriver. It all happened so suddenly. I was thinking to myself that as soon as he loaded them up I would climb down far enough to get his attention, and then he pulled up to the roof. All of a sudden there was a gun in his hand and he started shooting."

"What kind of a gun?"

"A pistol. He shot Whit first, and the women were so shocked they didn't have time to register what was happening before he'd shot them, too. Their bodies rolled into the water, and he just stood there in the boat watching until they sank."

Her voice was shaking, and tears were rolling down her cheeks as she set the iced tea aside.

Carroll grabbed the box of tissues from a side table and dropped them in her lap, then cleared his throat and waited.

Nola was shaking as she wiped her eyes and blew her nose.

"Do you know if their bodies have been found?" she asked.

"No, ma'am, I don't. I want to clarify some parts of your story, okay?"

She nodded.

"You say you were hidden in the high branches, and yet you could see this clearly through the leaves?"

"I was in the tree at least twelve hours before I even knew they were there. The water kept rising, and every time it did, I had to climb higher. It wasn't until the last time I went up that I saw them."

"Did they know you were there?"

"No, and I didn't call out to let them know. They couldn't have helped me any more than I could help them."

"Then what?"

"After they sank, he circled around and started back downriver toward me. I was scared to death that he would see me and climbed higher up into the tree. I saw him pass, but he was wearing a cap, and from my height, it concealed most of his face."

"What can you tell me about him?" Carroll asked.

"He was a white, middle-aged man, with salt-and-pepper hair and a big mustache."

"What was he wearing?" Carroll asked.

Nola gasped. "Oh, my gosh. I can't believe I didn't tell you that first! That was the most awful part of it all. He was wearing a parish police uniform."

Carroll leaned forward. "He was a cop? A cop was the one who shot them?"

"Yes. There was no mistake about that. I've lived there all my life. It was the same uniform the police wear in my parish."

"And yet you didn't recognize him?"

She shook her head. "No, as I said, the cap brim hid most of his face."

"Would you recognize him again if you saw him?"

"I don't know.... I doubt it."

"Too bad. Okay, then. I'll file this report and notify the authorities at Queens Crossing. If you remember anything else, don't hesitate to call."

"All right, and thank you."

"Yes, ma'am, and again, you really are something. Mind if I ask you a personal question?"

Nola frowned. "It's okay, I guess."

"What happened to your wrists? They're bloody and bandaged, and I couldn't help but wonder what happened to you in the flood to cause those injuries."

She glanced down at the bandages, then back up at his face.

"I was sick when I went up the tree. I tied myself to it because I was afraid I'd pass out and drown."

Carroll's expression shifted. "You were sick? Do you think you might have been hallucinating?"

Nola's anger was instantaneous. "Oh, my God, no, I didn't imagine it. If this is the best you can do, get out! I'll tell the police myself when I get home, and in the meantime if they fish any more bodies out of the flood, you can blame your damn self."

"I didn't—"

"I'm through talking to you! Get out!"

Carroll sighed. "Rest assured I will file the report, Miss Landry. I hope you get well soon."

When she folded her arms across her chest, Carroll knew she was done with him. He didn't know what he thought about the story, but he was obligated to report a witness statement regarding a murder, real or only marginally possible.

He drove back to the department, still doubting most of her story, and was at his desk writing up the interview when his captain came in and began tossing copies of a report on everyone's desk.

"Heads up, everyone. We just got a fax from the parish police in Queens Crossing. They've got seven dead bodies, all of whom were killed with a single gunshot. No suspects, but they were all killed with a pistol, probably the same pistol."

Carroll looked up in disbelief. "You're kidding!"

"No, I'm not kidding. Why?"

"I just took a report from one of the flood victims they brought in to Tidewater. She claims to have witnessed three people being murdered."

"Holy shit! Did she know them? Did she give any names?"

"Yes. Said they were her neighbors. Just a sec, I

have the names in my notes." He thumbed through the pages, then paused. "Here they are. Whitman Lewis, Candy Lewis, Ruth Andrews."

The captain's eyes widened. "Those names are on the list."

Carroll's pulse kicked. "We've got ourselves a witness, and get this. She said the killer was wearing a uniform like the ones from her parish."

"A cop? The killer is a cop?"

"That's what she said."

"Finish that report and fax it to Queens Crossing ASAP."

"Yes, sir," Carroll said, and made a mental apology to Nola Landry for doubting anything she'd said.

The killer's first victim had been in Dubuque, Iowa, after a tornado had swept through the town. When rescue workers began finding bodies with bullet holes, rather than wounds from storm damage, it didn't make sense. The police immediately knew they'd been murdered and began looking for a connection between them. But other than the fact that they'd lived through the storm before they were killed, there was none. News of the murders hit the papers, and all of a sudden the FBI was in Dubuque.

Special agents Tate Benton, Wade Luckett and Cameron Winger caught the case and had been following the killer's trail ever since. The next time he struck was after another storm hit. And the third time was in Omaha after a local flood in Missouri. Once it became apparent that his killings occurred directly after weather-related events, the media, being the media, dubbed him the Stormchaser.

During the past two months, the killer had begun taunting the agents through the media, mocking their inability to catch him and blaming them for the deaths.

Tate Benton's specialty was profiling, and he had picked up on the messages as being part of the killer's need to prove his superiority.

One of their first breakthroughs was figuring out that he didn't strike until after the Red Cross arrived. After clearing the actual Red Cross workers of any guilt, it led the team to suspect he was hiding among the hundreds of volunteers who came with any disaster, and that by working to assist, he was nullifying the sins of murder by helping minister to the ones he spared.

When the Mississippi River began to flood, the Stormchaser struck again, this time in Natchez, Mississippi. They were still working that scene when Special Agent Wade Luckett pulled into the parking lot of the Natchez Police Department and got out. His steps were hurried as he strode through the lobby, then down a hallway to the room that had become their field office. When he walked in, Tate Benton was on the computer and Cameron Winger was on the phone.

They both looked up.

"We have bodies in Louisiana," Wade said.

Tate frowned. "Damn. We were afraid of that. He's moving downriver with the flood. Where's the location?"

Wade hesitated, knowing this was going to be an issue for Tate.

"Queens Crossing."

A muscle jerked at the side of Tate's mouth. "Son of a bitch. How many?" he asked.

Wade glanced at the report. "Seven so far. The victims are male and female, no specific ages, and each of them dead from a single gunshot. The ballistics reports aren't in yet, but it's our man."

Cameron Winger ended his phone call and looked at Tate. "What's the issue with Queens Crossing?"

Tate's expression was grim. "I grew up there. Still have friends and family there. Do you have the names of the deceased?"

Wade glanced at his notes. "Yes."

"Can I see them?"

Tate took the list and scanned it quickly, relieved there was no one named Landry or Benton.

"How bad is the flooding?" he asked.

"At last count, twenty feet above flood level, and the river has yet to peak," Wade said.

Tate knew the location of Nola Landry's home and knew without question, it would be gone. It was bad enough that she and her mother would have lost everything. He didn't even want to think that they could have drowned. The last memory he had of her, she'd been crying and he'd been the cause. He sat down with a thump.

Wade frowned. "What?"

Tate shook his head, unwilling to get into specifics.

"I was just thinking about what-all has been lost and who might have died with it. So when are we leaving?"

"As soon as we can pack up," Wade said.

Cameron began gathering up his notes.

"I'll tell the Natchez police we're leaving," Wade said.

"We'll meet you in the parking lot," Tate said.

Two hours later they were on their way south to Queens Crossing and getting a firsthand look at the spreading devastation. It was midafternoon when they arrived to find a town in disaster mode.

The Red Cross was set up in the high school gymnasium. People who had been displaced by the flooding had not only lost their belongings but their homes, as well. Most of them had escaped with only what they could carry, and there were cars and trucks in a line outside the building, dropping off donations of what appeared to be food and clothing.

Tate searched the faces as they drove past, startled that there were so few he recognized, then remembered the place would be full of volunteers—one of whom could possibly be their killer.

"Hey, Tate, where is the police department, and will it be local or county?" Cameron asked.

"You're in Louisiana, remember? So it's parish, not county, and the law here will be local. Unless he's been replaced, the chief's name is Beaudry. Take a left at the bank and go down two blocks. It'll be the gray two-story building on the right."

"Two stories? That's a big building for a small town."

"It used to be the courthouse. The morgue is in the basement. The jail is on the first floor and offices are on the second."

"Got it," Cameron said.

A couple of minutes later they pulled up in the parking lot. When they got out, Tate led the way inside. He didn't recognize the officer at the desk and pulled out his ID.

"Special Agent Benton, FBI, and these are my partners, Luckett and Winger. We need to speak to the chief."

"Chief Beaudry is downstairs in the morgue," the officer said. "I'll let him know you're here."

"We'll meet him there. Just tell him we're on our way down."

The officer frowned. "Wait, you don't know where—"

"I know the way," Tate said.

He skipped the elevator and took the stairs two at a time, with Wade and Cameron right behind him.

"You've been down in the morgue?" Cameron asked.

Tate nodded. "My dad is the parish coroner. If they're doing autopsies, he'll be here."

"We've been partners for five years and I didn't know this," Wade muttered.

Tate shrugged. "Let's just say I'm not the favorite son, okay?"

"Ouch," Wade said. "Sorry."

Tate paused outside the main door, eyeing his partners. "It really has nothing to do with me. I just got caught in the middle of a thing between him and my mom."

"That's tough," Cameron said.

"It is what it is, and I'm telling you now only because my presence will probably impact his attitude."

Wade frowned. "Hell of a deal to put you in the middle of their troubles."

Tate shrugged it off and went in one door as Chief Beaudry entered the reception area from the other direction. The agents flashed their badges and made quick introductions.

Beaudry glanced at Tate. "I remember you. You're Don Benton's son, aren't you?"

"That's what my birth certificate says," Tate said. "Is he here?"

Beaudry nodded. "He's doing an autopsy on the

last body, although the bullet hole in his head looked pretty conclusive to me."

"You have firm IDs on all the bodies?" Tate asked.

"Yes, and they're all locals. It's sickening. Even though we found all of them in the floodwaters, none of them drowned. Is it true you think this is the work of that guy they call the Stormchaser?"

"It looks that way. Can we see them?" Tate asked.

"Yes, come with me."

Even though Tate was bracing himself for his father's antagonism, he was unprepared when, the moment they walked into the autopsy room, the familiar odors sent him into a free fall of memories—all of them painful. When he saw his father's face for the first time in eight years, he was startled. Don Benton had gotten old.

His father spoke without looking up.

"You know I don't like visitors in here, Beaudry."

"We're not visitors, Dad. We're working this case."

Don Benton froze at the sound of Tate's voice and then slowly lifted his head.

It was hard to tell what he was thinking, but Tate stood his ground.

"These are my partners, Special agents Winger and Luckett. We're working the Stormchaser murders. Do you mind if we take a look at the bodies?"

Tate could see his father struggling with the urge to argue, but his professionalism won out.

"Look, but don't touch. They're in drawers one through six."

Tate moved across the room and, one by one, pulled out the bodies to confirm their suspicions. Each one had a single bullet wound in the head.

"Excuse me, Doctor Benton, but have you recovered any bullets?" Cameron asked.

"Four were through-and-throughs, and three were not. I've already turned those over to the parish police," Benton said.

"We sent them off to Ballistics," Beaudry said.

Cameron nodded. "We have some comparisons with us. Let us know when you get results."

They moved to the autopsy in progress.

Tate had seen the process a hundred times, and yet it never failed to amaze him how doctors could be so skilled in the inner working of the human body that they could determine cause of death by what they saw.

"Are there any surprises here?" he asked.

Don Benton paused and looked up. "Other than you?"

Tate's face was expressionless.

Don shrugged. "If you're referring to the cause of death, then no, there are no surprises. This man died from a single gunshot wound to the head, although I would venture a guess that, judging by his enlarged liver, he had less than a year to live."

Tate heard the quaver in his father's voice and knew he was shocked by his arrival. So be it. He'd shocked Tate eight years ago when he'd rejected his existence.

Tate stared him down. "We'll be needing copies of all seven of the autopsies—at your convenience, of course. Chief Beaudry, if you'd escort us to where the Red Cross is set up, we will need to get names and contact info on anyone who's not a local."

Beaudry frowned. "Are you saying that the killer is someone in the Red Cross?"

Tate frowned. "No, and don't put words in my mouth, understand? If you would lead the way in your car, we'll follow. You can make the necessary introductions to whoever's in charge, and we'll take it from there."

Beaudry frowned. He didn't like being called down by anybody, but solving seven murders in their little town was out of his league, and he knew it.

Cameron saw the tension in Tate's shoulders and a similar stiffness in his father's manner, and wondered what the hell could have happened to cause their antagonism. Still, he gave Benton a courteous nod. "Sorry to interrupt you, Doctor Benton. Thank you for your information."

"You're welcome," Don Benton said, and just like that, he put them out of his mind as they walked out the door.

It didn't take long for the agents to get yet another field office set up. Beaudry gave them his only interrogation room, and after a quick visit to the gym, they had a list of Red Cross employees on the premises, and were running the name through their database to make sure they were cleared to be there. As for getting a list of the names of volunteers, it wasn't going to be that simple. They were coming and going with such a rapid turnover that the Red Cross officials on site had lost track days ago.

The men worked until after midnight, and with no motels or empty rooms available anywhere in town, they sacked out on some cots in a corner of the gymnasium with the other refugees. Tate could have asked his father to put them up. Lord knows the old Benton house had room to spare, but he didn't have the stomach to withstand his father's anger. Plus, he was afraid his father would bring up his mother's name, which would have been his tipping point, and the man was too old to fight.

Tate was still awake long after Cameron and Wade had gone to sleep, thinking of Nola and wondering if she was married. Finally he fell asleep from sheer exhaustion.

Babies cried throughout the night, disgruntled by the unfamiliar surroundings. People snored, some cried. Tempers were short, with the occasional argument popping up, followed by tears or angry silence.

Along toward morning Cameron opened his eyes to find a little girl about the age of three standing near his elbow. He had no idea how long she'd been standing there watching him sleep. Her hair had been in a ponytail, but during the night it had slid sideways until the ponytail was drooping somewhere between her right ear and her chin. Her clothes were a couple of sizes too big, which probably meant everything her family once had was gone and she was wearing donated clothing. She was also minus shoes, and had one sock on and the other one in her hand.

He rose up on one elbow and looked around to see if anyone was up and searching for a child, but everyone within sight was asleep. He grinned. They probably didn't even know she was gone. He swung his legs off the cot, and then leaned forward with his elbows on his knees.

"Hey, honey. What's your name?"

"Twicia."

"Need some help with that sock?" he asked.

She nodded and handed it to him. He slipped it on her bare foot and then gave her knee a quick pat.

"Where's your mama?"

She poked a thumb in her mouth and blinked.

"Are you lost?"

She nodded.

He got up, wincing at the cold floor on his bare feet, then picked her up in his arms.

"How about we go find her, okay?"

She nodded again, still sucking her thumb.

Cameron made his way between the cots and

sleeping bags, taking care as to where he stepped as he headed toward the only light in the place, a small office the Red Cross had set up near the door. By the time he got there the little girl had laid her head on his shoulder and was almost back asleep.

He saw a pretty young woman dozing in an old recliner on the other side of the desk and frowned. He hated to disturb her, but it was better for her to wake up now than to put the baby's mother in a panic when she realized her child was gone.

"Excuse me," he said softly.

The woman sat up with a jerk, blinking rapidly and obviously trying to gather her senses.

"Sorry to wake you," Cameron said. "But I woke up with this little elf standing by my cot. I don't know who she belongs to, but I'd sure hate for her mama to wake up in a panic."

"Oh, my goodness. Yes, you're absolutely right. I'm Laura Doyle, by the way. Aren't you one of the FBI agents?"

"Yes, ma'am. Nice to meet you, Laura Doyle. I'm Cameron Winger. And Sleeping Beauty here told me her name was 'Twicia' before she clammed up."

Laura smiled, trying to ignore how good this big hunky guy looked in gray sweats, and how adorable he was with the toddler asleep on his shoulder.

"Patricia, huh? Let me check the list of names. Hopefully there won't be too many little girls named Patricia on site."

Cameron waited, eyeing the way she chewed the edge of her lower lip as she scanned the list, thinking to himself that she was one of those women who looked good without makeup. He started to wonder if she looked as good without her clothes, and then she looked up and he blushed, thankful she couldn't read his mind.

"We're in luck. There's only one Patricia who's a juvenile. She belongs to the Metarie family. I think I know where they're sleeping. Follow me." She picked up a flashlight and led the way across the darkened floor of the gymnasium to the opposite corner of the room.

Once they reached the sleeping family, Laura tapped the father's foot and then softly spoke his name.

"Billy Joe, it's me, Laura."

The young father sat up with a jerk, blinking against the glare of the flashlight in his eyes.

"What's wrong?"

Laura was chuckling softly as she gave him the news, knowing they'd all had enough drama.

"Your daughter, Tricia, took herself a little walk. Mr. Winger here woke up and found her standing by his cot. We thought you might want her back."

"Oh, sweet Lord," he muttered, and came up off his cot as if he'd been shot from a cannon. He shook his head as he took the sleepy toddler from Cameron's arms.

"Thank you, thank you so much, mister."

"You're welcome. She's not much of a talker, but she's awfully pretty."

The young man smiled as he looked down at his daughter.

"Papa," the little girl mumbled, and then snuggled up beneath his chin and closed her eyes.

Laura smiled. "I do believe we've delivered her to the right place. Go back to sleep if you can. It's still a little while until morning."

"Yes, ma'am. Thank you, thank you both."

"You're welcome," Cameron replied, and then followed Laura back to the office. "Thanks for the help," he said.

She shrugged. "It's what I do. Just give me a shout if you need anything else, okay?"

He nodded, started to leave and then stopped.

"So I'm sure I'll see you around, right?"

She smiled. "I'm not going anywhere."

He was smiling, too, as he crawled back into his cot and closed his eyes, and he was still thinking about the way Laura Doyle chewed her lower lip as he fell back asleep.

Three

Beaudry showed up at the gym the next morning carrying a sack of doughnuts and a copy of the report his office had just received from the Tidewater P.D.

Tate had made an early visit to the boys' dressing room at the gym, and was already shaved, showered and wearing his last set of clean clothes. He distinctly remembered playing basketball in this gym and kissing Nola out behind the building when they were in high school, and now he was back in the same place, but investigating murders. Life was crazy. He'd known coming home on work-related business wouldn't be easy, but he'd had no idea how many memories it would evoke. He was sitting on the cot putting on his shoes when he saw the chief approach.

"Hey, guys, we've got company," Tate said.

Wade got off the phone and Cameron closed his laptop.

Beaudry was all smiles as he handed over the doughnuts. "Call it a mini-celebration."

"Thanks," Tate said as he took out a doughnut and then handed the sack to Wade. "What are we celebrating?"

"You have a witness to the shootings."

"You are kidding!" Cameron said. "Where? Who?"

"A flood victim rescued by the National Guard witnessed three murders. They took her to the hospital in Tidewater, and when she finally woke up from the fever she came in with, the first thing she asked for was the police. She gave her statement to the Tidewater P.D. that she'd seen her neighbors murdered, and they notified us."

"Where's Tidewater?" Wade asked.

"About forty miles south of here—and that's where we're heading next," Tate said.

"I'm coming with you," Beaudry said. "I know this is your case, but they were murdered on my turf, and I want justice as much as you do, maybe more. These people were my friends."

Tate nodded. "We'll be leaving in a few minutes."

"I'll take the cruiser back to the station. Pick me up there."

"Oh, hey…wait a minute," Tate said. "What's the witness's name?"

Beaudry paused. "Nola Landry. I believe you know her, right?"

Tate's stomach rolled the same way it had right

before he'd walked into the morgue yesterday, and for the very same reason. Everything bad that had happened between them was tied to what was wrong between him and his dad.

"Yes, I know her," Tate said. "See you in a few."

Cameron and Wade were waiting for an explanation, but when it appeared Tate wasn't going to volunteer any info, Cameron took the initiative.

"So, you know the witness. What's the big secret?" he asked.

Tate knew they would find out soon enough when Nola caught sight of him.

"She's why I don't date," he muttered.

Wade frowned. "Damn. Was she that big a bitch?"

Tate sighed. "No. She was that good. No one else ever measured up."

Wade glanced at Cameron, then shrugged.

"So what happened to screw it up?" Cameron asked.

"It's all tied into the mess between me and my dad. I'm driving. Get your things."

He walked out, leaving them to make what they wanted of that.

Wade looked at Cameron, shrugged and grabbed the sack of doughnuts as Cameron picked up his laptop. They were on their way out the door when Cameron saw Laura Doyle in the makeshift kitchen. She looked up and waved as they hurried past. He was still smiling when they drove away.

* * *

Nola washed her hair, then left it down to dry. Tate used to say it was the color of dark chocolate, his favorite treat, and it looked even darker when it was still damp, like it was now.

"I so need a hair dryer," she said, and then thought about what she'd just gone through and sighed. "No, I don't *need* a hair dryer, although a hair dryer would be nice. What I *need* is a house. Sorry about that, God."

The fact that she was talking to herself was immaterial. She'd been doing a lot of that since her mother's death. She continued to run her fingers through her hair, combing and fluffing it, until the door to her hospital room opened and four men walked in.

She recognized the parish police chief from Queens Crossing, but when she saw the three men with him, she went from shock to disbelief to anger so quickly it made her head spin. Unwilling to be caught in a vulnerable position, she hit the control on her bed until she was sitting completely upright.

Beaudry smiled as he headed for her bed.

"Hey, Nola, it's good to see you. I hear you had a rough time of it out there."

She nodded, but her gaze was fixed on the men behind him.

Beaudry could see she was as shocked by Benton's appearance as Benton had been when he'd found out she was the witness, but they were here on police business, not unfinished business.

"These men are from the FBI, and they're working a case connected to the recent murders in our area. We got a copy of the statement you gave Lieutenant Carroll about what you saw, but they want to talk to you some more, okay?"

She pointed at the men behind him. "What is he doing here?"

Beaudry frowned. "Uh, like I said, these men are from the FBI. That man is Special Agent Benton and—"

"I *know* who he is. I asked you what he's doing here."

Tate thought he'd prepared himself for this moment, but he was wrong. The girl he'd left behind had turned into a stunning woman. The soft round cheeks he used to kiss were firmer, the cheekbones more defined. Her eyes were still as blue, and the black winged brows above them were gathered into a mute statement of her anger. The abrasions on her face and hands were evidence of what she'd suffered. It hurt to think about what she must have endured before she was rescued.

"I'll speak for myself," Tate said. "Hello, Nola. This is a heck of a way to meet again."

Tate. Oh, Lord. I can't go there. Nola's heart was

beating so fast she felt faint, but it was anger that came up first.

"It's a damn shame people had to die to bring you back."

He ignored the anger. It was to be expected.

"These are my partners, Special agents Luckett and Winger."

"And that's *their* problem, not *mine,*" she muttered.

Cameron frowned. "Ma'am, excuse my bluntness, but whatever is going on with you and Agent Benton is going to have to be shelved. We're looking for a serial killer, and you're the first person who's gotten a look at him and survived."

Nola accepted the setdown. Her personal issues with Tate needed to take a backseat to finding a killer.

"Fine, Agent Winger. I'll answer any questions you ask, and if you're going back to Queens Crossing afterward, I would certainly appreciate a ride home." Then she sighed. "I need to rephrase that. I need a ride back to town. My home and everything I owned are gone."

"We'll be happy to take you, but will the doctor release you?" Tate asked.

She wanted to ignore him, but, as Winger had so clearly stated, there was more at stake here than hurt feelings.

"Yes, as of this morning. I just didn't have anyone left who could come get me."

"You don't have a husband?" When she glared without answering, he took that as a no and tried to ignore the relief pouring through him.

"What about your mom?" he asked.

"She died last Christmas."

"I'm sorry. I—"

Her voice was shaking as she cut him off. "So am I. You read my statement. I don't know what else I can tell you, but take a seat and ask me whatever you please. I'll do anything I can to help."

Wade took the first question to take the pressure off Tate.

"Miss Landry, I'm Agent Luckett. I read that you didn't get a good look at his face. Is there anything else you've remembered since you talked to Lieutenant Carroll?"

Nola shook her head. "No, I wish there was. I was stranded up that tree for nearly eighteen hours, and I know they were on their roof at least that long, too. We saw a helicopter once, but it was a long ways off, and then there was nothing to see but debris, bloated animal carcasses and the occasional gator swimming past us in the floodwater—which kept rising, by the way. I kept climbing up, hoping it would stop before I ran out of tree."

There were tears running down her cheeks, but she didn't seem to know it. The sight was tearing

Tate apart, but no one wanted to interrupt her train of thought, and so they sat, watching her relive the nightmare once again.

"The truth is, if I hadn't been sick I probably would have evacuated days earlier. But I guess everything happens for a reason, because if I'd been gone, I wouldn't have witnessed what happened. Once we all heard the outboard motor, we assumed it was the rescue we'd been praying for. When the boat appeared, there was only one man in it." She glanced at Beaudry. "When he got close enough, I could see he was wearing a uniform, but I didn't realize it was from your department until after he'd killed the Lewises and came by the tree where I was hiding, I'm positive about that."

Beaudry frowned. "The description you gave Carroll doesn't fit anyone who works for me, so it was obviously a fake uniform or a stolen one. We'll check that out."

"What happened after you saw him?" Tate asked.

"He saw the Lewis family and headed straight for the roof. Before I had time to make my move down the tree, he pulled out a pistol and just shot Whit in the head."

She paused, pressing her fingers against her lips to keep from breaking into sobs. She reached for the tissues.

"Whit was in the water when he shot Candy and her mother. After they sank, he gunned the motor and headed downriver toward me. I climbed higher, scared to death he would see me, but at the same time I felt like I just had to take the chance of getting a look at him. I tried, but I was too high up and the brim of his cap hid his face when he passed by. I'm sorry. I'm so sorry."

Even though it had nothing to do with their case, Tate had to know.

"How much longer were you up in that tree before you were rescued?" he asked.

Nola wouldn't look at him. She didn't want his damn sympathy. Not anymore.

"I have no idea. I was out of my head with fever. I finally tied myself to the tree because I kept passing out, and I was afraid I'd fall into the water and drown."

That explained the abrasions on the palms of her hands and what looked like rope burns around her wrists.

"What about the boat? What can you tell us about the boat?" Cameron asked.

She frowned. No one had asked her about that before. She had to pause and think.

"It was just a motorboat. Chief, you know what I mean? It was the kind people use to go fishing. A plain white boat with a big blue outboard motor." She closed her eyes, picturing it as it passed below the tree. Then all of a sudden her eyes were open and her voice was shaking. "There was a name painted on the back end of the boat. It was *Gator Bait.* Oh, my gosh, I just now remembered that."

Tate smiled. "Good job."

Nola almost returned the smile and then caught herself. They were not going to be friends, much less anything else, again.

Beaudry stood up. "I'm going to call the boat info in and get that registration check started. And then we'll get you out of here."

"Are you sure it's okay for you to leave?" Tate asked Nola.

She shrugged. "My fever is gone, and my scratched hands and face are hardly worthy of a hospital bed."

"Where will you go?" he asked.

"Where did the Red Cross set up?"

"The school gymnasium," Beaudry said.

"Is that where the other displaced people are at?"

Tate frowned. "Yes, but—"

"Then that's where I'll ask you to leave me. If the water was gone tomorrow, I still wouldn't have a place to live. The house was completely underwater, or maybe washed away. There's nothing to salvage, but I want to go home. I need to be with my people."

"Then you need to understand something first," Tate said. "Cameron already told you this man is a serial killer, and we've been trailing him for over two months. The media has dubbed him the Stormchaser, because he shows up at the same time the Red Cross arrives after a disaster. We think he conceals himself within the contingent of volunteers. You could be putting yourself at risk just by coming back into that environment, especially when he finds out there's a witness to what he's done."

The hair stood up on the back of her neck. "But I can't identify him."

"That won't matter. You're unfinished business," Tate said.

She slumped against the pillows, her chin trembling. "Just when I thought it couldn't get worse."

"Do you still want to go back?" Beaudry asked.

She took a deep breath. "I have nowhere else *to* go but back."

"Then do what you have to do to get yourself signed out," he said.

"I'll go find a nurse," Cameron said.

"Ask her if I can please have a pair of scrubs. They threw away the clothes I came here in."

"Yes, ma'am. Don't worry. We'll get you rigged out," Cameron said, and headed out the door with Beaudry behind him.

Nola looked at Tate, refused to acknowledge the plea in his eyes and turned away.

Hershel had taken the morning off to sleep in and was still debating with himself about going to the gymnasium to work. He'd been there until after 3:00 a.m. last night unloading supplies. Being a good guy was tiring.

Hershel, you need to get up. You've done very bad things, and you need to atone.

He groaned. "Damn it, Louise, you don't know what you're talking about, so don't be telling me what I have to do."

Hershel, Hershel, you break my heart. I don't want you to be like this. This isn't the sweet man I married.

"That man died when you did, Louise, so let it be. What I'm doing, I'm doing for you."

Don't blame this on me. You do not kill in my name. I won't have it.

Her anger was sharp, and he hated it when Louise was mad at him. His shoulders slumped as he leaned forward and buried his face in his hands.

"You don't understand," he whispered. "You went away and left me, and now you don't understand."

Nola was naked beneath the scrubs and very aware of that fact as she sat in the backseat between Tate and the chief. She had a running list going in her head as to what she was going to have to do when she got back. She had enough money in the bank to pick up some stuff at the Dollar Store in town, but where would she go after that? There was a trailer park, one small motel and a woman who took in boarders, but lot of people would have been displaced, so the chance of finding room in any of those places was slim. She knew things would eventually work out, but it was the not knowing that was so unsettling.

And then there was the killer among them. She'd seen him at work. That cold, calculated shot was something she would never forget. She leaned back in the seat and closed her eyes, and for the first time in years she regretted not leaving Queens Crossing with Tate Benton when he'd asked her.

It had been a long time since Tate had been this close to a woman he wanted, and pretending it didn't matter was next to impossible. He kept glancing at her when she wasn't looking. He had never seen her look this defeated. They'd spent their lives planning to raise a family in Queens Crossing. Having him do an about-face at the last minute must have shocked and, more than that, hurt her. He'd begged her to leave with him, but without being willing to offer an explanation. And she had refused to go without one. He'd been so hurt by his father's rejection, and Nola's rejection had only added to his pain. The only way he'd been able to function had been to get as far away from his father as he could. He should have trusted Nola then and told her—and he would have, if it had been his secret to tell. At the time, he'd felt he couldn't betray his mother, but given the way she was now, it was all water under the bridge—which, when he thought about it, was a horrible analogy.

Cameron was thinking of Laura Doyle as he drove

back to Queens Crossing and looking forward to seeing her again. He knew they were there to find a killer, not a new relationship, although it appeared Tate would be willing to rekindle his if the Landry woman would let him. However, there was no harm making friends with someone while working on a case, especially a woman as pretty as Laura.

Nola was asleep when they passed the city limits. She'd fallen over onto Tate's shoulder, and he'd let her lean all she wanted. If he didn't think too hard about it, he could almost believe it was just like old times.

Wade looked over his shoulder to the pair in the backseat, then frowned and pointed to Nola's wrists. One of them was seeping blood through the bandage onto the leg of her scrubs.

Tate nodded. They would get her bandaged up again at the gym.

Beaudry glanced out the window as they drove into town.

"All these strangers, all this chaos...it doesn't even look like home anymore," he said softly.

Tate followed his gaze, looking at his onetime home with new eyes. He and his partners spent most of their time in places just like this. Crime followed chaos, and it had been that way since the world began.

"Just drop me off at the station," Beaudry said.

Cameron took the turn at the bank toward the police station, let Beaudry out then drove to the gym.

Nola woke up just as they neared the gym. She was stiff and disoriented, and Tate saw the panic in her eyes.

"We're back in Queens Crossing," he said.

She scooted away from him, then saw the bloody bandage on her wrist and frowned.

"I have blood on my clean clothes."

"They have donated clothing at the shelter. I think they'll have something you can wear," Tate said.

She shoved her long hair out of her eyes. "That's good, and I think maybe I need to cut this stuff off."

Tate frowned. "Your hands will heal, and then you'd be sorry you cut your hair. You're bound to have friends in the gym. They'll help. I'll help. You aren't going through this alone."

"Yes, ma'am, Tate is right," Wade said. "It will all work out. You'll see."

"There's a really nice lady named Laura with the Red Cross. I'll introduce you," Cameron added.

Wade grinned. "Oh, yeah? Is she pretty, too?"

Cameron glared. "Shut up, Luckett. This is about helping Miss Landry, so get your mind out of the gutter."

Wade chuckled.

"I would appreciate it if the lot of you quit calling me Miss Landry and just stuck to Nola," she said.

"We're here," Tate said as Cameron pulled up and parked.

Nola stared. "Where did all these people come from?"

"Some with the Red Cross, others are volunteers and survivors of the flood," Tate said.

Her eyes welled. "The last time I was here was just a couple of months ago, for homecoming. Angie Durant's daughter, Bonnie, was crowned homecoming queen. They would have been flooded out, too. I wonder if they're here?"

"Let's go inside and find out, okay?" he said.

Nola ignored the hand he offered and got herself out of the car, then walked into the gym with her chin up and stopped, shocked into silence by the sight.

There were cots and sleeping bags in neat, crowded rows, and people everywhere. Tables stood against the back wall, loaded down with bottled water, and boxes and boxes of diapers.

"Oh, my God!" she said.

Tate put a hand in the middle of her back. "The good part is that you're alive, not down in the morgue."

She shrugged away from his touch.

He sighed. "Let's get you signed in at the office, so they can get you settled."

A baby cried nearby, and somewhere farther down in the gym another answered with a cry of its own. She wanted to cry with them.

Cameron was already in the office when they walked in. He smiled at Nola.

"There she is," he said. "Nola, this is Laura Doyle. I was telling her a bit about what you need. She'll get you some clothes and food, and a place to sleep, okay?"

Nola nodded as a pretty young woman with short blond hair approached.

"Hi, Nola. You come with me and, as my granny used to say, we'll let these men get back to their rat killing."

Nola smiled. "My aunt Frannie used to say the same thing."

Laura laughed. "The South is a fine place, is it not? Except maybe for floods and tornadoes, and hurricanes and gators."

When Tate walked away, he kept thinking he was forgetting something. And then it hit him, and he made a quick run back into the office and found the women in the back room where the clothing was stored.

"Hey, Nola, one more thing." When she waited for him to speak, he added, "In private."

She went to the doorway. "What?"

He ignored the snap in her tone and lowered his voice.

"Right now, all anyone knows about you is that you are just another flood victim. Don't talk about what you saw and hopefully it won't get out, understand?"

She nodded, her eyes widening fearfully, and just like that, she was reminded of her precarious position.

Tate felt her fear. "And don't worry. We're not going anywhere. We're staying here, too, so if you feel uncomfortable in any way, find one of us immediately. Okay?"

She looked away as her eyes filled with tears.

"Sorry," she mumbled. "All I seem to do these days is cry."

He cupped her face. Whether she liked it or not, he needed to touch her.

"Don't, Nola.... If I'd been through what you went through, I'd be crying, too. Don't apologize for anything, and remember, we've got your back."

She wanted to throw herself in his arms. She chalked the feeling up to being worn out and scared, but when he walked away, she struggled with the urge to follow.

"Nola?"

She jumped. She'd forgotten all about Laura and the clothes.

"I'm sorry. I'm coming," Nola said.

Four

Nola now had three pairs of jeans and an equal number of T-shirts, along with one lightweight jacket and a pair of tennis shoes. Walking back through the gym, making her way through the rows and rows of cots, carrying her secondhand clothes, dodging kids playing and waving at friends who were already there, she began to realize how really blessed they all were. They had survived what insurance companies would call "an act of God," knowing full well it was by the grace of God they had been saved.

The Red Cross had given her a pillow and a blanket, and assigned her to a cot in the corner next to the FBI agents. When she'd raised her eyebrows about the location, Laura had whispered in her ear that Agent Winger had requested it.

Nola didn't argue, and thankfully Laura didn't comment one way or the other about the oddity of the request. At the moment, all three of the agents were gone and Nola was relieved. Being around Tate was harder than she would have imagined. All these years she'd been so angry and hurt at the way they had parted. Now she was just disgusted with herself that the attraction was still there.

She'd heard enough conversation between them on the drive home to know that their field office was at the police station, so she assumed that was where they were.

As soon as she changed into a pair of jeans and a T-shirt, she stashed the rest of what they'd given her under the cot. She had one more task to finish and was going to need help, so she began walking through the crowded gym, looking for a familiar face. When she saw Delores Brim, who had been one of her mother's friends, she headed toward her.

Delores saw her coming and stood abruptly.

"Nola! Oh, honey, I worried about you. Did it take your house?"

"Yes, ma'am," Nola said. "What about you and Joe?"

"We don't know. We evacuated early on. We haven't been back."

"I need to ask a favor of you. Would you please braid my hair? Just one long braid down my back. My hands are still too stiff to do it myself."

Delores grabbed Nola's hands and turned them over, saw the abrasions and the bandages on her wrists, and began to cry.

"What happened to you?"

"I didn't get out in time. It was a while before I was rescued."

"Oh, honey, I'm so sorry. You must have been scared out of your mind. Of course I'll braid your hair. Come sit down on my bed. It won't take long."

Nola handed her the elastic band for her hair.

"I don't have a brush or comb. Just do what you can and I'll be happy."

Delores chattered as she worked, talking to Nola about how others had made it through the flood as she combed her hair with her fingers, and she soon had the braid finished and tied off.

"There you go, honey. You have the prettiest hair. Puts me in mind of your mama's when she was young. Thick and dark, and just a little bit of curl."

"Thank you so much," Nola said, and gave her a hug. "I'll see you around. I've got to run a couple of errands."

The braid bounced against Nola's back as she walked out. She paused to eye the sky for signs of rain and then headed uptown to the bank. When she finally arrived her legs were shaking, a sign she hadn't regained her full strength.

Betty Watts, one of her high school classmates, now worked as a teller. When she saw Nola come in, she waved her over.

"Hey, Nola, how's it going?"

"Hi, Betty. Actually, not so good. I lost my home."

"Oh, honey! I hadn't heard! I'm so sorry. Is that why your face is all scratched up?"

Nola nodded. "The National Guard pulled me out of a tree. I'm happy to still be here."

Betty reached for her hands and then stopped.

"Oh, my gosh. Your poor hands. Honey! Is there anything I can do?"

"I need to withdraw some money from my account, but I've lost my checks and my debit card... everything. Can you help me?"

"Absolutely."

Within a few minutes Nola had cash in her pocket and was on the way to putting her world back in order. Now that she had money, she walked up another block to the Dollar Store for underwear, new hair bands, a hairbrush and some toiletries. It wasn't her venue of choice, but in a small town, you took what you could get and the Dollar Store was it. It was nearing sundown when she got back to the gym. When she walked past the office, Tate all but leaped out of the room and grabbed her arm.

"Where have you been?"

She pulled her arm free. "The bank and the Dollar Store. Where have *you* been?"

He winced. "I'm sorry. That came out wrong. I just... We didn't..."

She grabbed his arm and pulled him outside. Every local person in the gym knew the history between them. She'd already caught some curious glances, and what she had to say didn't need to be overheard.

"Look, we don't owe each other anything. I appreciate the reason you're here, but I don't think I'm in any danger in broad daylight. I have enough sense not to get in cars with strangers and no one knows what I saw, so you do your thing and I'll do mine. When it's over, you'll be gone just like before."

Tate wanted to shake her, but he could tell by the jut of her chin that she wasn't going to budge. He'd burned his bridges with her and had no one to blame but himself.

"Fine. I hear you. Now *you* hear *me*. The Tidewater police know what you saw and they told the police here. And secrets like that don't stay secret long. The Stormchaser isn't someone to fuck with, Nola. So all I'm asking is if you leave the gym, let someone know so I won't have to imagine you with a bullet hole in *your* head, too. Deal?"

"Yes. Fine."

She walked past him and inside, carried her purchases to her cot and stowed them under it, then went to find Laura.

"Hey, there you are," Laura said as she saw Nola walking through the gym.

"I'm a little shaky, but I don't like to sit and do nothing. Is there anything I can do to help?" Nola asked.

Laura pointed at a pair of middle-aged women

who were standing over a small four-burner stove in the concession area.

"Ask Peg or Mary. They're in charge."

Nola eyed the women, noting their matching curly perms and copper-red hair. If the number of wrinkles on their faces had anything to do with their ages, their hair was obviously dyed. She walked in and leaned across the counter.

"Excuse me. Laura said I should ask Peg and Mary if there's anything I can do to help."

The taller woman turned around.

"What's your name, girl?"

"Nola."

"Hi, Nola. I'm Peg. She's Mary. We look alike because we're sisters. She's older, which is why I'm prettier, but she's smarter, which is why I'm chopping onions and she's not."

Nola laughed out loud.

Both women laughed with her, and then Mary noticed the condition of her hands and wrists.

"Since you're still bandaged up, you can't be handling food, but when we begin to serve, you can hand out water bottles. Okay?"

"Okay."

"As for right now, take a seat and talk to us. We haven't heard a good story all day. What's yours?"

Nola sat. "I spent the flood up a tree. How does that grab you?"

Both women turned around. "For real?"

"For real."

"What about your home?"

"Gone, same as most everyone else who's here."

"Sorry, honey," Mary said.

Nola shrugged. "Me, too."

Peg grabbed another onion. "What do you do? For a living, I mean."

"I'm an artist. My work is in a half-dozen galleries in the state, and I work on commission, too."

Both women stopped again. "For real?"

Nola grinned. "For real."

"Do you paint naked people?" Peg asked.

Nola's smile widened. "I'm sorry to say I've never had the pleasure."

"I might have you do a nude of me. I could give it to my husband, George, to hang over the bar in his man cave," Peg said.

Mary giggled.

Nola grinned.

When it came time to serve the food, Nola felt as close to normal as she had in a week. She moved to the far end of the food line and was waiting for the first diners to reach her when a sixty-something man wearing black sweats and an Alabama T-shirt came out of the storage room pushing a dolly loaded with more cases of bottled water. He had a crescent-shaped scar on the side of his neck and dimples in his cheeks, and his head was as shiny as his face.

Another man in jeans and a long-sleeved T-shirt

was following him. He was stocky and middle-aged, with a gray ponytail and a smile that didn't reach his eyes.

The bald-headed man spoke first.

"Hey there. You're a new face. I'm Bill, and he's Leon," he said, and he and Leon began unloading the cases behind the table.

"I'm Nola."

Leon just nodded, but Bill smiled.

"Nice to meet you, Nola. Peg sent me over here to help you. She said you're not to be lifting stuff, so when you need new stock, Leon or I will get it for you."

"Okay," Nola said.

He grinned. "No problem. Truth is I'm a little scared of Peg and Mary. When they tell me to do something, I bust a move to make it happen."

"They're both amazing," she said, including Leon in her comment, but his gaze was blank as he turned away.

Bill tapped her shoulder, then pointed down the line.

"Here come our customers. Since their hands are full, all you have to do is place the bottle on their tray."

"Okay, thanks."

Bill opened extra cases three times during the meal, and Leon set them up until the line of people straggled to an end.

"Now *you* eat," Bill said. "Grab a bottle of water and go back to the kitchen. We'll pack up what's left."

"Thank you for the help," Nola said.

"No problem."

She took the water as she started toward the kitchen when Wade Luckett waved her down.

"What's up?" she asked, as he caught up with her.

"Tate said you like shrimp po'boys. If you haven't already eaten, we brought you one. We appreciate being able to bunk here, but we don't want to use up the food that's been provided for the victims, so we get our own. If you don't want it, I'll eat it along with mine."

She wondered about the wisdom of fraternizing with Tate and his agents, then thought, what the hell. She was sleeping beside them. Surely she could share a meal, as well.

"I do like them, and I'll take it, if you don't mind."

"I don't mind…but I'm not too proud to eat leftovers, either, if you can't eat it all."

Nola grinned. She liked Wade. He was easygoing and funny—like Tate used to be.

"Follow me," he said, and led the way back to the cots.

Tate and Cameron had turned a box upside down to make a table and were digging sandwiches out of a big sack when they walked up.

"She wants one," Wade said. "I tried to talk her

out of it, but she stayed firm. However, I called left-overs if she has any."

Tate accepted the jealousy he was feeling as inevitable and turned away.

Cameron handed her a sandwich. "Here you go. Have a seat. We have things to talk about."

Back in the kitchen, Peg was looking for Nola as Leon took a bowl of chili from the counter and sat down away from the others.

"Where's the girl? Doesn't she know to come back here to get her food?"

"I told her," Bill said as he added salt to his own bowl.

"That doesn't need salt," Mary said.

"Does so," he said, and covered it liberally.

Mary glared.

Peg walked to the doorway and looked out across the gym, saw Nola sitting with the FBI agents and then went back inside.

"She's eating with the Feds," she said.

Mary frowned.

Bill snuck an extra handful of crackers, crushed them on top of his chili and quickly stirred them in before the women saw him.

"Why are the Feds here?" he asked as he took a big bite.

"I have no idea," Peg said as Laura walked in.

"Do we have any left?" Laura asked.

"Enough for you," Mary said.

A minute later Laura took a bite of her chili and then reached for the salt.

Bill laughed when Mary gave Laura a hard look, too.

"What?" Laura asked.

"Nothing," Mary said. "So why are the Feds here?"

Laura shrugged. "It has to do with some of the bodies they recovered from the flood, but other than that, I'm not sure."

Leon glanced up. "They're here because of that Stormchaser dude. They were in Natchez, too. I saw them on the news."

"So why is Nola eating with them?"

Laura smiled. "Now that I *do* know. One of the agents grew up here. They're friends."

Peg nodded. "That makes sense."

"So, Laura, what's on our to-do list tonight?" Bill asked.

"Just carrying out the garbage and that's it for the evening. You've both been working like slaves, anyway. We're expecting a new shipment of supplies tomorrow, so we'll have to unload that when it arrives."

Bill nodded. "Okay, thanks. At my age, I can use a couple extra hours of sleep."

"Yeah, me, too," Leon said.

"Where's Judd Allen?" Peg asked. "He usually helps you with the lifting."

"I don't know," Bill said. "I haven't seen him all day. Have you seen him, Leon?"

Leon shook his head.

"Well, when he shows up, tell him I need to talk to him," Peg said.

Bill waved his spoon to acknowledge the order and finished off his food. He dumped the plastic bowl and spoon in the trash, and headed out into the gym with Leon at his heels.

Mary eyed him curiously. "Leon's a strange one, but Bill isn't a bad-looking guy, if you don't mind a bald head and a few wrinkles," she added.

Peg frowned. "Bill is a little bit bowlegged."

"And what does that have to do with anything?" Laura asked.

Mary giggled. "Peg's first husband was bowlegged. He cheated on her, so she doesn't trust bowlegged men."

Laura grinned. These two women made her day. "I have some reports to write up, so I'm going to take my food back to the office. Great job, you two." She grabbed an apple on her way out.

Across the room, Cameron saw Laura leaving the kitchen and watched her walk all the way through the gym until she disappeared around the corner before he turned back to the conversation in progress.

"After you eat, we want to show you some pictures," Tate was saying to Nola.

She frowned. "I already told you I wouldn't recognize him."

"It's still a shot we have to take," he said.

"Fine, I'll look. Are they here, or do I have to go to the police station?"

He tapped his laptop.

She sighed and took another bite just as Tate's phone rang. When he saw the caller ID was the hospice in Washington, D.C., he frowned. She remembered that look. Something was up.

"Excuse me. I have to take this," he said, and walked away.

She watched, telling herself it was curiosity and not a desire to sneak extra glances. It was obvious by his body language he wasn't happy, but when he ended the call, she made a point not to stare.

Wade glanced up as Tate sat back down.

"Is it your mom again?"

Tate nodded.

"Sorry, man."

Nola frowned. "What's the matter with your mother?"

Tate's shoulders slumped. "She has Alzheimer's. They just called to let me know she fell and broke her hip. They're taking her into surgery in the morning."

Nola gasped. "Oh, my God. I am *so* sorry. How long ago was she diagnosed?"

He hesitated, then decided what the hell. "Almost nine years."

Her mouth opened, and then she leaned back without saying a word. It had been eight years since their breakup. And she'd found out only after Tate was already gone that his mother had left with him. It hadn't made sense then, and this made it even more confusing. At the time, everyone had wondered why Julia Benton had left her husband, and Nola had already been confused as to why Tate had all of a sudden wanted to leave town, so how did that tie in with what had happened, and what, if anything, did it mean?

"Uh…Tate."

He heard the question in her voice and was afraid of what she was going to ask.

"Yeah?"

"Why didn't you say anything?"

"Because I didn't know."

"Did your dad know?"

Tate pointed at her sandwich. "Are you through eating?"

"Yes."

"I called dibs on the leftovers," Wade reminded them.

She gave it to him.

Tate opened his laptop and then handed it to Cameron.

"Show her the photos. I need to run an errand."

He strode out without looking back, leaving Nola

with more unanswered questions. When she looked back at his partners, they both shook their heads.

"Don't ask us. We didn't even know his dad was a coroner," Cameron said.

"I got the impression that his father was dead," Wade added. "It's sure a shame about his mom. So, scoot over here by me. They're obviously mug shots, and we don't want anyone to wonder why you're looking at them."

She did as Wade had asked, looking carefully through the array.

"I'm sorry, but none of these look even remotely familiar. Is that all?"

Cameron nodded. "It's okay. We had to try. You've been up all day on shaky legs. Why don't you have an early night? If you can sleep in this racket," he added.

Cameron was right. The gym was like a nest of ants, so many people going in different directions and doing different tasks, with lots of noise and none of it decipherable.

"That sounds like a plan," she said, and after a quick trip to the bathroom with her toothbrush and a washcloth, she emerged with dragging steps and all but collapsed onto her cot. She didn't think she would be able to sleep with the constant murmur of voices, but when she rolled onto her side and pulled the blanket up over her shoulders, it felt so good to be horizontal that she was out before she knew it.

Five

Tate's despair at the latest news of his mother's condition quickly turned to rage. He knew the minute he started toward the house that had once been his home it was going to be an ugly confrontation, but the whole thing was ugly and way past due, so what the hell.

The light was still on in the living room, which was a sign his dad was still up. He skidded to a stop in the driveway, and in seconds was out and headed toward the house in long strides, wanting to get this over before he changed his mind. The moment his feet hit the steps, the hair stood up on the back of his neck. He hadn't been here since the night his dad kicked him out, and this was a hell of a way to come back.

He rang the doorbell, then doubled up his fist and hammered on the door until the porch light came on and he heard the lock click.

The door swung inward. His father was standing there with his reading glasses halfway down his nose and the sports section of the newspaper dangling from his hand.

"What is the meaning of this?" Don snapped.

Tate pushed him aside and strode into the foyer.

"I didn't say you could come in!" Don yelled.

Tate turned around and stabbed his finger against the button on his father's shirt. "I didn't ask!" he shouted.

"I'll call the police!" Don shouted back.

A slow smile spread across Tate's face.

"I *am* the police. Now shut the hell up and listen, because I'm not going to say this twice. I doubt that you give a damn, but Mom is dying. The nursing home just called me. She fell and broke her hip. They're taking her into surgery in the morning, but in the long run it won't matter, because she'll be gone before the bone can ever heal."

The newspaper fell from Don's fingers as he staggered, then steadied himself with a hand against the wall.

"Is it that disease?"

"By *that* disease, are you referring to the one you refused to acknowledge she had? 'That disease' has already destroyed her, but it isn't what's killing her. She hasn't known her name—or me—for over two years. She moaned and cried over you for five years, and then her Alzheimer's kicked into high gear and she forgot the son of a bitch she'd married even existed, then she forgot me, and *then,* even worse, she forgot how to tell someone that she hurt."

"Stop!" Don said. "Stop talking. I don't need to hear this. She left me. I didn't leave her."

Tate's hands curled into fists. "If you weren't old, I would hit you where you stand. You know what you did. You are a self-serving, sanctimonious bastard who doesn't deserve peace of mind. Mom had end-stage breast cancer before anyone figured out she was sick, and that was four months ago. The doctor who called me tonight isn't sure she'll live through the surgery, but they have to try."

Don's face was as white as the shirt he was wearing.

"Why are you telling me this?"

"I can't believe you even asked me that," Tate snapped. "I told you because you're still her legal husband, you asshole. She made me promise years ago that when she died, I would tell you face to face."

Don's hands were shaking. "She's not dead. You said she wasn't dead. Why are you telling me now?"

"Because of a fucking serial killer, that's why. There's every chance we will be called away to a new location at any time, and when we're through here, I won't be back. Unlike you, I don't break my vows."

"She lied to me!" Don screamed. "And even then, I forgave her! I told her she could stay! I told her we would get past it! But she packed up and left me, anyway."

"You lost her when you threw me away, and I hope the rest of your life is as miserable as your soul."

Tate pivoted angrily and headed for the door.

"Wait!" Don shouted. "Wait!"

Tate turned around. "What?"

"Where is she?"

Tate shook his head slowly. "Oh, no, you don't get to play that hand. You don't get to make a last-minute run to her bedside to assuage your guilt by being there in the end. It doesn't matter where she's at."

Don's hands were trembling. "But you're bringing her home to bury, right?"

"She issued orders years ago that she wanted to be cremated. It was her way of destroying the disease that was destroying her. I'm done here. Have a nice night."

Tate slammed the door behind him when he left, but by the time he got in the car he was crying. He drove through the streets with tears on his face. He couldn't go back to the gym like this, and he hurt so bad it hurt to breathe. Then he saw the spire of St. Andrew's and headed toward it. He hadn't been in church in years, but he had a sudden need to give his confession.

It was just after 8:00 p.m. when he pulled up to the church and got out. The lights were still on. The door was unlocked. When he opened the front door and stepped inside, it felt like coming home. He didn't recognize the priest walking toward him, but it didn't matter.

"Welcome, my son," the priest said. "How can I serve you?"

Tate took a deep breath, wanting the rage in his heart to be gone.

"Good evening, Father. I know it's late, but would you hear my confession?"

"Of course I will. Follow me."

It was nearly midnight when Tate got back to the gym. The doors were shut, but the light was still on in the office. A stocky gray-haired man with two full sleeves of tattoos was on guard duty. He looked up as Tate walked in and stepped out to question him.

"I'm sorry, sir, but we're shut down for the night. I need to see some ID."

Laura was asleep on a cot in the back and heard the voices. She got up just as Tate was pulling out his badge.

"He's okay, Judd. He's one of the federal agents working the murders here."

Tate eyed Judd curiously. "I haven't seen you here. What's your name?"

The man frowned. "Why?"

"We're checking everybody out, that's why. Can I see some ID?" Tate asked.

All of a sudden the tables were turned and the

man was fishing out *his* wallet instead. "This is a hell of a deal," he muttered. "I come here to help out these poor people, and all of a sudden I'm a suspect?"

Tate frowned. This was the first person they'd talked to who had complained. They were going to take a harder look at him.

Tate took down his full name, address and driver's license number; then, before the man knew it, Tate had snapped a picture of him with his cell phone, too.

"Hey!" Judd said, then turned around and stomped back into the office and shut the door.

Laura frowned. "That was weird."

"Do you know him?" Tate asked.

"Not really. He's just one of the volunteers, but he was cleared by the home office before he showed up. He's missed a couple of shifts, but we can't complain. They don't get paid, so we take what we can get. Is there anything you need?"

Tate sighed. He was tired—so tired. "Just a place to sleep, and I already have that, thanks to your generosity. And, don't hesitate to tell us if you ever need the space we're taking up. We'll find somewhere else to bunk."

"There are no other places to bunk. The motel in Queens Crossing is full, and there are no bed-and-breakfasts. It's these beds or try and rent a motor home from some other city, then find a hookup at the trailer park, which I hear is also full," she said.

"So, you're welcome to bunk here with the rest of the displaced."

He smiled. "And we thank you very much."

"You're welcome. See you in the morning," she said, and went back into the office as Tate headed toward the back of the room.

There were a couple of night-lights along each wall and one at the far end where the bathrooms were, so it was easy to see where he was going. His focus was the woman asleep on the cot between his bed and the wall. It wasn't going to be easy, lying next to her tonight with his emotions this raw and exposed. He felt vulnerable, which wasn't good for the job he'd come here to do.

Cameron roused as Tate approached.

"It's just me," Tate whispered.

Cameron gave him a thumbs-up and lay back down as Tate took off his jacket. He sat down on his cot, kicked off his shoes and then stretched out gratefully and pulled up the blanket. After a few uneasy moments he gave in to the urge and rolled over on his side to face Nola, and then lay watching her sleep.

Once he'd known every nuance of her facial expressions and what every hitch in her breath meant when they made love. Now she was an enigma. They had a past, but his parents had screwed up their future. Now he was just a man in the middle with a heart full of pain.

As he watched, her forehead began to furrow and

her jaw clenched. She was dreaming—God only knew of what, but she'd been through hell, and if he could help it, he didn't intend for her to be in danger again.

When she started crying, he reached out across the narrow aisle and took her hand.

She flinched as her eyes flew open and she found herself looking at Tate.

"You were crying in your sleep," he said softly.

Cognizant of her crowded surroundings, she was embarrassed that someone might have heard.

"Sorry," she whispered, and then closed her eyes. It never occurred to her to object that he was holding her hand.

Hershel was amped. He'd just had his first up-close-and-personal glimpse of his Fed buddies, and they didn't even know it. They had popped up quietly in Queens Crossing, just like they had in Natchez. He'd left them plenty of bodies to play with there, but no clues as to how to find him. And he'd given them plenty to work with here, too. Seven bodies. His most in one location—so far.

It is a sin, Hershel, not something to brag about. You should be on your knees praying to God for forgiveness, not gloating about getting away with murder.

Hershel frowned. "Hush, Louise. It's time to rest. I have a lot of work to do tomorrow. Just because you don't sleep anymore, doesn't mean I don't need mine."

And just to prove he was in charge, he pulled a cell phone out of his pocket and typed a little message to his pals, just to say hello, then sent it to Tate Benton's cell phone. It would be a nice way for Benton to start his day tomorrow.

It wasn't as if they could trace the message back to him, because the phone belonged to one of his victims from the tornado in Dubuque. What they *would* know from the cell towers it pinged off of was that he was here, which was what made it so perfect. He tucked the phone away for the next time, and then kicked back and closed his eyes.

The first news crew showed up just after daylight. The flood was one story, but finding out that the Stormchaser had struck again was bigger news. They got info on a time and place for the news conference being held at midmorning, then headed for the Red Cross station hoping to get personal stories from people who knew the victims, and the more dramatic the better.

It was a baby crying that dragged Nola up from the depths of sleep. She opened her eyes, only to find that Tate had pushed his cot even closer to hers and fallen asleep holding her hand. She was so shaken by the sight that she quickly closed her eyes, willing herself not to move.

She heard him stir, and moments later the weight of his hand was gone and she could hear him pulling the cot back into place. She waited until his footsteps moved away before she dared another peek. As soon as he disappeared into the men's bathroom, she jumped up and headed for the women's restroom.

When she came out, she heard a commotion near the entrance and wondered what was happening. All of a sudden Tate was behind her, whispering in her ear.

"The media is here. Don't talk to them, and don't acknowledge that you know me. Someone here may reveal that you were a neighbor of three of the victims, but all you have to say is that you don't know anything about what happened to them, because you've been sick and just got out of the hospital. Then walk away. Don't let them draw you into a conversation, okay?"

She nodded, but her heart was racing. Reality was catching up with them, making her situation even more precarious.

"What if someone at the Tidewater P.D. slips up and tells them about me?"

Tate shrugged. "We'll deal with that if it happens. Just do what you were going to do today and pay them no mind. The Red Cross won't let them in here, but if you go out, just beware, okay?"

Nola sighed. "All things considered, thank you."

He nodded. "All things considered, you're welcome."

"Tate?"

"What?"

"Why did you and your mother leave town?"

"It doesn't matter anymore."

There was a knot in the pit of her stomach. She had a feeling that if she'd known the answer eight years ago, it might have made a difference in her decision.

She frowned. "That's not fair. It mattered to me then. You abandoned me, and I still don't understand why."

"I didn't abandon you," he said softly. "I had to leave town, but I asked you to go with me. You're the one who rejected me."

Nola gasped. "I didn't reject you! You came out of nowhere with the news that you were leaving, which changed every plan we'd made together for the entire length of our college years, and you wouldn't tell me a damned thing about why. I don't know what was going on, but I know I deserved a better answer."

There was a lump in her throat as she walked away, but she refused to let him see her cry.

Tate was sick at heart. In retrospect, she was right, but he couldn't change the past. He felt for his phone, then realized it wasn't in his pocket and headed back to his cot. It must have fallen out in the night. He found it beneath the covers.

"Want some coffee?" Cameron asked as he stretched, then stepped into his shoes and wandered in the direction of the food tables.

Tate nodded as he sat down to check messages and missed calls. He was scanning through the list when he noticed a familiar number that made his skin crawl. It was the stolen phone that the Stormchaser had been using ever since they came on the case. They'd taken over paying for the number to make sure they had a way to stay in touch with him.

"The son of a bitch," he said softly.

"What's wrong?" Wade asked as he walked up behind him.

"The Stormchaser just sent me a text. He knows we're here, which means *he* must be, too."

"Well, hell," Wade muttered. "What did he say?"

Tate read the message aloud. "'I've been having all this fun without you. What took you so long?'"

"The bastard," Wade said.

"Who's a bastard?" Cameron asked as he walked up and handed Tate a coffee.

Tate handed him the phone, letting Cameron read the message for himself. Cameron's thoughts were the same as his.

"If he's here, why the hell can't we recognize him? We've been at every kill site from the second one on, and we know he's been there watching us. We have crowd shots and film footage from every press conference we've held, and there are no repeat faces in the crowd. What is he, a chameleon?"

Tate blinked. "Actually, that's something we haven't thought about."

"What do you mean?" Cameron asked.

"A man of a thousand faces? Makeup. Disguises. Nola said he was wearing a parish police uniform, remember? That's information we never had before, that he shows up prepared to pass as someone else. And she said he was middle-aged, with salt-and-pepper hair and a mustache. All of that could be a disguise to go with the clothes he was wearing. Go ask Beaudry if he ever ran that info down about a missing uniform. If our killer's turning up with a good ID and a new face at every scene, that explains why we never see a familiar face."

"On another note and speaking of press conferences, who's going to handle the one this morning?" Wade asked.

Cameron pointed at Tate. "He needs to. He's the profiler. We just need to figure out what to say that can force the bastard to get careless."

"Or we'll only make him kill again just to prove he can," Tate muttered. "I need to think."

Cameron left to talk to Beaudry, and came back a few minutes later.

"The chief says the local cleaners reported a robbery just after the river went over its banks. The only thing missing was a uniform belonging to a local cop."

"I don't suppose they dusted the scene for finger-prints?" Wade asked.

Cameron shrugged. "Nothing was destroyed, and the uniform was the only thing missing, so no. They didn't even know it was a crime scene."

"Then how did they know it happened?" Tate asked.

"The cop came in to pick up his dry cleaning, and when they realized his uniform was gone, he did a little investigating, found scratches on the door plate where the lock had been picked and went from there. It was too late to bother looking for prints, though."

Tate frowned. "How did our killer even know there might be uniforms there? He has to be com-ing on scene far earlier than we imagined, using the weather reports to lead him to likely disaster scenes. So where would he stay? How would a total stranger blend into the scenery without sticking out like a sore thumb?"

All of a sudden Tate stood up.

"What?" Wade asked.

"Travel trailers, motor homes. Laura Doyle men-tioned it earlier. There are volunteers from around the state who come to help out at disasters. Some-times they bring their own accommodations. This is the first site he's struck that was so small. All the others were in larger cities and we assumed he was moving from motel to motel. But that isn't possible here, so he could be traveling in a motor home or with a camper. Could have been doing that all along, and we just didn't know it."

"Is there a trailer park here?"

"Yes," Tate said. "A pretty large one, actually. It's cheaper to pay a mortgage on a trailer home than a regular house. So why don't we find out how many volunteers showed up early and see if something pops?"

"You're working on the press conference. I'll do it," Wade said. "Does the owner live on site?"

"He used to. It would be a big white double-wide with a front porch along the front. His name is Jonesy."

"I'll go talk to him and be back later," Wade said. "I've got the SUV. Call if you need me."

Six

By the time the press conference began, a half-dozen news crews from across the country had gathered in front of the police station. Some were airing clips of interviews they'd done with friends and relatives of the seven victims, while others were doing live, on-the-spot feeds.

Hershel was in the crowd of people waiting for news, visiting with strangers and Red Cross workers alike. He saw Leon Mooney lurking at the edge of the crowd and turned away. He didn't want to be bothered with Leon today. It gave Hershel a high to know this news conference was because of him, and he wanted to savor it alone. He liked causing grief to the people in power, just as they'd caused his despair. Then he heard someone call out his name and turned around. It was Laura Doyle.

"Hey," she said as she walked up behind him.

He frowned. He didn't want to have to go back to work right now.

"What's going on?" he said.

"Nothing, really. I'm here for the same reason you are, I guess. I want to hear what they have to say. But, since I'm seeing you now, I'll let you know that there's a truck coming in around ten o'clock tonight with donations. Will you be available to help us unload?"

Relieved that they didn't want him now, he happily agreed.

"Sure. No problem."

"Great. Oh, I think they're about to start. I'll see you later," she said.

Hershel turned toward the bank of microphones, and moments later Chief Beaudry came out, followed by two of the FBI agents. They looked very solemn—a good look when you're the law and you can't catch a killer for beans. He resisted the urge to smile.

Beaudry opened the news conference by introducing himself and then telling the media that Special Agent Tate Benton from the FBI would be taking the podium.

Tate was watching faces as Beaudry spoke, and was surprised to see his father standing at the back of the crowd. It was strange, but now that the dreaded confrontation was over, he felt nothing. The man no longer had the power to hurt him. When he saw Laura Doyle in the crowd, he spent a couple of frantic moments making sure Nola wasn't there, as well. When Beaudry said his name, Tate forced himself to focus and stepped up to the podium.

"Good morning. As you already know, the Stormchaser has struck here in Queens Crossing. To date, we have seven new victims. All seven have been identified, and their families have been notified. A list of names is available on the website of the local paper. I will take a few questions, but we will not comment on the progress of the case."

"Agent Benton! Agent Benton! Can you tell us if you're any closer to identifying the killer than you were before?"

Tate eyed the reporter, recognizing him from Natchez and Omaha.

"Hello, Avery. I see Channel 25 is still keeping you employed."

A few chuckles rolled through the crowd as the reporter stood firm.

"Agent Benton, I repeat, are you making any headway?"

"I just answered this question, but for you, I'll answer it again. We will not comment in any way on the progress of this case, because if I tell you, then you'll put it in the paper, and then the Stormchaser will know what we know and that's obviously self-defeating."

Another reporter shouted out. Tate recognized him from a national news crew.

"Agent Benton, is there any connection between the victims here?"

"Other than the fact that they are all locals, no," Tate said.

Another reporter chimed in. "What about the method of death? Are they all gunshot victims?"

"Still the same," Tate said.

"We already know that the Stormchaser sends your team texts. Have you heard from him here?"

"No comment."

The reporter persisted. "Does that mean you have?"

Tate smiled. "Just because you don't like the answer, it doesn't mean you'll get a different answer if you ask the question again."

Again laughter rippled through the crowd.

Hershel was furious. Instead of focusing on him and his skill, Benton had them laughing like he was a stand-up comedian. This wasn't a laughing matter, damn it! He would give them something to laugh about.

All of a sudden there was a commotion at the back of the crowd. Everyone turned to look as another news crew pulled up. A reporter got out on the run, pushing his way through the crowd until he was all the way up front.

"We've just learned from a reliable source that

you have a witness to several of the most recent murders. Who is it? Is it a local? Can you give us a name?"

Tate didn't blink. He had only seconds for damage control. If they knew this much, it wouldn't be long before Nola's name leaked, too.

Hershel was in shock. He couldn't believe what he was hearing! They were wrong. There was no way they had a witness. Every one of his kills had been out in the flood zone, and he'd killed everyone in sight.

"That's certainly very interesting. What's your name?" Tate asked.

"I'm Jason Arnold, Channel 12 News. What do you have to say in light of this new information?"

Tate smiled. "That I miss days when the media had to verify facts before they said anything to the public," Tate drawled.

More laughter rolled out from the crowd. Hershel's fingers curled into fists.

"I repeat, what do you have to say to this?" Arnold asked

"That you don't have your story straight," Tate said.

"So you're saying there was no witness?"

"There is no one—let me stress that again, *no one*—who saw the killer's face. There is no one who can identify him."

"What about the woman the National Guard

pulled out of a tree near where three victims were killed?"

Tate swallowed the bile that surged up his throat. *Damn it to hell.*

Tate kept his expression emotionless. "Are you talking about the woman who was sick when she crawled up a tree, tied herself to the trunk and passed out?"

Arnold frowned. "I guess."

"Well, that would be the same woman who was still out of her head after they brought her in, talking about everything from aliens to aardvarks, so there is no witness to aid us in any way. Let's hope you haven't already filed that report with your news desk, or you're going to have egg on your face."

This time Hershel laughed along with everyone else, but *he* was laughing out of sheer relief.

The news conference died a natural death after the air went out of Jason Arnold's bombshell. The moment things were over, Tate and Cameron went back inside to find Wade at his laptop running names through a database.

"Did you get any names from the trailer park?" Tate asked.

Wade nodded. "About ten."

Tate frowned. "That many?"

Wade nodded. "Beaudry also ran down the owner of that boat the killer was in. He's a local. He said the boat came loose from his dock when the river flooded and he assumed it was lost, so that lead didn't go anywhere."

Once again what had seemed like a quick fix was turning into another muddle. Tate was frustrated, not to mention worried about Nola.

"I'm going back to the gym. Nola has to be warned about what's happening. If her name comes up, those parasites will come looking for her."

"She needs to be anywhere but here. Doesn't she have any family in the area?" Wade asked.

Tate shook his head. "Not since her mother died."

"What about friends?"

He frowned. "We can't foist her off on innocent people and take the chance of getting them killed. The downside of this whole thing is that she did see the murders, but without an ID on the killer, we're helpless. And she's a target simply because he would want to tie up loose ends."

Tate started to leave, and then stopped.

"Wait. Did we get anything back on the info I gave you about that guy named Judd Allen? The one I ran into last night at the door?"

Wade dug through the faxes that had come in. "Nothing yet."

"Something's up with him, even if he's not our guy," Tate said.

Cameron stood up. "I arranged for film footage of the crowd, so I'll go get that. Never can tell when we'll see a familiar face from another location pop up, although at this point, there's no way to tell a good Samaritan from the killer."

Tate's phone rang. He glanced at the caller ID and frowned. "I have to take this. Hang on a minute."

He tossed a couple of files onto the table and then sat down on the corner of it to talk.

"Hello? Yes, speaking. She did? Good. Is she conscious? Yes, okay. Thank you for letting me know."

He disconnected, then dropped the phone in his pocket.

"Was that about your mom?" Cameron asked.

"Yes. She made it through the surgery, although she's not conscious. I don't know whether to be relieved, or sorry." He took a deep, shaky breath. "Either way, it's a hell of a way to feel."

Wade thumped him on the shoulder. "I'm really sorry, man."

"I know. Thanks. Okay, I'm going to find Nola," Tate said. "When you come back, bring burgers, and get one for her with mayo and no onions."

They both grinned at him. "When are you going to admit you still love her?" Cameron asked.

Tate shrugged. "I don't deny that, and it was never the issue."

The smiles slipped. "Then what the hell, buddy?" Wade asked.

Tate just shook his head. "I'm taking the SUV. If you want a ride later, give me a call."

"We'll be fine. Go take care of your girl," Cameron said.

* * *

Hershel watched as Tate came out the door. He'd been lingering to see where Benton went when he finally emerged. Hershel was of the opinion that if there was more to that witness story than the Feds were willing to admit, Benton might lead him to her. When he saw the man heading for his government SUV, he got in his own truck and followed from a safe distance. He was disappointed to realize that Benton was only going back to the gym. He stayed back, waiting in his truck to make sure Benton was inside, before he pulled up and parked. The less eye contact he had with any of them, the easier it would be to stay under their radar.

The first thing Tate did when he got inside was look for Nola. It was almost noon, and when he didn't see her lying down resting or visiting with any of the other people, he headed for the kitchen.

She was there. He paused for a moment, breathing easy that for the moment she was safe and most likely unaware that her poorly guarded secret was out. He stood, watching her laughing and talking, and remembered she'd once been that free and happy with him.

Then she turned her head and caught a glimpse of him in the doorway, and with a single nod of his head, he told her he wanted her to follow him.

He went out a side door without looking back, and

the moment she exited, he pulled her around behind the gym, just like he used to do to sneak a kiss before her mama came to take her home. The trees were bigger now than they had been when they were in school, the shrubbery thicker, concealing their presence from anyone who might be passing by.

"What's going on?" she asked.

He put a finger to his lips, indicating quiet, and then lowered his voice to a whisper.

"Someone leaked the news about a witness. One of the reporters threw it out at the press conference. I did what I could to squash the information, but it's only a matter of time before they come up with a name."

Nola felt all the blood suddenly rushing from her head. Tate's face was getting blurry as her legs suddenly went out from under her. She grabbed hold of his jacket, struggling to stay upright as he caught her, holding her close against his chest.

"Breathe, honey, breathe. We won't let anything happen to you," he said.

"You can't stop him," she whispered. "You don't even know what he looks like."

Tate was as frustrated as she was afraid.

"I told them the person they think was a witness was actually just a sick woman who was feverish and hallucinating when she was rescued. I said the woman was out of her head, and there was no witness to the killer's identity."

"Do you think they believed you?"

"You know how some of the media are these days. If they don't have a story, they'll make one up."

She groaned. "What do I do?"

"Don't put yourself out there, for sure. I'm not going anywhere. Go about your normal routine inside. Don't behave as if you're spooked, or someone will put two and two together, especially when they see us keeping tabs on you."

She was silent, her mind scrambling to find a quick solution. And then it hit her.

"The locals know we used to be a couple, right?"

"Yes. So?"

"Well, one excuse for us being in each other's pockets would be that we're resuming our relationship. Unless that messes you up as a federal agent or something. I don't know how all that works."

Tate was silent. She actually had a good point. It would allay suspicions and leave everyone to assume they were just renewing their relationship.

He tilted her chin until their gazes were locked. Her eyes were glistening with unshed tears, and he could see her pulse throbbing at the base of her throat. Her mouth was slightly parted, like there was something more she was about to say, but he didn't give her a chance.

He lowered his head, and when their lips connected, he heard a sigh and then her eyes went shut.

He didn't know how she felt, but for him it was like coming home.

When he finally pulled back, she stifled a groan, her eyelashes fluttering as she finally looked up.

"Why did you do that?"

"If we're going to convince people we're a couple again, that is bound to happen. I had to make sure you wouldn't slap my face."

Nola frowned. "After the week I've had, I'm way past slapping faces. I'm just happy to be here, Tate. I'll follow your lead. Whatever you do or say about us as a couple, I'll back you. That way I won't overstep your government bounds, okay?"

Tate smiled wryly. "We're federal agents, not priests. We're allowed personal lives."

"Even on the job?"

His expression hardened. "I'll handle it. Just stay where I can see you."

She wrapped her arms around his waist and hugged him.

"What was that for?" he asked.

"I keep thinking what kind of trouble I'd be in right now if you and your team hadn't showed up when you did."

He frowned. "I don't even want to go there. You're damn lucky you're still alive. Let's get back inside. We'll play this slow. It'll be more believable if we don't become too familiar too fast."

"Like I said, I'll follow your lead."

"You go back in now. I'll come in another door and we'll take it from there."

She nodded, and then slipped back around the building and went in the side door.

Tate circled the gym and went back in the front door as if he was just arriving.

Hershel entered the gym just as Peg came out of the office.

"Oh, good, a pair of strong arms. Do you have time to help me?" she asked.

"Sure. Lead the way," he said, keeping an eye out for Benton, but he was nowhere in sight.

Peg pointed him toward the back door. "Help the other guys finish unloading. It's all baby formula and diaper donations. The driver is on a tight schedule to get the rest of it downriver. They're as hard hit as Queens Crossing is."

This is how you need to be living—helping others. You have to quit this need for revenge. I don't like it.

He ignored Louise's yapping and jumped in to help. The next time he looked up, he saw Nola and Laura sitting in a corner talking and laughing, but still no sign of Benton.

A couple of minutes later, he spotted the man out in the gym drinking a bottle of pop and talking to some locals, and he reminded himself that the guy had grown up here. That was when it hit him that

Benton wouldn't actually stash a witness here, and it was a stupid assumption on his part.

As soon as he finished unloading, the truck driver signed off and drove away.

Leon walked up behind him and tapped him on the shoulder.

"Did you go to the press conference?"

Hershel nodded.

"What do you think about that Fed? Do you think he was lying? That Stormchaser has the sorry bastards jumping through hoops. He's sharp as hell, that's all I got to say."

Hershel's eyes widened in surprise. *I've heard about people who get hard-ons for serial killers. It seems I have myself a fan.*

Shame on you, Hershel! You should not be proud of the fact. What you're doing is a sin and you know it!

Hershel ignored Louise and glanced at his watch. It was almost noon. Laura had already asked him to be on site late tonight to unload another shipment. He had half a mind to grab a burger and go back to his travel trailer to get some sleep when he saw Nola get up and leave the kitchen.

He watched her just because he knew she was a link to Benton and toyed with the idea of killing her, too, just to show the hotshot what real grief was about. He was still watching her when he noticed Benton separate himself from the people he'd been talking to and walk across the gym to meet her. Hershel's eyes widened as he watched them embrace. Their kiss was brief, but a kiss was a kiss. He was still mulling over what he'd seen as he walked out of the gym.

He drove through town to the local café. Calling the place Eats didn't show much creativity, but he knew from experience that while the food was basic, it was good. He walked in, nodding to the people he passed, and went straight to the register to put in an order to go.

"Hey there. I see you came back," the waitress said.

Hershel smiled. "Good food always brings a hungry man back."

She laughed. "Do you know what you want, or do you need to see a menu?"

"Burger and fries, and a piece of that apple pie to go, please."

"You got it," she said. "Do you want something to drink while you wait?"

You like a Pepsi with your burgers, Hershel. Order yourself a Pepsi.

He frowned. *I can make my own decisions about what the hell I drink.*

Don't you curse me, Hershel Inman.

Go away, Louise. You're dead. You don't belong here anymore.

I won't leave you, Hershel. I can't. It's your

fault I'm still here, because you're killing people in my name.

"I'll have a Pepsi," Hershel said, and then rolled his eyes when the waitress went to fill the order. Louise was dead and still running his life.

He took his Pepsi and sat down at a nearby table to wait for his food. As he did, he noticed that the people at the table next to him were from one of the news crews. He sat back, sipping his drink and honed in on their conversation.

"What do you think about the Feeb's excuse?" one man said.

"You mean about the witness not seeing anything?"

"Yeah, that."

"I don't know. It's possible. I mean, the hospital verified that she came in unconscious, with a fever."

"Yeah, but they also said they heard her mumbling something about a shooter."

"It could be that she'd heard about the murders and was just afraid it would happen to her, but since she was out of her head sick, that's how it came out. We don't work for a tabloid, and I'm not into spreading lies for the sake of a half-assed scoop."

That made Hershel feel even better, and he kept drinking his pop with one eye on the kitchen, waiting for his order to come up. He wanted to go home and kick back, watch a little TV as he ate, but his neighbors at the next table were still arguing the point.

"Look, he and the woman they pulled out of that tree, the one who must be the witness, what's her name...? Landry. Nola Landry. They used to be an item. What if he spun that story to protect her? What if he lied?"

"He's a federal agent."

The guy laughed. "I repeat...what if he lied?"

Hershel choked on his pop and it came out through his nose.

"Son of a bitch," he muttered, as he grabbed a handful of napkins and cleaned himself off.

The waitress came back to the counter carrying a brown paper bag.

"Here you go, honey. Your order is ready."

Hershel whipped out a twenty-dollar bill.

"Keep the change," he said as he grabbed the bag and headed for the door.

Hershel! You didn't wait for your change. Why did you tip her that much? What were you thinking?

He slid into his truck seat, slammed the door and started the engine.

"Louise, I need you to stop talking now. My head hurts. I'm tired, and I'm hungry. Go away."

You're going to be sorry one of these days that you didn't listen to me. Mark my words. You're going to be sorry.

"I already am!" he shouted. "Now shut the fuck up. I mean it."

He drove the rest of the way home in blessed silence, ate his food without tasting it and showered before crawling into bed. He set the alarm to make sure he didn't oversleep and miss his night shift, and was out within minutes.

Cameron and Wade showed up just before 5:00 p.m. with fresh bandages and antiseptic for Nola's wrists, and a bag of burgers and fries from Eats. They spotted Tate and Nola sitting on a cot, talking.

"Honey, we're home!" Wade said as he set the bags on the upturned cardboard box and began digging out the food.

The kitchen had just started serving the evening meal, and most of the people in the gym were either standing in line to get their food or sitting outside at the dining tables, already eating.

"Smells good," Nola said.

"We got some medicine for your wrists, but wait until after you eat to use it. It stinks," Cameron said.

Tate grinned. "Thanks for the heads up."

Wade and Cameron suddenly stopped, looked at the couple and then at each other. Their eyebrows went up, but it was Wade who spoke.

"You two are sitting together. Nola said something positive, and Tate smiled. What the hell's going on?"

Nola looked to Tate to explain.

"Sit," Tate said, and then lowered his voice. "It was Nola's idea. After the news broke about a witness, with us hovering around her...well, you know where I guessed that would lead. She suggested we let people assume we were renewing our relationship to explain that away."

Cameron eyed her closely. "That's actually a good idea, especially since the identity of the witness who wasn't a witness has pretty much been revealed."

Nola's smile disappeared as she cast a nervous glance in Tate's direction, but he shrugged.

"It was only a matter of time. However, this is the best we can do, and the less said the better."

"Am I in a lot of danger?" Nola asked.

"Maybe. Hang with us," Tate said, going through the burgers until he found the one with mayo and no onions. "Here, this one is yours."

She took the burger and unwrapped it. "Is there any—"

Tate handed her a packet of salt.

Wade grinned. "Well, isn't this something? Just like an old married couple. Knows what she likes to eat and knows she's gonna ask for salt before the words come out of her mouth. What do you think, Cameron?"

Cameron pointed at the sack. "I think you need to hand me my burger. It's the one with double cheese and ketchup. And don't forget fries. I ordered fries."

"I ordered fries for everyone," Wade muttered.

"Yes, but that doesn't mean you won't eat them all, anyway," Tate said.

When the three partners laughed, Nola laughed

along with them, even though she didn't really feel like it. She'd told Tate she would follow his lead, and if this was it, she was game. She took a bite of her burger and dipped a French fry in the ketchup Tate squirted on the paper. She'd never thought about what she might want her last meal to be, and she sincerely hoped this wouldn't be it.

Cameron Winger was kicked back on his cot with his laptop open, but he was watching the Red Cross crew back in the kitchen while the facial recognition program continued to run.

There were a half-dozen or so people back in the kitchen area, talking and playing cards as they waited for the last delivery truck to show up so they could unload it and go home.

Judd Allen was shuffling the deck, while Bill Carter and Laura appeared to be arguing, something about dealing from the bottom of the deck. Two men Cameron knew only as Brad and John were watching a small television set up in the corner of the room, waiting for their new cards to be dealt. Leon Mooney was sitting by himself eating a bag of chips and drinking a Coke, while a woman named Patty was refilling everyone's coffee cups.

Cameron had one eye on his computer screen and the other on Nola, who was at the far end of the gym talking to friends. Tate was at their field office, which they'd set up in the police station, finishing up some reports, and Wade was somewhere outside.

All of a sudden the program signaled a match, and Cameron jumped. It was Judd Allen's face, but the name under the photo was Grady Bell. Tate had been right. Bell had done time, and there were two outstanding arrest warrants on him, one for armed robbery, the other for assault, both from the state of Washington. He frowned. The man only matched a couple of markers on the profile of their killer, and Cameron couldn't see anything in his rap sheet that would lead anyone to think he would start committing random murders. He was, however, a wanted man. Cameron closed the laptop, and then got up and walked to a more secure place to call Tate, who answered on the first ring.

"Hello."

"It's me," Cameron said. "We got a hit on Judd Allen, just like you thought, only his name is Grady Bell. He has two outstanding arrest warrants from Washington State, one robbery, one assault, but I don't think he's our killer. You need to let the chief know. Maybe they can get him out of here without alerting anyone to what's going on. I'd hate to do anything to scare these people. They've been through enough."

"I knew he was jumpy about something," Tate said. "I'll tell Beaudry. Is Nola okay?"

"Yes. She's at the far end of the gym visiting with some friends."

"Okay. I'm just about done here. I'll be back before long."

"See you soon," Cameron said, and hung up.

When he walked back into the gym area he checked on Nola, then glanced toward the kitchen. The truck they'd been waiting on must have arrived. The card game had been abandoned, and the back door was open. As he watched, the crew began wheeling in dollies loaded with freight. He walked back that way and caught Laura coming in with an armload of paper products.

"Can I talk to you a minute?"

"Sure," she said. "Let me put this stuff down and I'll be right with you."

Cameron shoved his hands in his pockets and smiled, then nodded at Brad and John as they came in carrying boxes.

"How's it going?" he asked.

"Long day," Brad said.

"Not bad," John added. "I had a nap earlier."

Patty was unloading a dolly just inside the storeroom.

"Who slept?" she asked, as she poked her head out the door.

"John did," Brad said, and laughed.

Patty shook her head. "That beauty sleep didn't

do you much good. Come help me put this stuff up on the shelf. I'm too short to reach."

"Why sure, shrimp. I'll just take my ugly self right in there and help you out."

They all laughed, which was good, because when Allen came in, he looked startled to see an FBI agent in the kitchen.

Cameron didn't look at him. He didn't want to spook him. And as soon as Laura came out, they walked away.

"So, is there a problem?" she asked.

"Yes. Your Judd Allen has two outstanding arrest warrants from the state of Washington, only his real name is Grady Bell. Beaudry should be on his way over here to take him into custody. I'd like to do it with as little fuss as possible."

She groaned. "Oh, no. I can't believe he slipped under our radar. We've just been so overwhelmed that we gladly take any semi-local help we can get."

"I don't think he's a local," he said.

She frowned. "Oh. Well, I know he's been staying at the local trailer park, because he's one of the volunteers who came in early. He was already here when we arrived. Said he was down from Natchez. Said he'd heard some of the Red Cross there talking about setting up down here, as well, so I just figured that's where he was from."

Cameron's heart skipped a beat. "You're serious?"

"Yes, why?"

"Don't let on about anything. Just find a log sheet or something from your office and carry it back like you were checking on what just came in. I've got to get hold of Tate and Wade."

"Wade is outside where we're unloading. I was just talking to him."

"Thanks," Cameron said. "I've got to go. If we're lucky, this could be it."

Seven

Cameron checked on Nola's whereabouts one last time, then put in a call to Tate as he headed outside.

Tate answered on the first ring. "I'm already on my way."

"I was just talking to Laura, and she said Allen was one of the volunteers who came in early and is staying at the trailer park. He told her he'd been in Natchez and heard them talking about setting up farther downriver, so he thought he'd come lend a hand."

"Son of a bitch," Tate muttered. "Keep an eye on him. We don't want him to get away."

"Will do," Cameron said as Wade appeared around the corner of the building. Cameron waved him over.

"What's going on?" Wade asked.

"We may have a break in the case. Judd Allen, real name Grady Bell, has two outstanding warrants for armed robbery and assault in Washington State.

Beaudry is on his way to arrest him now, and Laura just told me the man came in as one of the early volunteers, that he was in Natchez and heard they were going to be setting up here, so he came ahead to help. He's staying at the trailer park, too."

"He was on the list the trailer park manager gave me, but I didn't get any hits on the name Judd Allen. Now I know why. So what's our plan?"

"You go around back and make sure he doesn't leave that way. I'll watch him from in here, and when Tate and Beaudry's people get here, we'll take him into custody."

Wade nodded, and headed around to the back of the gym.

When Cameron went back inside he caught sight of Nola going into the women's restroom, so he headed to the kitchen.

When he walked in the room was empty, and for a moment, he thought Bell had gotten away. Then Laura and Bill walked in from outside, laughing at something Brad and John were saying as they came in behind. Last was Judd Allen, who went to the sink to wash his hands. Leon and Patty were nowhere in sight.

When Hershel saw the Fed standing in the doorway, the hair rose on the back of his neck. He wasn't in any criminal database, and he had never left any DNA behind—not that it mattered, anyway. That was the perk of committing murders in the middle of a disaster site. Everything was contaminated, including his crime scenes. But seeing the Fed immediately reminded him of Nola Landry. He was convinced now that she had seen him committing murder, and even though no one believed her and she would never be able to identify him, it was still a mistake. He couldn't have mistakes. The last time he'd made a mistake, Louise had died. He needed to get rid of her now and, as an added bonus, destroy Benton, as well.

His pistol was in the truck, hidden in a secret compartment, but he couldn't use it here, anyway. They would be on him in seconds once they heard it go off. He thought of the switchblade under the seat. A silent weapon, that was what he needed—that and a few seconds alone with her. One slash across her throat and she would be history.

"Hey, Laura, what time do you need me to come in tomorrow?" he asked.

She glanced at her clipboard.

"Why don't you sleep in? We have enough help already on the schedule for the breakfast shift, so how about we see you at noon, okay?"

He nodded. "Sounds good to me. I could use a little extra sleep."

He picked up his jacket, then strolled out the back door as if he didn't have a care in the world. The moment he reached the parking lot, he hurried for his truck, which he made a habit of parking under the pole with the broken light, got in and drove away. But instead of going back to the trailer park, he made a quick turn at the end of the block, came in through a back alley and parked in the shadows.

He grabbed the switchblade, then took off his jacket and shirt, and traded them for a black hooded sweatshirt. He changed his work boots for black tennis shoes, and dug through another box for a quick facial disguise. He chose the same thick mustache he'd used with the stolen uniforms, and got the same wig. There wouldn't be much of it visible under the hood, but just in case someone spotted him, he would fit what little description Nola Landry might have given.

He still didn't know how he was going to get her away from the cops, but he was willing to wait for the opportunity. He already had a hiding place in mind and knew he could get there without being seen. Confident that he was prepared, he palmed the knife and headed for the gym, taking care to stay away from the streetlights and inside the shadows.

He walked in with a group of men, and then separated from the crowd and moved along the side wall with his head down. He didn't look any different from most of the others, with their hand-me-down clothes and weary steps, and he was almost at the janitor's closet when he heard a commotion in the back, toward the kitchen.

People were standing up near their cots to see what was happening, while others began running to get their children. He saw Judd Allen—the police on his heels—make a run for the front door, shoving people out of his way as he raced through the gym.

When people began screaming and running, Hershel didn't know whether to follow through with his plan, or wait for a better time. But when Nola Landry came out of the ladies' restroom, he had his answer. His target had just been delivered straight into his arms.

Nola was in the bathroom when she heard the uproar, and when people began screaming, she ran out to see what was going on. She could see the police, and someone running, and she got a glimpse of Tate before the crowd moved in front of her. She was debating whether to stay where she was or try to get back to her cot, when a masculine arm suddenly snaked around her neck and yanked her backward. She saw the knife from the corner of her eye, and without thinking, she rammed an elbow in her attacker's belly, then stomped hard on the top of his foot.

When her assailant grunted in pain, she leaped forward, trying to twist out of his grasp. Just as she broke free, the back of her arm began to burn. She ran out of the gym screaming Tate's name, and didn't look back.

Beaudry and his deputies had Allen in handcuffs and were taking him to the patrol car when Nola came running out of the gym, screaming.

Tate spun toward the sound, saw her running and covered the distance between them in seconds. As soon as he caught her up in his arms, he saw the blood.

She was shaking, both from the shock and the pain.

"Behind me. He was behind me," she gasped.

Tate's heart sank. She'd just given them confirmation that Bell wasn't their killer.

Cameron was already running back into the gym, trying to get past the people who were spilling out in panic.

Tate grabbed his cell phone.

"Wade! He just attacked Nola. He's in the gym." Then he thrust her into a deputy's arms. "Call an ambulance. Put her in a squad car ASAP, and don't leave her alone."

"Yes, sir," the deputy said.

Nola couldn't stop shaking, and watching Tate running into the gym with his gun drawn only added to her panic.

Another deputy appeared with some towels and wrapped them around her arm before they put her into the squad car.

By the time Tate got into the gym, Wade and Cameron were coming to meet him.

"There's no one here!" Wade shouted. "He ran out with the crowd."

They did a one-eighty and flew out the door, but

there was nothing to see, no one to chase, just a huge crowd of anxious parents and crying children.

Furious, Tate turned and headed around the building to the patrol car. Nola was in the backseat, in obvious pain.

"Where's the ambulance?" he asked.

"Already on a run outside of town, and something's wrong at the hospital. They lost power and are having trouble getting the backup generator going," the deputy said.

Tate opened the door of the squad car, picked Nola up in his arms and headed for the government SUV. Wade was already behind the wheel, and Cameron was holding the door open for them to get in.

Cameron looked back. Laura was trying to quell the panicked crowd. He felt sick. It was their presence that had caused this. They couldn't stay here again.

Tate could tell Nola was in shock and made a decision he hoped he wouldn't regret.

"Power is out at the hospital and the backup generator isn't working. Drive to the police station," he said.

"But what about her arm?" Wade asked.

"Just drive," Tate said, and pulled out his phone. He punched in a number and waited for it to ring.

Don Benton had fallen asleep in his recliner watching the late-night news, and when his phone began to ring, he jumped. It had been a lot of years since he'd gotten a call in the middle of the night, but his reaction was instinctive as he grabbed it on the second ring.

"Hello?"

"Dad, it's me. Don't hang up. The killer attacked Nola at the gym. Her arm is cut badly. It needs stitches, and the power is out at the hospital. We're on our way to the police station. Bring your bag. Please. It's not for me. It's for her."

Don didn't hesitate. "I'm on my way."

Cameron glanced over his shoulder at Tate's face. "Is he coming?"

Tate nodded. The towel the deputy had wrapped around Nola's arm was soaked with blood.

"I think I'm going to be sick," she mumbled.

"Close your eyes and take a deep breath, then exhale slowly," Tate said. "You can do this, honey. We're almost there."

Seconds later Wade skidded to a stop in the parking lot and jumped out, his gun drawn. There was no way of knowing if the killer was hiding somewhere with a gun, waiting to finish her off.

Cameron came out armed, as well, opened the door for Tate and then covered them as he carried her inside the station.

Allen aka Bell was being booked as they came in the front door. The chief took one look at the woman in Tate's arms, then the blood and the weapons, and pointed at a deputy.

"Put the prisoner in holding," he commanded, and had his hand on his weapon as he headed toward the door. "What happened?"

"The killer just attacked her inside the gym. He got away in the chaos. The power is out at the hospital, and Dad's on the way here to stitch her up. We'll be in our field office. When he gets here, bring him up."

"Lord, Lord," Beaudry mumbled, and headed down the hall to make sure they got Allen in a cell before anything else came loose.

Nola barely knew where she was and couldn't stop shaking, but she heard Tate's voice and knew she was safe.

"Move all that stuff off the table," Tate said as they entered their office.

Wade and Cameron began stacking files and moving equipment. When the table was clear, Tate laid her on it. She moaned.

"Nola, can you hear me?"

"Yes."

"Did you see him?" he asked.

"No. He was behind me. All I saw was an arm and then the knife. It happened so fast."

Tate was furious. No matter what they did, the bastard stayed one step ahead of them. He was trying to stop the flow of blood from her arm when his father arrived, issuing orders without bothering to say hello.

"There are clean towels in this bag, and a large bottle of antiseptic wash. Put a couple of towels under her arm. Tate, you know what to do. Clean the area so I can see what we're up against. If he cut deep into the muscle, she may need surgery."

Nola groaned.

That was when Don realized she was conscious and patted her shoulder.

"I apologize, Nola. My usual patients aren't able to hear me. I'm afraid I've lost my bedside manner."

She heard him, but she was shaking so hard she couldn't answer.

"She's going into shock," Don snapped as they rolled her over onto her stomach to get easier access to the wound. "Hurry."

Tate was working as fast as he could, swabbing the arm with the antiseptic wash to clean the area around the wound.

"There's a bleeder here somewhere," he muttered. "Take a look."

Don was already gloved up and had his instruments at the ready when he moved into place. He began injecting the area with Novocaine to numb it against what he was about to do. His patients weren't the kind who felt pain, and it was all he could get his hands on at this time of night. He hoped he had enough to do the job.

Nola moaned and then passed out.

"Good. Maybe I can finish before she comes to," Don said. "Somebody bring me some more light."

Cameron grabbed a large flashlight from their gear and aimed it down into the wound.

"A little to the right and up," Don said.

Cameron adjusted the angle.

"There. I see it," Don said, and moments later clamped the large vein that had been slashed and tied it off.

The ensuing minutes were almost silent, except for Don's occasional request or demand. The other men stood motionless around the table, watching him work.

Beaudry came in, but he stood back and kept silent, too.

"She's waking up," Tate said briefly.

"I'm almost finished," Don said.

Nola moaned. Tate grabbed her other hand and squeezed it lightly to let her know he was there.

"You're okay. Lie still."

She blinked and then opened her eyes.

"Where am I?"

"At the police station," he said. "Dad is sewing up your arm."

She moaned. "It hurts."

Don frowned. "I gave her all the Novocaine

I had—sorry. Just two more stitches and we're through."

Nola moaned as the needle went into her flesh.

Tate frowned. "Dad. Stop!"

"No...just finish it," Nola begged.

Don didn't hesitate. Moments later he clipped the surgical thread, then wiped the surface again with antiseptic swabs.

"It's the best I can do under less than sterile conditions," he said, and then began bandaging up the wound.

"I can do a decent field dressing," Tate said. "Do you have something you can give her for pain?"

"I don't have a regular doctor bag, you know. I just gathered up what I could find. Nola, are you allergic to anything?" Don asked.

She groaned again as another wave of pain wracked her body. "No, not allergic."

He peeled off the surgical gloves, then dug around in his bag until he found something that would work, filled a syringe and gave her a shot.

"This should knock her out."

"Write the prescriptions for whatever you think she needs. We'll get them filled," Tate said.

Don frowned. "Happy to oblige if I can find a prescription pad. I keep repeating myself, this is not what I do for a living." He dug around in the bag again, then shook his head. "I'll go see if there's one down in the morgue. I'll be right back." He hurried out of the room.

A few minutes later, he was back. He handed Tate one for an antibiotic to combat infection and one for pain, then gathered up his things. He paused, adding as an afterthought, "You have my number," and walked out.

"That was weird," Cameron said. "Nice of him to help out, but weird."

Tate didn't care. Nola had gotten what she needed. The braid in her hair was coming down and there was blood all over her, but she was alive. He leaned down and brushed the hair from her forehead.

"Hey, honey, is that shot kicking in yet?"

"I feel like I'm floating."

"That's good. Just hang in there with us while we figure out what to do with you."

Cameron shoved his hands in his pockets, remembering the chaos they'd left Laura in the middle of when they'd driven away.

"We can't go back to the gym, it's too dangerous for the families," he said.

"That goes without saying," Tate said. "But we need to put her someplace safe."

"I have four empty cells," Beaudry said.

"Where's Allen? I don't want to sleep next to him," Wade muttered.

"In a holding cell just behind the front desk. The other cells are in the back, down on the first floor."

"We'll take you up on that," Tate said.

"Give me some time to make sure it's clean enough to bring her down," Beaudry said, and left again.

"Cameron and I will go to the gym and get our things," Wade said.

"So sorry…" Nola said.

"It's not your fault. None of it is your fault," Tate said.

But she kept remembering the people running, scared out of their minds, and all because of her and the man who wanted her dead. Her thoughts were beginning to muddle, and it was hard to come up with the right words.

"Scared them."

"We know that, but if anyone is to blame, it's us for putting you there," Wade said. "We knew the killer was irrational. Finding out there was a witness to his crimes probably pushed him into taking a chance in a public place. Now wait here. We'll be back soon."

"Hey!" Tate said, and pulled the prescriptions out of his pockets. "Find the pharmacist, even if you have to get him out of bed, and get these filled."

"Will do," Cameron said.

As the two agents left, Nola reached for the bandages on her arm.

"No," Tate said. "Just close your eyes and let go."

"Stay with me?"

"I'm here," he said.

She clutched his hand and took a deep breath as her grip loosened, then went limp.

He ran a finger down the curve of her cheek, where the abrasions were healing, then leaned down and whispered in her ear, "I *am* here, baby, and I'll never leave you again."

She sighed but didn't move, and he didn't care. He would say it again, when the time was right.

Hershel pulled up to his motor home and got out on the run. The moment he was inside, he locked the door and began to undress. He yanked off the wig and mustache, and tossed them on his bed, pulled the hooded sweatshirt over his head, then stripped and tossed everything in the little washer and started it up. His switchblade was as bloody as his clothes, and he took it to the kitchen, threw it in the sink and covered it with bleach.

He was so pissed he couldn't think. Even though he'd cut her, it wasn't life-threatening. His first mistake had been in leaving a live one behind. He wondered where she had been, and which victims she had seen him kill. He knew she was up a tree, but there had been half-submerged trees all up and down the flooded river.

And now, when he'd tried to eliminate her, she'd escaped him once more, and that was *not* okay. Mistakes had to be corrected. It was how you lived life. When you know better, you do better.

That's what Oprah always said. When you know better, you do better. Remember, Hershel? Remember how I always liked to watch my afternoon shows?

"Stop talking to me, Louise. Oprah can't help me, and I need to think."

You did something bad again, didn't you? Answer me, Hershel! Did you hurt someone again? Did you commit another murder?

Hershel walked from one end of the motor home to the other, with Louise going on and on in his ear. As soon as he got in the tiny shower stall, he proceeded to scrub every inch of his body until all the blood was gone and his thoughts were clear. When the time was right, he would grab Nola Landry and take her back to the place where she should have died with the others, and that was where he would shoot her. If he did that, then all the other mistakes would be erased.

Hershel, that's silly. You can't make stuff go away with do-overs. People are already dead. You can't take back what you've already done.

"They don't know who I am. They don't know

where I am or what I look like. I can do anything I want, and I want Nola Landry to go away. She messed everything up, and I have to fix it."

He put on a pair of sweats, then stowed his wig and mustache and got his other cell phone. He'd put the knife in Tate's woman. It was time to twist the blade.

Eight

The jail cells were small and smelled of industrial-strength cleaners. The floors were still damp where they'd been recently scrubbed down, and the stained and cracked commodes were vivid reminders of the temporary inmates who would have used them, but for the time being, it was the safest place in Queens Crossing they could put her.

Tate had pulled a mattress from another cell and put it on the floor in front of her cot, then spread the sleeping bag he traveled with out on top. Wade and Cameron were in the other cells in their sleeping bags, but no one was sleeping except Nola.

Tate had just emailed a full report of the latest incident to the director and was about to log out when his cell signaled an incoming text. His gut knotted as he recognized the number.

"Hey!"

His partners looked up.

"We've got another text."

Wade ran over, and Cameron followed.

"What's it say?" Wade asked.

The message was like a fist to the gut. He glanced at Nola. Even though she appeared to be out, he didn't want her hearing any of this and handed them the phone.

How does it feel to know your bitch nearly bought the farm?

"Oh, shit," Cameron said softly.

"Up until now, everything he's done has been random. Now he's making it personal," Wade said as he handed the phone back. "He's never done that before."

Tate glanced at Nola. "That's because the only witness to what he's doing happens to belong to me, or at least that's how he sees it. The woman I had a relationship with saw him in action, therefore it *is* personal. And the easiest way to stop me, stop us, is to hurt someone I care about."

"What do you think he'll do? Maybe he'll just move downriver. The flood hasn't crested yet."

Tate shook his head. "He can't. Up to now, everything has been going his way. This is his first stumble, and with his mind-set he'll need to correct it before he *can* move on."

Wade frowned. "She's in a hell of a lot of danger. We should send her away somewhere."

"That wouldn't keep her safe," Tate said. "She's the problem, not me. He sent this message to remind us—*me*—of who's in charge. If she leaves, he'll go look for *her*. In a way, he considers her his jinx. He'll be afraid to continue until he makes sure the mistake has been corrected. The only way I'll know for sure she's safe is if she's with me."

"What will the director say?" Cameron asked.

Tate shrugged. "I don't know. I just sent the report. I can guarantee he won't like it that a personal connection has developed between us, but I've already stated in my report that replacing me on the team won't impact what the Stormchaser does. Nola will be his entire focus until, in his mind, his mistake is fixed."

"Well, my focus is on getting us some new digs. I've never spent a night in jail in my life, and I want this to be the first *and* last time it ever happens," Wade muttered.

Nola moaned.

Tate reached out and laid a hand on her shoulder. Moments later, she quieted down.

Tate eyed his partners. "Go back to bed. We're good here."

Nola was dreaming that her arm was on fire. She kept trying to pour water on it to douse the flames, but the water wouldn't come out of the pitcher. She was screaming for her mother when she woke up in Tate's arms.

"You're okay, you're okay. It was just a dream," he kept saying, as he cradled her in his lap.

She moaned. "My arm was on fire, and I couldn't put it out. I couldn't find my mom. Oh, my God, it was so real."

"It's from the pain meds," Tate said. "They hit people like that sometimes."

But her focus had already shifted to the cot and the iron bars.

"Are we in jail?"

"Yes, but not as in arrested. We're here because, after what happened to you at the gym, we can't go back there. It puts everyone else in too much danger."

"Did the Stormchaser really try to kill me?" she whispered.

"Yes."

She swiped a shaky hand across her face.

"Oh, my God, why is this happening? I can't identify him."

"In his eyes, you're the first loose end he's ever left. You're a mistake. He's trying to fix it."

"I'm scared, Tate."

"I know you are, baby. But we're here, and we won't let him hurt you again."

Nola knew he meant what he said, but there was no way he could keep that promise. Her thoughts were scattered. Her body ached, and circumstance had thrust her back into Tate Benton's life in a way she would never have imagined. Her anger at him was still there under the surface. There was so much about their past that she didn't understand. But now, sitting in his lap with his arms around her and her cheek against his chest, she felt whole again.

"Is there a bathroom anywhere close by?" she asked.

"You mean besides the one over there?" Tate asked, pointing at the toilet in the corner, and then grinned when she wrinkled her nose. "Just kidding. I'll take you," he said.

"I can walk, but I'm going to hang on to your arm. I feel dopey from the medicine. Is that the bag with my stuff?"

He nodded.

She looked at the bloody shirt she was wearing.

"I don't want to look at this shirt another minute. Would you please find something else in there for me? It doesn't matter what. They're all a little bit too big, which is actually a good thing now."

Tate dug through the clothing they'd given her at the Red Cross center, pulled out a large, oversize LSU T-shirt and held it up.

"Will this work?"

She eyed the width of the sleeves and neck against the bandages on her arm and nodded.

Tate walked her out of the jail area, then up the

hall toward the receiving desk. Allen was asleep on the cot in the holding cell as they passed by, and they continued on without speaking until they'd reached the ladies' room.

"This is it, but I don't know how clean it will be."

Nola sighed. "As long as it's private, I can manage."

"You're not too dizzy or anything?" he asked.

"I'm okay. Wait for me?"

"Absolutely. Here's your shirt."

"Thank you," she said, and went inside.

He was still standing in the hall when Wade and Cameron came down from the field office upstairs.

"Where's Nola?" Wade asked.

Tate pointed to the bathroom. "What have you been doing?"

"Talking to Jonesy out at the trailer park," Wade said. "When I was out there the other day I remembered him saying he's a night owl, so I called and told him our dilemma. He has two trailer houses he rents out and one just turned up empty. The people who'd been staying there were in the same fix as Nola. Jonesy said they just left to go stay upstate with family, since their home is underwater. The trailer is the deluxe model, whatever that means, and he's already cleaned it out, so if we want to take a chance on staying there, given the fact that our killer could be there, too, we have a place to go tomorrow."

Tate shrugged. "Truth is, we don't know where

the bastard is. We took her to the Red Cross shelter and look what happened. At least we'll be more isolated in the trailer park and can see who's coming and going. It's the best we can do under the circumstances. Good work."

The bathroom door opened, and Nola came out carrying her bloody shirt.

"What's going on? Is something wrong?" she asked.

"We were just telling Tate we found a new place to stay out at the trailer park," Wade said.

"I thought they were all full."

"A trailer house just came up empty. Jonesy offered to rent it to us," he said.

Nola's eyes widened. "Jonesy offered us a place to stay?"

"Yes, why?"

"It's not the deluxe model he rents out is it?"

Cameron groaned. "What don't we know?"

"It's supposed to be haunted," she said.

Wade frowned. "Well, shit."

"As long as our killer isn't in residence, I'm good with it," Tate said. "It's after 2:00 a.m. and you, young lady, need to lie back down."

"Can I take another pain pill?" she asked.

"Yes."

"Then I'll follow you anywhere."

A few minutes later she was back on the cot in her jail cell, tucked safely inside the sleeping bag and waiting for the pain pill to kick in. Tate positioned himself between her and the door, and Wade and Cameron were settling down in the other cells.

She finally fell asleep, and so did the others.

Except for Tate. He wasn't sleeping. He wasn't even lying down. He was sitting up with his back to the cot, his pistol in his lap, watching the door.

Every so often he heard Nola mumbling in her sleep and guessed she was dreaming again. Those pain pills were kicking her butt.

Just before dawn his cell phone vibrated, signaling a call. He saw the number, jumped to his feet and ran out into the hall to answer.

"Hello. This is Tate Benton."

"Mr. Benton, this is Doctor Andreas. I'm sorry to tell you that your mother passed away about an hour ago. She did not suffer. She took a deep breath, exhaled and never took another."

Tate had been expecting this, and yet he felt the bottom falling out of his world. In every way that mattered, she was all the family he had left, and even though she hadn't recognized him for years, he was surprised by the depth of his grief. His voice was shaky.

"Did you call her husband?"

"Yes. He's on record as one of two notifications that were to be made. You are the other one."

Tate was grateful. That meant he didn't have to talk to his father again.

"Thank you for taking care of her all these years."

"Of course. I'm sorry this was how it ended…with her breaking her hip, I mean."

"So am I," Tate said. "I assume you know the situation I'm in."

"Yes, yes. You and I have spoken about this at length. Have no fear. I will carry out your mother's last wishes. The crematorium has been notified. They will pick up her body in the morning and will wait for you to claim her ashes."

"Thank you for calling," Tate said.

"She is no longer suffering, Mr. Benton."

"I know, and that's the only thing that makes this bearable," Tate whispered, then disconnected.

He dropped his cell phone in his pocket, then turned to the wall and closed his eyes, glad he'd had the foresight to go by and see her before they'd begun this chase. Hot tears rolled down his face, but he wasn't crying for the woman who had died. He was crying for the woman she had been. It was finally over, and she was at peace. Now he had to find his own.

He stood for a few minutes until he got his emotions under control, then wiped his face with the heels of his hands and strode back into the jail.

He watched everyone sleep and thought how strange it was that life could be this way. One person's world was crashing, one was being stalked by a serial killer, and everyone else went on as if nothing was wrong.

Don Benton was bereft. It was an old-fashioned word that his mother had been fond of using, and it fit his feelings perfectly. Even though he hadn't seen his wife in over eight years and had never forgiven her, he had not been able to stop loving her. It was a joke life had played on him, but he wasn't laughing.

Despite himself, his thoughts turned to Tate. He would be devastated, but that was none of his concern. He poured himself a stiff drink and downed it like medicine. His hand was shaking as he set the glass on the bar, so he poured one more and then tossed it back, letting the burn roll all the way down his throat.

His last responsibilities to Julia were over. He had not betrayed his wedding vows. He'd kept her as his wife, even when she had abandoned him. He was full of self-righteous anger as he strode into the kitchen and began a pot of coffee, then turned on a burner to heat a pan to fry his eggs. When he saw the flame, he remembered Tate telling him she had asked to be cremated. He stared at the fire, imagining the beautiful woman he had known being consumed in such a manner, and all of a sudden bile rose in his throat. He made it to the bathroom just in time, then retched until his belly hurt and there was nothing left to come up.

"Ah, Julia…damn it…damn *you*," he whispered, and began splashing cold water on his face.

He could smell the coffee when he walked back into the kitchen, but he didn't want food anymore and turned the burner off without looking at it again. He poured a cup of coffee and walked out onto the back porch to watch the sunrise.

His career had been built on his skill as a coroner. The condition of a body often spoke a much-needed truth on behalf of the deceased. But there was no one to speak for Julia. He knew what had killed her, but she had never spoken the words he needed to hear, and now it was too late.

A siren sounded at the far end of town. He listened for a moment, then relaxed. It wasn't an ambulance, it was a cop car. Hopefully they wouldn't be bringing him any bodies later to autopsy. There had been too much death here already and he wanted everything back the way it was before the flood—and before the killer came, bringing Tate back with him. Seeing him was a reminder of wasted years and all he'd lost.

Beaudry entered the jail area just after 7:00 a.m. with hot coffee for the team, eager to check on Nola's condition, only to find everyone up and packed and getting ready to leave.

Tate was quiet and unusually solemn, but the chief chalked it up to the seriousness of the situation.

"Hey, where are you guys headed?" he asked.

"We have another place to stay," Tate said. "But thank you for your help last night. It was a lifesaver."

Beaudry handed out coffee while eyeing Nola's pale face.

"I'm real sorry about what happened to you," he said.

"So am I," she replied. "It's a nightmare that keeps getting worse. I keep wishing I would just wake up and find out it was all a bad dream."

"I thought you should know that the media found out you were attacked last night. Everyone at the Red Cross center was talking about it and now they're looking for you all over town for an interview."

She frowned. "Well, that's just great."

"Face it. When you're the first witness to his murders, and then the first person to live through an attack, you're big news."

"But I can't identify him. Not from either time," she said.

"I guess he doesn't know that," Beaudry said.

"It doesn't matter to him," Tate said. "She's a mistake, and this man doesn't allow himself to make mistakes."

Nola sat back down on the cot, cradling her arm, but she was getting mad.

"I am *not* a mistake, damn it. I am a survivor.

I should have drowned and I didn't. I should have been shot down out of that tree, but I wasn't. I should be lying in the morgue with my throat cut, but I'm not. So get me out of here and go find him. I do not intend to live the rest of my life, however long that may be, hiding from a madman."

The men blinked.

Then Tate smiled.

"There's the woman I remember. Chief, again, we appreciate your help. We'll go out the back way and hopefully miss the news crews."

"Where are you going? You're not leaving town are you?"

"We're staying in one of the empty rentals at the trailer park," Tate said.

Beaudry frowned. "I hope it's not the deluxe trailer. It's haunted."

Nola rolled her eyes, as if to say, *I told you so.*

Wade cursed beneath his breath.

Beaudry shuddered. "Better you than me. Anyway, if you need me, you know how to get in touch. And, Nola, take care of yourself, honey."

"Thank you, Chief."

"I'll drive the car around back," Wade said.

"I'll let you out the door we use when we load up prisoners for transport," Beaudry said.

A short while later they were in the SUV and headed to the trailer park. As they drove, Tate was trying not to think of what was happening to his mother's body and forced himself to look ahead to the rest of the day.

"When we get settled," he said, "I want you two to go out to the gym, make sure everything is okay again, express our apologies to Laura Doyle and, without making a big deal of it, find out if any of her regular workers failed to come in this morning."

"You're still thinking it could be one of them?" Nola asked.

"It's our best guess," Tate said. "If there's anyone who failed to show up this morning, we'll make a personal call on him and see what shakes out."

He stopped at Eats long enough for Cameron to go inside and pick them up some breakfast sandwiches, then they took the back roads through town to get to the trailer park.

Jonesy was standing on the porch of their rental waiting for them when they drove up.

"That's a nice-looking trailer," Cameron said.

"Well, it *is* the deluxe model," Nola reminded him, and then grinned.

Wade glared. "This isn't funny."

"Actually, it is," she said.

"If it's really haunted, you won't be laughing," he said.

Tate frowned. "Enough. You guys get the stuff. I'm going to get Nola inside as quickly as possible. The fewer people who know where she is, the better."

"Right," Cameron said, and he and Wade started

gathering up their things as Tate walked Nola up the steps.

"Hi, Jonesy," Nola said.

"Hey, sugar. Sorry about your troubles, but you can rest easy here. This is a really nice trailer. It's the deluxe model, you know."

Nola grinned. "Yes, we know. You remember Tate Benton, don't you?"

Jonesy grinned. "I'll say I do. You turned into a fine-looking man, and you're an agent with the FBI now, huh? That's really something."

"Thanks," Tate said. "Lead the way."

"Will do, and you can sign the rental agreement inside." He went in ahead of them, stopping at the kitchen island to spread out the papers. "I crossed out the monthly agreement part, and we'll just take it a day at a time until you don't need the place anymore. Is that fair?"

"It's perfect, and thank you," Tate said, and signed his name.

"Here are the keys. There are three on the ring. The front and back doors open with the same key, and if something doesn't work, I'm just four trailers down. My number's on the lease, so either give me a call or come knock on the door. I turned the refrigerator on, so it will already be cold, and there are some dishes and a few pots and pans. I brought in some towels and washcloths for y'all, and there's some laundry soap on a shelf in the utility room.

There are sheets on the beds and extra blankets in the linen closet. I try to keep the place move-in ready, but if you need anything, just let me know."

He started out, then stopped and held the door open for Wade and Cameron, who were carrying their things inside.

Wade eyed the interior as if he expected ghosts to pop out of the walls at any minute, then gave Jonesy a cautious look.

"Is this place really haunted?" he asked.

Jonesy frowned. He wasn't happy that the place had garnered such a reputation. It made it hard to keep it rented.

"I've never seen anything," he said, and shut the door behind him as he left.

"Nice kitchen," Nola said, eyeing the black, up-to-date appliances, the onyx laminate countertops and the silver backsplash.

The floor tiles were black-and-white hexagons, and the cabinets were white. For modular housing, it did have an extra flair.

The adjoining living room was fairly spacious, and the hardwood flooring was shiny and clean. The furniture was turquoise sectional, and there was a nice-size flat-screen TV. The color palette, an homage to the '70s, beat the jail cells all to heck.

Nola eyed the small utility area where the washer and dryer were situated and was glad she would have a place to wash her bloody clothes, then wandered down the hall, checking out the three bedrooms.

"This one will be yours," Tate said as he came up behind her.

"But it's the largest. You should give it to Wade and Cameron."

"No, because it's at the farthest end of the house, and for anyone to get to you, they have to come past all of us."

It was a startling way to think, and then she realized it was the only way any of these men *would* think. Their focus would always be on safety and accessibility, and how easy it would be to deter the bad guys.

"I didn't think about that," she said.

He gave her shaggy braid a soft tug.

"That's why you have us. And while I'm thinking about it, if you'll find a hairbrush, I'll fix this braid for you."

She didn't hesitate. "I won't say no. Give me a second to find it."

"All the stuff is in the living room," Cameron said. "We're heading to the gym to talk to Laura."

Tate nodded, then took two of the keys off the key ring and handed them over. He took out a couple of the breakfast sandwiches and handed the sack to Wade. "Get some groceries on your way home."

They locked the door behind them as they left.

Tate began going through the house, checking

windows to see if they were locked, checking the back door and the amount of shrubbery nearby, making sure there weren't any places that would be advantageous for someone to hide in.

"Found it!" Nola called, and then winced as she bumped her stitches. "Oh, my Lord, that hurts," she said, cupping the bandages over the wound.

"I'm so sorry," Tate said, and grabbed a chair from the dining room set and turned it around. "Sit here and eat while I take down your hair."

She peeled the paper back from the sausage-and-egg biscuit and took a bite, while Tate pulled the hair band off the end of her braid and then began undoing it, combing his fingers through its length until her hair hung loose.

"Tell me if I pull," he said.

Nola took another bite as he began brushing her hair.

"Can I ask you something?" she said.

Tate frowned. There were any number of things she might ask that he didn't want to deal with, but it was past time to set some things right.

"Yeah, sure. What's up?" he said as he continued to brush out the tangles.

"What's up with you and your dad? He never used to be so cold."

"I guess you could say we had a parting of the ways."

"Did it have something to do with me?"

"No! Lord, no. Why would you say that?"

"I don't know. He used to be friendly when he'd see me, and after you left, he wouldn't even speak to me. He'd usually make a point of doing something else if we ran into each other."

"That was probably because you reminded him of me, and I was what he didn't want to think about."

She waited for him to explain further, but when he didn't, she sat and finished the rest of her sandwich as he began to rebraid her hair.

"Tate?"

"Yeah?"

"Are you ever going to tell me the truth?"

His fingers were trembling as he wrapped the hair band around the end of the braid.

"All done," he said. "I'll reheat our coffee in the microwave."

"Thank you," she said, and then got up and threw the sandwich wrapper in the trash.

When the microwave dinged, he took out the cups and handed one to her.

Nola accepted it without comment and took a small sip to make sure it wasn't too hot, then carried it to the living room and sat down. With the open concept of the trailer, she could see everything he was doing in the kitchen. He ate his sandwich while looking out the windows.

Once again, she felt as if he had slammed a door

shut between them, and from the stiff set of his shoulders, it was obvious he didn't want it opened.

When his cell phone rang, he answered quickly, obviously grateful for a reason not to have to talk to her. This was the same way he'd acted eight years earlier, and she still had no idea what the hell had gone so wrong. What she did know was that it hurt her feelings, and it made her mad. She had deserved better than this then, and she deserved better now, too.

Her eyes narrowed as she watched him pacing as he talked. From what she could hear, it sounded as if he was talking to his superior, and someone wasn't happy. Well, neither was she. She walked out of the room, going down the hall to her bedroom, and closed the door. He kept shutting her out. Maybe he needed to see what that felt like.

Nine

Tate knew he'd hurt her feelings. Again.

While he'd been trying to figure out how to tell her about the quagmire that was his personal life, the director's call had interrupted his train of thought. When the call finally ended and he turned around, she was gone. He stood in the silence of the room knowing he'd put this off long enough, then followed her down the hall and knocked.

"What?"

He winced. If she was crying, he was done for.

"May I come in?"

A few moments later the door swung inward, but she turned away and walked back to the bed, where she put her arm up on the pile of pillows she was using as support.

Tate closed the door behind him and then stood with his hands in his pockets, searching for words.

"Mom died this morning."

"Oh, no," Nola said, and then started to cry.

Tate sat down on the bed beside her and reached for her hand.

"I haven't said anything to the guys yet. I just told the director."

"Are you leaving?" Nola asked, and blew her nose on the tissue he handed her.

He shook his head. "She didn't want a funeral. She didn't want to be buried."

"She wanted to be…to be—"

"Cremated? Yes."

"Oh. Oh, Tate. I'm sorry. I'm so sorry."

He nodded, struggling not to cry along with her.

"This may sound cold, but I can't say I'm sorry. This is one of those times when death really *was* a blessing. She hasn't been living for years, only breathing."

"Does your dad know?" Nola asked.

A muscle in his jaw suddenly jerked, as he nodded.

"Legally, they were still married. The hospital called him, too."

She reached for his hand and just held it. There were a thousand questions to be asked, but now was not the time, so she began talking about losing her own mother.

"I remember after Mama died, for the longest time I kept thinking it wasn't real. I can't tell you how many times I got up to go look for her to tell her something about my work and then remembered she was gone."

Tate frowned. During all the confusion, he had never once thought about how she supported herself.

"What's your work? What do you do?"

"I'm doing exactly what I always wanted to do," she said.

His eyes widened. "You're painting?"

She nodded. "*Was* painting, anyway. Everything is gone except the work I have in galleries. It will take a while to replace my equipment and supplies."

For a moment the sadness on his face was gone.

"That's wonderful, Nola. You were so damn good in college. I'll bet your mama was really proud of you."

"No more than your mama was of you," she said.

He shrugged. "She had a couple of good years after I joined the FBI, but then she became so confused, half the time she thought I was Dad, and the rest of the time she didn't know where we were or who I was."

She shook her head. "That had to be terrible. Your dad should have been there to help you. I just can't get over the fact that all this happened the way it did."

"I guess you're still pretty mad at me," he said.

Nola hesitated and then opted for the truth.

"It's a mixture of anger and confusion. It never

made sense why you left, so every lame answer you gave me felt like a lie."

Tate ran a finger down the side of her face, staying clear of the healing scratches, and wished this conversation was already over. It made him sick to his stomach just thinking about reliving the past, but it was time.

"So, you already know Mom was diagnosed with Alzheimer's a year before I left, but I didn't know it. Only she and Dad knew it, and he was in denial. She didn't want to tell anyone until she got worse. Said they would all treat her differently if they knew, and she was probably right about that."

"When did you find out?" she asked.

"The same night I came and told you I was leaving. The night I asked you to go with me."

She frowned. "How did you find out?"

"When I got home that evening they were in the middle of a fight. Mom was crying hysterically, and Dad was throwing my clothes down the stairs."

"*Your* clothes? Why in the world would he do that?"

He sighed. "That's pretty much what I wondered, too. I asked him what the hell was going on, and he looked at me with such hate I was stunned. I asked Mom what was going on, and she just kept crying, saying something about secrets."

Nola could feel the tension in his body and tightened her grip on his hand for moral support.

"I started picking up my clothes and went to take them back upstairs when Dad met me halfway up, doubled up his fist and cold-cocked me. I fell backward down the stairs with the clothes in my hands, and Mom went ballistic. I thought they'd both lost their minds. They were screaming at each other again, like I wasn't even there, but I got the drift. It was hard to miss. Dad was screaming, 'He's not my son, and I don't want him under this roof!'"

Nola gasped. "He said you weren't his son? But what—"

"That's what he kept saying. Then Mom told him if he threw me out, she was leaving, too. He said he didn't want her to leave, that he would forgive her. And her last words to him were that she would never forgive him for what he'd just done to me."

Nola felt sick to her stomach. "And you came to me, and *I* rejected you, too."

Tate sighed. "That's what it felt like at the time, but once I calmed down, I realized how crazy I must have sounded. I didn't know what to tell you, because Mom wouldn't explain, and Dad just kept shouting, 'He's not my son!' If Mom had an affair and I was the result, I didn't know how to tell you without giving away a secret that was hers alone to tell. It wasn't until Mom and I were on our own that I figured most of it out, then guessed the rest."

"Guessed what? Who your real father was? What?"

Tate's smile was as cold as the expression in his eyes.

"Oh, Don Benton *is* my father, he just doesn't know it. Whatever Mom said that led him to believe he wasn't, it came from one of her earliest hallucinations. Whatever she was rambling about that set him off, it wasn't real. And he was in such denial over her diagnosis that he wouldn't ever have considered that what she was saying might not have been true."

Nola nodded. "I see what you mean. Like, who would willingly lie about having an affair when it didn't happen?"

"Exactly, and to satisfy myself, I had a DNA test to prove it."

"But how did you get a sample? Weren't you already gone?"

He nodded. "It was actually Mom who furnished the sample and she didn't even know it. The night she packed, she was throwing things into bags and accidentally took Dad's hairbrushes instead of her own. I submitted my DNA and the hairbrush to a laboratory. It came back 99.99% positive that he was my father."

"And you didn't want to confront him with the truth?"

"No."

"But why, Tate?"

"After what he'd done, I no longer wanted him."

"I'm stunned! I'm hurt you didn't trust me

enough to tell me and so sorry for you all at the same time."

"I handled it badly, but all I can say is that I was in shock. I kept thinking I needed to get away to survive it, and naively, I just assumed you would go. When you began pushing me for answers, I didn't even know how to begin explaining."

Nola got to her knees, then put her good arm around his neck and laid her head on his shoulder.

Tate wrapped his arms around her without saying a word, and before he knew it, he was crying.

She crawled into his lap and held him tighter.

After last night's chaos, Laura Doyle was still trying to put the bits and pieces of their rescue center back in order. They had just finished serving breakfast, and during the meal she had explained the basics of what had happened. Everyone had been sympathetic to Nola Landry's plight and stunned by Bell's arrest, but at the same time concerned she would come back and put their families at risk. Once they learned that she was gone, the mood shifted and a new calm began to spread.

But Laura's troubles were just beginning. Because of what had happened, she'd lost three volunteers who were now too spooked to return, and another volunteer had called in sick, and she didn't know if he was actually ill or too scared to come back. When

Cameron and Wade showed up in her office, her concern increased yet again.

"If you have bad news, don't tell me," she said.

Cameron frowned. "I'm so sorry about all this. We just wanted to let you know we won't be staying here anymore."

Laura sat down in her chair and managed a shaky smile.

"Well, that's good news and bad news."

"Does that mean you might miss us?" Cameron asked, trying to tease her.

"I might," she said, and then waved a hand as if dismissing the topic. "So, was this visit just an apology, or is there something I can do for you?"

"Have any volunteers quit after last night?" Wade asked.

"Yes. Three quit and one called in sick. I don't know if he's really sick, or if he just doesn't want to admit he's too scared to return."

"We need a list of names and contact information," Wade said.

Laura nodded. "Give me a couple of minutes. I need to pull up the info." Then she added, "You do realize that this list only verifies their driver's licenses and the fact that they don't have a criminal record. I know Bell slipped past it, but in traumatic situations, no one expects a bad guy to come help the Red Cross, so I can't say how carefully the results are monitored."

"I understand," Wade said. "Right now I just need the names of the people who were here and either quit or didn't show."

She got out her cell phone and scanned her contact list, making notes as she came to the names, and then handed the page to Wade.

"Thank you," he said.

"You're welcome and good luck," she said.

"Take care," Cameron added, and then they were gone.

Hershel had been running a fever ever since he woke up. He'd taken aspirin, but it wasn't doing much good, and he hated taking himself out of the picture at such a vital time. He wanted to know what was going on, but being stuck here in bed, he had no way of knowing.

You're sick because God is punishing you.

He rolled over in bed and thumped his pillow.

"Louise, stop talking. I'm sick. The least you could do is take pity and stop talking."

You didn't have any pity when you killed all those people in cold blood. If I wasn't already dead, I would divorce you. This isn't the man I married.

"You're right. I'm not the man you married. That man lost his mind when he lost you, and this is what's left. Now either shut the hell up or bring me something cold to drink. I'm on fire."

You know I can't help you anymore. You have to help yourself.

Hershel moaned, then threw back the covers and staggered to the bathroom to get a drink and take more aspirin. He made it to bed and collapsed, trembling in every joint. It occurred to him that he could have caught some disease from being in the floodwaters. Every nasty thing he could imagine had been in that water, and after finding that motorboat caught in some debris up against the riverbank, he'd been in that water, too. He'd considered the boat a little gift from the Fates, but now he wasn't so sure.

"Maybe I got typhoid fever or something," he mumbled, and then rolled over and closed his eyes. "And maybe I'll die."

One of the volunteers who'd quit was a woman, and the agents quickly cleared her. It wasn't the arrest of Judd Allen that had put her off, it was the attack on Nola Landry. Until the Stormchaser was arrested, she was sticking close to home.

They understood, didn't blame her and moved on to the next person on the list: a man named Russell Warren. They found him in the backyard of his house, working on his truck. When he saw them drive up, he put down his tools and went to meet them, wiping grease from his hands as he went.

"Russell Warren?"

"That's me," Russell said.

"I'm Special Agent Luckett, and this is my partner, Special Agent Winger. Do you have time to talk to us a bit?"

"Sure. How can I help you?" Russell asked.

"After everything that happened last night, we were checking in with everyone on site, and Miss Doyle informed us that you quit."

Russell nodded. "Yeah, I did. I hated to let her down like that, but the wife was pretty rattled when she heard what went on, and she was afraid the killer might come after her and I wouldn't be here. So, bad as I hated to do it, that's why I quit."

Cameron nodded. "I can understand that. Have you lived here long?"

"All our lives, and we've known Nola and Tate all our lives, too. Sorry about what's going on, but my family comes first."

"Do you know Leon Mooney?" Wade asked.

"Well, I know who you're talking about, but I only met him up at the Red Cross setup. Didn't know him beforehand."

"So he's not a local?" Cameron asked.

"Naw…don't rightly know where he's from."

"Do you know where he's staying?"

"Not for sure, but I think he said something about a travel trailer once. You might ask Jonesy. Mooney could have ended up there."

"We'll do that, and thanks for your help," Cameron said.

Russell nodded, and they headed back to the SUV and drove away.

"So, let's head back to the trailer park. We can get the groceries for Tate on the way, and then talk to the last two men."

Hershel, wake up! You need to get up and take your medicine or you're gonna die like I did.

Hershel moaned. "I'm too sick to get up."

Get up now and get some water or you're gonna dehydrate and have a stroke.

"Oh, for the love of God, Louise. I'd rather die than move."

Well, that's exactly what's gonna happen. Mark my words!

Hershel moaned again. His eyes were burning. His skin was so hot it felt sunburned, and he was so parched that his tongue was stuck to the roof of his mouth. He knew Louise was right, and he didn't really want to die, so once again he threw back the covers and swung his legs off the side of the bed. But the room was spinning, and instead of getting up, he braced himself, waiting for the world to settle.

Finally the dizziness passed and he felt steady enough to stand up. He headed toward the front of the motor home to get some water and was almost there when there was a knock at the door.

"Oh, hell no," he muttered, and kept on moving toward the refrigerator.

But the knocking persisted, and then someone shouted his name. He looked out a window and recognized two of the three federal agents, and sighed. Whatever this was, better to get it over with.

He staggered to the door and then braced himself against the frame as he opened it.

"Yes?"

"Sorry to bother you, sir, but I'm Special Agent—"

Hershel waved off the introduction with a shaky hand.

"I know who you guys are. What do you want, and if you don't mind, talk fast, 'cause I'm pretty shaky on my feet."

Wade could see the guy was sick. His skin was flushed and his eyes were glassy.

"We were just checking on everyone who was at the gym last night when the ruckus started."

"What ruckus is that?"

"When the police were there, and when Miss Landry was attacked."

Hershel staggered, then steadied himself again.

"Good Lord. Didn't know anything about any of that. I left right after we unloaded the last truck. I was already feeling bad, but I thought it was just a passing thing. I came home and pretty much passed out, and I've been in bed off and on ever since."

"So you didn't see a stranger out in the parking lot when you were leaving?" Cameron asked.

Hershel frowned. "Well, yes, I see lots of strangers every day. I'm not from here, you know. I couldn't have said who belonged and who didn't. Look, guys, I'm real sorry, but I gotta go lay back down before I *fall* down."

"Sorry to have bothered you," Wade said.

Hershel closed the door in their faces.

You lied, Hershel. You're gonna have to stop that. Your mama didn't raise you to lie.

Hershel didn't bother answering. He needed to get that water and then get back into bed.

Wade looked at Cameron and shrugged. "That's three down and one to go. What's the last name on that list?"

"Leon Mooney. He's supposed to be in Lot 9. He has a Dodge truck and a travel trailer."

"Lot 9 it is," Wade said.

They got back in the SUV and drove down a few lots, and then came back up on the other side, but to their dismay, the lot was empty.

"Damn," Cameron said.

"We'll stop by Jonesy's again and get the tag numbers on the truck and travel trailer, then put out a BOLO to the Louisiana Highway Patrol. All things considered, this guy took off pretty fast. You'd think the least he would have done was sleep in before getting back on the road."

"But his absence leaves us with yet more questions. Is he our killer or just a man fed up with the flood and all that came with it?" Cameron said.

"I guess we'll know for sure if more bodies show up somewhere else," Wade muttered. "Tate isn't going to be happy to hear this."

"What do you mean?" Cameron asked.

"All you have to do is look at him. He's fallen hard for that girl all over again. He's not going to want to leave her behind if we get sent to a new crime scene, especially with this threat hanging over her head. I mean, who's to say the killer won't sneak back and try to finish her off while we're checking things out downriver?"

"One thing at a time, partner. Leon Mooney might not be our man, just like Judd Allen wasn't," Cameron said.

Wade nodded. "Okay, let's stop at Jonesy's, then notify the highway patrol."

Nola was lying down in the living room, watching Tate sorting through the groceries and thinking of the time they'd lost that they would never get back. If things had gone the way they'd planned, they would have most likely had children by now, and Tate would have been working with Chief Beaudry, or maybe even have become chief himself. Or…they would have eventually left town together and started a life somewhere else. She was sad for what was gone and sadder yet about what had happened to their families. She didn't have any parents left, and the one he still had didn't want him. It was crazy.

Then Tate turned around and caught her staring, and for a moment their gazes locked. They'd come a long way toward reconciliation in a short while, but the future was still shaky. They had to get past this episode with the serial killer before anything else could take place.

"You know what?" he said.

"What?"

"Even though you look like you went twelve rounds with Mike Tyson, you are so damn beautiful it makes me ache."

Breath caught in the back of Nola's throat.

"Oh, Tate, I—"

The front door opened, bringing a brisk wind, and Wade and Cameron with it.

Nola stifled a groan as Wade walked in, talking in his usual bullet-point format.

"Three checked out clean. One checked out of Queens Crossing."

It wasn't easy, but Tate made the shift from Nola to business without giving himself away.

"Which one?" he asked.

"Leon Mooney."

"I remember him," Nola said. "He was that stocky, middle-aged guy with a gray ponytail, right?"

Cameron nodded. "Right. Good eye. Anyway, we got the tag number of his truck and travel trailer, and put out a BOLO to the Louisiana Highway Patrol. If they find him, they'll detain him for us to question."

"And if they don't?" Nola asked.

"Then we wait," Tate said. "If it's him, bodies will show up somewhere else, but if they don't, there's every reason to assume our killer's still here."

That was a kick-in-the-belly answer she didn't like.

"So what now?" Cameron asked.

Nola glanced at Tate, and then got up and walked out of the room. They were partners and he was going to tell them about his mother. They deserved that time together without her.

Laura Doyle was running shorthanded to the point that people who'd come seeking shelter finally stepped up and stepped in for the ones who'd quit.

Peg and Mary were stirring up their usual nonsense with the chili they were making for the evening meal. As if operating shorthanded wasn't enough to cope with, the weather was turning on them again. Another storm system was sweeping through the state and bringing yet another round of thunderstorms, which meant the flood was going to worsen.

People who had been holding firm on their land had given up and were coming into Queens Crossing seeking shelter, and there was nowhere left to put them. The gym floor was packed to capacity with cots, and after a few frantic phone calls Laura had two churches volunteering their dining areas as new refugee centers. She was shuffling supplies and bedding to both places in hopes they had enough on hand to meet the increased need.

And then the storm hit.

Ten

The first clap of thunder rattled the windows in the deluxe model trailer, waking Wade up with a start. Then he heard the wind and thunder, and relaxed. As long as the noise was nature-made instead of ghosts, he was fine.

Cameron had just finished up the report on the day's activities and hit Send when the lights flickered. He groaned as he looked down at the laptop, but the backup battery had saved him. The report had gone through. Relieved, he got up to refill his coffee cup and see if there was anything left to eat.

Nola woke up crying and realized her arm was aching.

The bottle of pain pills was on the nightstand, but her water bottle was empty. She shook out a pill and headed down the hall, meeting Tate coming out of his bedroom.

He smoothed the scattered wisps of hair away from her forehead and then cupped her cheek.

"Are you all right?"

"I need to take this, and I'm out of water."

"I'll get it for you," he said, and loped to the kitchen, with her walking more slowly behind.

Cameron looked up and smiled when he saw them coming.

"Sounds like that storm front finally got here," he said, and poured the last of the coffee into his cup and then palmed a couple of cookies. "Want me to make some more coffee?"

"Not for me," Nola said.

"I'm good. I'll settle for a cold Pepsi," Tate said.

"I just want water…and the pain to go away," Nola said, and downed her pill when Tate handed her a bottle of water.

Cameron gave her braid a gentle tug.

"You've had a rough week, girl, but you're as tough as they come. All we need is a break to catch our man so you can get your life back to normal."

Nola didn't want *normal* back, because it had been too damn lonely, but she couldn't look at Tate without giving away her feelings, so she changed the subject.

"Would you please pass the cookies?"

Tate pushed the bag toward her just as the lights flickered again. Another round of thunder and lightning swept across the sky as the first drops of rain hit the roof. They swiftly progressed to bulletlike pings easily heard within the trailer.

"Great, more rain. Just what we don't need," Nola muttered. She started back into the living room and then paused. "Do you mind if I stay here to eat? I can't go back to sleep until the pain pill kicks in."

"You don't need to ask permission to do anything," Tate said. "Of course you can." He eyed the sweatpants and the LSU shirt she was still wearing. "Are you cold?"

"No, I'm fine."

Cameron emptied his coffee cup and then set it in the sink.

"I'm beat. I'm going to bed," he said. "See you guys in the morning."

"Night," Nola said.

"See you tomorrow," Tate added.

Rain was pounding against the windows now as Nola settled into the easy chair with her cookies and water. She eased her elbow up onto the arm of the chair for support, set the water bottle between her legs and bit into a cookie.

Tate grabbed a cookie and his Pepsi, and followed her into the living area.

"Better check the weather reports," he said, and reached for the remote.

Nola popped the last half of the cookie into her mouth, and then settled back and allowed herself the privilege of watching him when he wasn't looking.

His shirt was unbuttoned halfway down the front, and he was barefoot and in jeans. His short dark hair was standing up in spikes, as if he'd run his fingers through it more than once.

She watched the muscles in his jaw as he chewed and swallowed, studying the bone structure of his face and picturing how she would paint him one day. She'd known him once like the back of her own hand, and now this man was almost a stranger—but a stranger she wanted back in her life. The issue here was, did *he* want *her* back, as well? She desperately wanted to know, but he had more important things to worry about than her feelings, and she had to survive the Stormchaser before she could deal with the possibility of a future with Tate.

"Are you okay?" she finally asked.

He turned to face her, remembering what it had felt like to be holding her in his arms earlier that day.

"Yeah, I'm okay. How about you? Still mad at me?"

"No. Do you still feel like I rejected you?"

He shook his head. "I came to terms with my fault in all that years ago."

She nodded. "Good."

He sat there for a few moments more, watching the changing expressions on her face.

"What are you thinking about?" he asked.

"Wondering if I'm going to live through this."

Anger followed shock.

"Hell yes, you're going to live through this. And then you're going to live a long and happy life."

"It hasn't been all that happy lately."

His chin went up, and his eyes narrowed. "I could change that...if you were interested."

She'd just gotten an answer to her question without having to ask. Her voice was a little shaky, but that was because her heart was beating so fast.

"I'm interested."

"Thank God," he said softly.

A weather warning began scrolling across the bottom of the television screen. They both read it in silence, and then Tate spoke.

"Well, this could amp up the Stormchaser's kill rate."

She frowned. "What do you mean?"

"If he's still in the area, the river will rise even more, and more people will become stranded. He could make a second sweep, which means we'll have new bodies turning up."

"Do you think he's still in the area?" she asked.

Tate hesitated, and then realized she needed the truth. It was her life on the line, and becoming too complacent could get her killed.

"Yes, I believe he's still here."

Her shoulders slumped. "Because of me?"

"Yes, because of you, but we will make sure you are safe."

Nola's eyes narrowed angrily. "You don't have

to sugarcoat anything. I *saw* him at work, remember? Coldhearted, methodical bastard that he is. He pulled up beside that roof and raised the gun, and then—" All of a sudden she leaned forward. "Oh! Left-handed! I just now remembered! He pulled the gun with his right hand, then traded hands and shot with his left!"

"Are you sure?"

"Positive."

Tate flew out of the chair and ran to grab his laptop. He booted it up, then went to a file that held the killer's previous texts.

Nola got up and followed him to the table where he was working, watching as a page opened.

"Son of a bitch!" he said. "Okay, I was right. Now how does this…?"

"What is it?" Nola asked.

"He's been sending us texts almost from the first. His personal relationship with us has become part of his thing. It's like he considers us partners in how his game plays out."

Her stomach suddenly rolled. "Does he know about our prior relationship?"

Tate nodded.

"Is that part of why he's after me?"

"No, and I can say that with assurance. It may be just an added way to dig at me personally for not being able to catch him, but no matter who witnessed his acts, he would need that moment erased."

"Then how does being left-handed mean anything?"

"It's in one of the texts he sent. It was biblical, and it made no sense at the time."

"What did he say?"

"It's from the Book of Matthew. I'm paraphrasing, but it's the one about 'if your right hand offends you, cut it off.' On the surface, it meant nothing. But… this changes his personality profile."

She shook her head. "I don't get it."

"As a profiler, we look at all kinds of things to help us understand a perpetrator. This gets into the psychology of a killer's brain, but for instance, if killing randomly in some way disturbs him psychologically, he *could* convince himself that his sin was absolved by using his other hand."

She was amazed. "How did you learn to do all this?"

He shrugged. "Studies on human behavior and a pretty good instinct. How did you learn to paint?"

"Okay, I get it. Part of it you're born with, and part of it you learn."

He smiled, then slid an arm around her waist and pulled her into a gentle hug.

"It's close to 3:00 a.m. You need to get some rest."

She shivered as a flash of lightning shot across the sky.

"The last time I slept in weather like this I woke up in the water."

He hated the anxious expression on her face and once again was in awe of what she had survived.

"Where, exactly, was that tree you climbed?"

"Remember that grove down past the barn?"

He frowned. "That was a long way from the house. You walked that far while you were sick?"

"Up to my knees in water, out of my head with fever, in the dark, with live critters bumping against my legs, every time imagining it was a gator."

"Sweet Lord," Tate said, and then pulled her close, grateful she was still with them. "Just remember, you're not alone anymore," he said. "How's your arm now?"

"Better. I guess the pill kicked in."

"I need to get you to a doctor tomorrow, and make sure there's no infection and get the dressing changed. That was done under pretty rough circumstances. Is Doc Tuttle still practicing?"

"Yes."

"Then I'll give him a call and get you in a back door or something. Don't want to alert the media where you are and have them camping out here at the trailer park."

"Okay."

"Go to bed, baby. Sleep while you can," he said softly, then leaned down and brushed his lips across her mouth.

"I will. Might be wishing I wasn't sleeping alone," she added.

He groaned. "Don't tempt me."

Nola wrapped her good arm around his neck and gave him a hug.

"Night, Tate. Sleep well."

"I will," he said, and watched her go down the hall until the door closed to her room. Then he checked the locks on the doors, turned the volume down on the television and stretched out on the sofa. He had a clear view of the front door as he laid his handgun on his belly and closed his eyes.

Hershel's fever broke at daybreak leaving him weak and shaky. It was still raining, which meant more people would be stranded, but he was in no physical condition to get out in such weather. He made himself some coffee and had just sat down to watch the morning news when his cell phone rang.

"Hello?"

"Hi, it's me, Laura. I'm just checking to see if you're coming in today."

"No, ma'am, I'm sorry, but I don't think I can. I'm still pretty shaky, and my fever didn't break until an hour ago. If I don't have a setback, and I get some food and rest today, I should be able to come in tomorrow, at least for a half day or so."

"That's okay. I'm glad to hear you're feeling better," she said. "I don't want you to think I'm bugging you, but we really appreciate your help. I'm just trying to allocate the volunteers I have between all three rescue stations."

"Three? What happened?" he asked.

"We've added two churches to handle the overflow, because the gym just can't handle all the new people coming in. You take care, and I hope you feel better tomorrow."

"Yes, ma'am, and thank you for calling," he said.

"No problem. If you need anything, a ride to the doctor or anything like that, give me a call. I'll find you some help."

"I appreciate that," he said, and hung up.

See, Hershel. That's how decent people behave, offering to help their fellow man, not putting bullets in their brains. You got sick because God was punishing you.

He frowned. "Hush up, Louise. I did not get sick because God is punishing me. If He was going to punish me for killing people, He would have just struck me dead, don't you think?"

God works in mysterious ways.

"Well, there's nothing mysterious about my fever, and it's already left me, which is what you should do, too."

I can't leave you, Hershel. Not until you pay for your sins.

Hershel upped the volume on the television because he didn't want to listen to Louise anymore. After a while he decided to try eating a little food and opened a can of chicken noodle soup. When he was a kid, his mother always fed him noodle soup when he wasn't well, and he had a need for comfort. That it came in a can didn't matter. It served the purpose of the memory.

As soon as he ate he felt stronger—strong enough to shower and get out of the clothes he'd been sleeping in ever since he got sick.

He showered quickly, but by the time he shaved, he was already shaky again, and he hurried to get some clean sweats. He happened to glance out the window as he was dressing, and then stopped and stared.

That car up the street looked like the Feds' SUV. But why would—

He sat down on the side of the bed with a grin. They weren't at the gym any longer. Probably kicked out because of all the commotion. So the Feds were his neighbors. He cackled, then slapped his leg with glee. They had been chasing him all over the United States and couldn't find him. If they knew he was only five lots down and could wave at them from his front door, they would break their necks getting down here.

The longer he thought about it, the funnier it became. Every time he went past a window and looked out, he laughed all over again. He wondered if the woman was still with them or if she was in a hospital. He'd cut her good. Hell, they might have shipped her out of the state.

The moment he thought that, he panicked. She couldn't be gone, because that would mean he couldn't fix his mistake. And he had to fix his mistake or he couldn't continue, and if he couldn't continue, then Louise's death would never be avenged.

He began to pace. How was he going to find out if she was with them? Maybe he could just keep watch on the trailer. They wouldn't stay there all day. Surely they had stuff to do. He would just keep an eye out and see what transpired before he let himself panic.

Nola woke up and went to the kitchen for coffee, walking into a very visual image of what their field offices looked like.

They had pictures of bodies taped up on one wall, a stack of files knee-high on the floor and a couple more files open on the coffee table. Cameron was working on his laptop, Wade was on the phone and Tate was pouring coffee.

"Good grief," she mumbled as she walked into the kitchen.

Tate eyed the expression on her face and pointed to the crime scene photos.

"Are you going to be okay with these?"

"Well, I'll never be *okay* with them, but they're not going to make me run screaming out into the yard. Do what you have to do. I just won't look, okay?"

Cameron grinned, shook his head and went back to his work.

Wade winked, and then continued with his conversation.

But it was Tate she wanted, and she went straight into his embrace and gave him a one-armed hug.

"Good morning to you, too, sunshine," he said. "Cereal okay with you?"

"Sure. You pour and I'll eat."

She scooted up onto a bar stool at the kitchen island, laid the pain pill down on the counter and waited for the cereal. When Tate set it in front of her, she hungrily took her first bite. Then he gave her a glass of water and a cup of coffee.

"Water for the pill. Coffee for you," he said.

"Did you put—"

"Two sugars and a shot of milk? Yes."

She grinned. "Thank you."

His phone rang just as she was taking another bite. Beaudry's number.

"This is Benton."

"Morning, Tate. It's me. I got in touch with Doc Tuttle. We'll take Nola in through the delivery door at the clinic, and we'll take her in my cruiser. The media already recognizes your SUV."

"Thank you. When he can he see her?"

"Whenever we get there. You tell me when to come."

Tate eyed Nola's hair and outfit, and knew she wouldn't leave looking that way.

"She isn't through with breakfast. Give us about forty-five minutes and we'll be ready."

"Will do. See you then."

"What?" Nola asked when he hung up.

"Beaudry is going to drive us to Doc Tuttle's office. Hopefully that way we can keep the media from finding out."

She began to fidget, feeling her hair and looking down at a spot on her shirt.

"When? I'm a mess."

"Forty-five minutes. You have lots of time to get pretty. Finish your cereal, and I'll help with the rest."

"We'll all help," Wade added, grinning.

Nola rolled her eyes. "One of you is more than enough."

Cameron laughed, and Tate gave both of them a look, but they ignored him. They'd already figured out that he was long gone on the woman and thought it was funny when he got all territorial.

As soon as she was through eating, she headed for the bathroom.

"I'll yell when I'm ready for help," she said.

Tate nodded.

The other two grinned at him when she left.

He grinned back and flipped them off.

* * *

Hershel was sitting in a chair by the window, sipping coffee, when he saw a Queens Crossing cop car pull up beside the Feds' SUV. Moments later the trailer door opened and Benton came out, flanked by the other two agents. It took him a second to realize there was someone else walking between them, and then he grinned. *She was there.* They had just delivered her up to him on a platter and didn't even know it.

"Hang tight, missy. You and I have a trip to take upriver."

Nola took a dive into the backseat of the cruiser and then scooted down. Tate slammed the door and then got in the front seat with Beaudry. The other two waved and walked back inside.

The chief looked up in the rearview mirror and caught her eye.

"Stay down. A news crew followed me all the way to the front gate of this place."

Nola got on her knees and curled up in the floor as Beaudry drove off.

Tate kept his focus on the news people at the gate, wondering if the killer was with them.

One of the vans loaded up and took off after the chief's cruiser.

Tate eyed them in the side view mirror. "We've got a tail," he said.

Beaudry looked up in the rearview mirror again, and then smiled.

"I've got this," he said, and called up a deputy to stop the van for a broken signal light.

Within a block another police cruiser shot out of an alley and hit the siren in a series of short blasts. Beaudry watched as the driver of the van threw up his hands in frustration and then pulled over to the curb.

"Clear sailing. That's what I'm talking about," Beaudry said.

"Chief, you are getting way too much fun out of this," Nola said.

Tate grinned as Beaudry accelerated across an intersection, then turned down an alley and drove the back way to Tuttle's office. By the time they pulled up behind the office, Nola's leg was cramping. She was trying to get up without much success when Beaudry got out and headed for the delivery door. As planned, it was already unlocked.

Tate scooped Nola up off the floor and into his arms, and carried her inside. The whole maneuver took less than ten seconds.

"My leg, my leg. Put me down, Tate. I need to walk out a cramp."

He set her on her feet and then dropped to his knees, ran his hands down the back of both legs, felt the cramp and immediately put pressure on it, then began kneading it out.

"Oh, that feels good," she said as the pain began to ease. "Thank you, thank you."

He stood, patted her backside and grinned.

"You're welcome."

"Well, hello, Nola. I hear you've had yourself quite a time."

Nola hadn't seen Doc Tuttle since the night her mother died, and hearing his familiar voice brought all the memories flooding back. She was suddenly struggling with a lump in her throat as she saw his familiar face.

"Hi, Doc. Really good of you to help us like this."

He patted her head as if she were still a kid and then nodded at Tate.

"It's been a while since we've seen you around here, Tate. Good to see you again."

"Thanks, Doc."

"Follow me," Tuttle said. "I've got everything set up in the back examining room. Let's get you checked out."

They followed him into the room, and then Tate leaned against the door as Nola climbed up on the exam table.

"Let's see what we have here," Doc said as he began removing the bandages. "Who stitched this up, by the way?"

"Dad," Tate said. "It happened the night the hospital lost power. We had to make a quick decision. He got the short straw."

"Not bad," Doc said, eyeing the stitches, then began cleaning up the wound.

Nola winced as he wiped across the stitches, but it was nothing to the pain she'd felt when it had happened.

"Any infection?" Tate asked.

"Doesn't appear to be. It's healing up pretty well, considering. Was it deep?"

"There was one bleeder, up toward the shoulder," Tate said.

Doc nodded, and then began putting on the new bandages.

"Are you on pain meds and antibiotics?"

"Yes."

"Do you have enough?"

"Two weeks' worth," she said.

"That should suffice, however, I'd like to see you back here in a week, just to be sure."

"I like to be back here in a week, too," she said.

Doc Tuttle looked up. "What's that mean?"

Tate sighed. "The serial killer we're hunting has targeted Nola."

Doc's eyebrows arched. "Seriously? Why?"

Nola sighed. "Because I watched him kill Whit and Candy Lewis, and Candy's mom. I can't identify him, but he knows he has a witness."

"But if you can't identify him, then why does he care?"

"Ask Tate. He's the wizard of crazy people," she muttered.

"It's a long story," Tate said.

Doc shook his head. "I'm so sorry, Nola."

"So am I."

Doc finished the bandages and then helped her down.

"I'll say a prayer for you, honey."

Nola's eyes blurred with quick tears.

"Thank you, Doc."

Tate opened the door, glanced out into the hallway then motioned her out.

Just as she stepped out into the hall a man jumped out of another exam room, swung a camera up and began snapping pictures in rapid motion, then made a run for the front door.

"Son of a bitch!" Tate said. He couldn't run after him without leaving her unattended and had to let the guy go.

Nola groaned.

"How did he get in here?"

"Good question," Tate muttered.

"What happened?" Doc asked.

"A photographer just jumped out of an exam room and took a bunch of pictures."

The look of shock on Doc's face shifted to anger as he strode up the hall yelling at his receptionist.

"Lucille! Lucille! Come here this instant!"

A little blonde came storming around the corner, waving her arms as she ran toward them.

"I didn't let him in! I didn't do it! I swear! I stepped away from the desk to go to the bathroom. I'm sorry! I'm sorry! What did he do? Did he steal drugs?"

Doc's anger was gone as quickly as it had come.

"Okay, okay, I should have known. It was just a shock. Damn news junkie." Doc turned to Tate and asked, "What kind of damage will this do?"

"I guess we'll find out soon enough," Tate said. "Come on, honey. Let's get you home."

She rolled her eyes. "Home?"

"Where are you staying?" Doc asked.

"I guess it's not a secret any longer," Tate said. "We're out at the trailer park."

"At Jonesy's? I hope he didn't put you in the deluxe model trailer. It's haunted."

Nola looked at Tate and burst out laughing.

He rolled his eyes.

"Come on. Let's find the chief and get you out of here. Thank you again, Doc."

"You're welcome. See you next week, remember?"

"She'll be here," Tate said.

When they got to the back door, he pushed her behind him.

"Stay behind me all the way to the car."

"I will."

Beaudry was at the cruiser with the door open and his gun drawn.

"Get in!" he yelled. "There's a car coming up the alley."

Nola bolted for the backseat and ducked inside only seconds before the car coming up behind them sputtered to a halt.

Tate slammed the door the minute she was inside and swung around with his gun aimed.

A young man jumped out with his hands up, screaming, "Don't shoot! Don't shoot! Get Doc Tuttle fast! I found a guy hung up on some debris down at the river. He's still breathing!"

Beaudry bolted toward the car and looked in the backseat.

"There's a body in there! Why the hell didn't you take him to the hospital?"

"I was running out of gas. I coasted down the alley!" the kid said, and then started crying.

Tate pointed at Nola. "Stay there!" he shouted and opened the back door. "Doc! Doc!"

Tuttle came running out. "Put up your guns. That's Jeff Wilson. I delivered him just like I delivered you."

"Doc, come quick," Jeff said, and opened the back door of his car so the Doc could lean in.

Tuttle made a quick assessment of the victim.

"This man has been shot!"

"Load him up in the cruiser," Beaudry said. "It's faster than calling an ambulance."

Nola bailed out of the backseat and ran back into the doctor's office with Tate at her heels. He handed her his phone.

"Call Wade. He's 2 on the speed dial. Tell him to come get you."

"Where are *you* going?" she asked.

He needed her to understand the seriousness of the situation and not think he was abandoning her.

"I have to go with the victim. If he comes to, even for a minute, it may help us catch the killer."

"Then go," she said, and ducked into the exam room as he ran out the door. She closed the door behind her and quickly made the call. Wade answered on the first ring.

"Yeah, what's up?" he said, thinking it was Tate.

"Wade, this is Nola. Tate said for you to come to the doctor's office to get me. While we were here, someone arrived with another victim, and he's still alive. Tate went to the hospital with the chief in hopes the man wakes up."

It was clear from his voice that he understood the urgency of the situation.

"Stay inside and don't budge. I'll be there in five minutes."

"Okay," she said, and then dropped Tate's phone in her pocket and started to pray that this was the beginning of the end of the killing spree.

Eleven

Somehow the news vultures had glommed on to the fact that another victim had been found and this one was alive.

Hospital security had already run them out of the E.R., and Beaudry had finished things by banning them from the hospital property altogether. Now they were camped out on the other side of the street with their long-range lenses, hoping for a scoop.

Tate was concerned that the paparazzi types were arriving in the wake of the legit media, because that was how the guy from Doc Tuttle's office had come across. And now, without a phone, he had no way of knowing if Wade had already rescued Nola up, plus he was worried the latest victim wouldn't wake up.

Beaudry had already left the hospital to interview Jeff Wilson, the young man who'd found the body, and Tate was pacing the floor when Cameron showed up, bringing Tate's phone with him.

"Your girl's safe and sound with Wade," he said as he put the phone in Tate's palm. "Beaudry called. He said he'd take us out to the recovery site whenever we're ready. What's happening with the vic?"

"They're still working on him," Tate said.

"Any idea as to when the attack happened?"

"They made a guess that it was sometime between midnight and daybreak today."

"Damn it. So he *did* start up again after the storm, just like you thought."

Tate shook his head. "I'm not sure. This one is different."

Cameron frowned. "What do you mean?"

"He wasn't shot in the head. He has a chest wound. And all of the others were clean kills. Would he be that far off?"

"Well, he used a pistol on all the others, then used a knife on Nola," Cameron said.

"But circumstances could have forced him to change his M.O. He could hardly use a gun in such a crowded environment and not be noticed. And speaking of Nola, is she really okay?"

"I told you, she's fine. She said she wasn't used to doing nothing, and since she didn't have her art supplies, she was going to cook."

Tate nodded. "She's a good cook. That's something to look forward to."

"What happened with the photographer in the doctor's office?"

"I don't think he's with any of the legit news outfits. He snuck in when the receptionist stepped away from the desk. I think he's paparazzi. Those guys are wily, and gutsy enough to do anything for a photo they can sell."

"Other than create more drama for Nola, it can't really hurt us, because the killer already knows about her."

Tate nodded, but his eye was still on the E.R. bay where the victim was being worked on. As they were waiting, the doctor stepped out.

"Agent Benton, we're taking him to surgery. I can tell you that his name is Bobby PreJean. He's a local, and still unconscious. You won't be able to talk to him for several hours, if at all. I'm sorry."

Tate sighed. "We understand. Thank you, Doctor. We'll check back later."

"Now what?" Cameron asked.

"Let's take Beaudry up on his offer to take us out to the scene."

Jeff Wilson was twenty-six years old and had gone to check the water level, as he'd done every day since the flood began, to see how much closer it was to his home. That was what he'd told Beaudry, and that was what he was telling the two federal agents as he sat in the backseat of his own car and directed Tate out of Queens Crossing, with Beaudry following behind in the cruiser.

Jeff was still rattled and shaking; telling the same thing over and over was stressing him out.

"I live with my mama. Daddy's been gone for nearly two years now, and Mama's been scared about the water, so I go out and check it twice a day. Man, when I saw that body lying on that pile of debris, I nearly dropped dead myself." Then he pointed. "Take a right here at this road. It leads to our place."

Tate nodded.

"How far is your house from the river?" Cameron asked.

"Normally, two miles, but now? Not nearly far enough," Jeff said. "Mama's probably worried herself into a fit. I've been gone a lot longer than she would have expected."

Tate took the turn. "How far from here," he said.

"Another half mile on this road, and then about a half mile back in the woods. Daddy didn't much take to town living."

When they finally reached his house, Jeff was fidgeting.

"I need to let Mama know I'm okay before we go down to the river."

He parked and got out on the run as Beaudry pulled up behind them.

Tate and Cameron got out as an older woman exited the house, obviously upset. They could see Jeff talking and hugging her, obviously reassuring her that he was fine.

"That's a good boy," Beaudry said. "His mama got widowed, and he moved home to take care of her."

"Where had he been living?" Tate asked.

"New Orleans."

The mention of a boy taking care of his mother brought a lump to Tate's throat. He looked up as Jeff came running back to the car.

"We'll take my cruiser," Beaudry said.

"Okay," Jeff said, nodding. "Drive past the barn and follow that road through the woods."

"Am I going to get stuck?" Beaudry asked.

"No, sir, not if you stay on the road."

They got into Beaudry's cruiser and drove through a small clearing, then turned onto a narrow road that led through the trees until they reached a stopping point.

"We walk from here," Jeff said.

"Got the camera?" Tate asked.

Cameron nodded.

They followed Jeff, but by now they could have found the river for themselves. The sound of rushing water was loud, and the closer they got, the louder it became.

Tate thought about Nola stranded up in a tree, hearing all this below her, and thinking at any moment the tree would give way and she would be washed downriver. Once again he was struck by the strength of her determination to survive.

Jeff walked a ways ahead, talking and pointing.

They were within fifty yards of the river when they saw a pile of debris caught in an old fence row.

"That's where he was," Jeff said. "If his shirt hadn't been bright blue, I might have missed him and just thought he was part of the debris."

"Walk with me," Cameron said. "Show me exactly where the body was and how you got to him."

Tate was watching the ground as they walked, looking for footprints other than Jeff's. He'd already identified them from seeing the prints Jeff was leaving now, so any footprint larger or smaller, with a different tread could belong to the shooter.

Cameron was taking pictures as Tate slowly walked the area in a large, expanding circle. When he saw footprints coming out of the woods and then going back into them, he stopped and yelled back, "Hey, Jeff! Were you over here?"

"No, sir. I parked where we parked just now, and I walked in a straight line to the debris pile, and then I grabbed the guy, threw him over my shoulder in a fireman's carry and ran back to the car. I wasn't ever over there."

"Hey, Cameron," Tate shouted. He was about to tell him to bring the camera over when a shot rang out from the woods behind him.

Jeff's hat flew off his head as Cameron shoved him down to the ground and pulled his weapon.

Beaudry's gun was in his hand as he began running for cover.

Tate pulled his weapon as he turned and dropped, frantically searching the tree line. A tiny snake slithered out from under some leaves and took off toward the brush as a large crane took flight from the river.

When a second shot rang out, Beaudry went down. Tate saw the flash of fire from the shooter's rifle and began firing off shots in that location.

He heard a cry of pain, and then a flash of blue as someone took off through the trees in a sprint.

"I'm going after him!" Tate yelled. "Call it in!"

Jeff was on the ground, crying and praying.

"Stay down!" Cameron yelled, and ran to check on the chief.

"It's just my shoulder. I'm still breathing," Beaudry said.

"Hang tough, Chief. I'll get help," Cameron said, and ran through the woods toward where Beaudry had parked the cruiser. As soon as he reached the car, he was on the radio. "This is Special Agent Cameron of the FBI. I have an officer down at the Wilson place. I do not have a specific location, just follow the road through the woods 'til you hear the river. I need an ambulance and backup. Over."

The dispatcher's voice came over the radio.

"I have your location via satellite. Am dispatching backup and ambulance ASAP. Over and out."

Tate was running through the trees without caution. He couldn't get a clear shot at the shooter, and didn't want to stop and take aim for fear of losing sight of him in the heavy woods. The man was at least thirty yards ahead and running in an awkward lope. Tate's legs were longer, though, and he was gaining ground when all of a sudden the shooter spun and got off a half-dozen rounds.

Tate sidestepped a fallen log and took cover behind a tree to return fire, but the man had already disappeared.

"No, you don't, you son of a bitch," Tate muttered, and bolted forward.

Within seconds he caught sight of his quarry again, now running in an easterly direction toward Jeff Wilson's house. Tate's heart skipped a beat as he thought of the vulnerable old woman alone in that house. She would have heard the gunfire and no matter what she did to protect herself, she would either be the killer's next target, or his hostage. Tate needed to get there first. He started running parallel to the route he'd seen the shooter take. He had to either catch up or cut him off before he claimed another victim.

The shooter ducked behind a trio of pines to see where the Fed was, and when he no longer saw him, he grinned, thinking he'd either lost him or winged him, too.

They would be calling in backup, though. He needed to get out before they showed up, but to do this right, he wanted to make his mark, just like the Stormchaser. They would be talking about him on the news, too, when they found the old woman. He would put a bullet right between her eyes. That would put him on the map.

His hip was burning, and he could feel the blood running down his leg. One of the Feds' shots had creased him, but he wouldn't let that slow him down. He lengthened his stride, assuming the chaos he'd left behind him would give him enough time to do the deed. The ground was soft and the brush was thick, but he knew where he was and kept moving in a straight line. When he got his first glimpse of the house through the trees, his pulse kicked.

He burst out of the woods and into the clearing around without caution. His entire focus was on the old woman standing on the porch. He could see her staring off toward the river with her hands clutched up against her belly.

He grinned. Just a little bit closer and she would be victim number three. A few seconds later he stopped, shouldered the rifle and took aim.

Shots rang out, one almost on top of the other.

The old woman screamed as a bullet hit the wall of her house about six feet to her left. She ran back inside and locked the door behind her.

The shooter found himself belly down on the ground, the rifle only inches away from his fingers, but he could no longer feel them. Then all of a sudden someone rolled him from his front to his back. He looked up into the face of the Fed and groaned.

"You killed me," he mumbled. "I would'a been better than him."

Tate was breathing hard as he stared down into Leon Mooney's face. Here was the missing volunteer, but the moment Leon opened his mouth, he realized this was not the scenario they'd expected.

"Better than who?" Tate asked.

"The Stormchaser. I would'a been better than him."

Tate's gut knotted. A copycat killer. Damn it. He knelt down and felt the man's pulse. It was thready and uneven.

"I'm cold," Leon said. "Did you call an ambulance for me? I don't wanna die."

"Neither did the people you shot," Tate said.

Leon's eyes were glazing over. "He was the best. If I could'a had more time, I might have beat him. I just didn't have Katrina."

"Beat who, Leon? Did you know him? Do you know who the Stormchaser is? Who's Katrina? Who is she?"

"Guessed. Saw him watching. Saw him cut your woman."

Tate grabbed him by the shoulders. "Who? Say his name! Who is he?"

Leon shook his head. "Can't. That's not how you play—"

He took a deep rattling breath as his eyes rolled back in his head.

"No!" Tate shouted. "Say his name. Say his name!"

Leon exhaled once and never took another breath.

Tate stood abruptly and then walked away from the body, struggling with rage and frustration. So close, and yet once again, the lead was gone. He heard a siren, then looked down the road toward the river and saw the police cruiser coming toward the house at a fast clip. Cameron was driving. He stopped just feet short of the body and then got out on the run.

"Who is...hey! Isn't that Leon Mooney?"

A muscle jerked at the corner of Tate's eye. He couldn't look at the body without wanting to scream. This close, and they still didn't have a name.

"Yes, it's Mooney, but he's not our killer. He's a copycat. He said he was trying to outdo the Storm-chaser. He saw the man cut Nola. He knew who it was, but he wouldn't tell me, said that's not how you play the game and died without telling."

Two police cars came into view, lights flashing and sirens screaming, with an ambulance right behind them.

Jeff was already out of the cruiser and running toward the house to check on his mother.

"Beaudry took one in the shoulder," Cameron said. "The ambulance is for him."

Tate shoved a hand through his hair in frustration.

"I had to shoot him. He was aiming at Jeff's mother when I took the shot."

Cameron clapped him on the shoulder. "It is what it is, partner. You saved the kid's mother, and that's good enough."

The ambulance pulled to a stop, and Cameron directed them to Beaudry as Tate began filling in the officers arriving on scene.

Hours later, they rode back into town in Beaudry's cruiser with a deputy driving. He dropped them off at the trailer park, then headed back to the hospital to check on the chief.

Tate walked into the trailer with steps dragging, Cameron right behind him.

Wade took one look at the expressions on their faces and knew it wasn't good.

"What happened?"

"It's a long story. I need to change and wash up," Tate said as he walked past his partner and headed straight for Nola, who was stirring something at the stove. He noticed she'd taken her hair out of the braid, and it moved with the motion of her body, like wind across water. Without explanation, he wrapped his arms around her and buried his face against the curve of her neck.

"I'm sorry. I'm so sorry," he said.

That he was upset was frightening enough, but the tremor in his voice made it worse. She hugged him back, even though the stitches pulled, and because she was afraid to ask what was wrong.

Wade frowned. "What happened, damn it?"

Cameron shrugged. "Well, we found Leon Mooney right where Jeff found the victim. He must have been lying in wait for the cops to arrive. He was trying to pull a copycat, wanting to outdo the Stormchaser. He took a shot at Jeff and shot Beaudry in the shoulder. Tate took off after him, then wound up having to shoot him to keep him from killing Jeff Wilson's mother. The kicker was that Mooney knew who the Stormchaser was. He saw him attack Nola. He recognized him, but he died refusing to tell."

Nola gasped.

Tate felt sick. They'd been so close to solving this mess, and he'd taken out their only real witness without knowing it, leaving the man to his killing spree and Nola still in danger.

"Don't be like this," Nola said. "You didn't have a choice. He didn't give you a choice. I know Jeff's mother. She's a sweet lady. Thank God you saved her. I'm sure Jeff is grateful. Now go clean up. I have just created a silk purse out of a sow's ear here in this kitchen, and I expect high praise and kudos for my effort."

"That's for sure. I'm the official taster, and it's amazing," Wade said.

"Go," Nola said. "Get cleaned up."

Tate walked away, still frustrated and more than

a little anxious. He was in the bathroom when his cell phone beeped. He recognized the number and got pissed all over again after he read the text.

When wrong is done and never acknowledged, it takes many wrongs to make it right.

Tate's eyes widened. Yet another clue to their killer's identity. Somewhere in this man's past, he had suffered at the hands of law enforcement or possibly people in power. But suffered what? And where?

Twelve

Tate had washed up, changed out of his muddy clothes into jeans and a long-sleeved T-shirt, and then headed back to the kitchen in his bare feet.

Cameron had cleaned up, too, and was in the process of giving Wade a blow-by-blow account of what went down.

When Tate walked in, he could see by the look on Nola's face that she was rattled. Hell. He didn't blame her. So was he.

"I'm here. Show me the silk purse," he said.

She glanced up. She hadn't heard him come in, and now she wondered how long he had been watching her. If he only knew how angry she was becoming at the whole incredible situation, he wouldn't worry so much that she might have an emotional meltdown. She was too pissed for that. She waved her hand toward the table, which had already been set.

"Sit. While you and Cameron were playing in the bayou, Wade and I created this amazing feast."

Wade carried a big cast-iron skillet over to the table and set it on a magazine they were using for a trivet. Nola got out a bowl of salad and handed that to Wade. Her arm was aching, but it wasn't anything she couldn't bear, and she didn't want to take a pain pill until bedtime. Still, when she sat down at the table, she cupped her elbow to keep the stitches from pulling.

Tate saw her wince.

"How long since you took a pain pill?" he asked.

"I'm fine."

"Where are they?"

"I'll take one after we eat, okay? For once, stop trying to orchestrate everything and relax."

"It's in my DNA," he said.

"Like I don't already know that," she muttered.

Still, when Cameron dug into the casserole, the aroma shifted their attention.

"What do you call this?" Cameron asked.

"Feeb feed," Nola said, and then grinned. "Isn't Feeb another word for FBI?"

"In some circles," Tate drawled, as he took a big bite. "Oh, my Lord, this is good! What on earth did you put together from that crazy assortment of groceries to make this?"

"Frozen hash browns, sliced ham from the deli, an onion, a can of corn and a can of peas. I made a white sauce from milk, butter and biscuit mix for thickening, and diced up some cheese for a topping."

"I watched her doing it and still can't believe she thought to use all this stuff together," Wade said.

Cameron took a big bite. "It's really good, Nola. If you're available, I might be in the market for a girlfriend."

"She's not available," Tate said shortly.

The men laughed, but Nola ignored them, dipping out a helping onto her plate, along with a serving of the salad.

"Hey, what about that pretty Laura Doyle at the Red Cross Center? I thought you had a thing for her?" Wade asked Cameron.

Cameron grinned as he took another bite. "She *is* really pretty, but I don't know if she can cook."

More laughter filled the room until Tate finally began to turn loose of regret. He'd been in this business for a while now and knew better than to take things personally. It was all because of Nola that he'd let this get under his skin.

"Even the salad is good, but we didn't have any salad dressing," Wade said.

"I used salt, pepper and some lemon juice. In fact, this meal used up just about everything we had to eat."

"We'll get more," Tate said. "I need to go by the hospital and find out if our victim came out of surgery okay."

"I called," Wade said. "He did survive the surgery, and the doctor thinks he's going to make a full recovery."

A little bit more of Tate's guilt lifted, and he told them about the latest text, a genuine clue to what was driving the killer.

"Now if the chief comes out of surgery okay, then we can call this a good day," Cameron said. "Wade and I will go check on him, then get more groceries, after we eat."

"And I would like to swing by the Red Cross Center," Cameron said, and then suffered their teasing in good-natured silence. He liked Laura Doyle and wasn't ashamed to admit it. "I have a method in my madness," he added. "Now that all the shouting has died down, I thought we might talk to the people there and see if someone might have seen what happened to Nola, or even have seen the killer making an escape. It's worth a shot."

"What about the news crews? Have they left town yet?" Nola asked.

"Unfortunately, no," Tate said. "They're all over the place. Murder always makes the news. When they get wind of a copycat killer, it's going to get even crazier."

"I can't believe that all this started because of a flood," she muttered.

"Actually, it began in Iowa, because of a tornado,"

Tate said. "When the Mississippi flooded, he—" Tate stood abruptly. "Oh, man, how did I miss that?"

"Miss what?" Cameron asked.

"One of the last things Mooney said was that he'd never be as good as the Stormchaser because he didn't have Katrina. I thought he was talking about a woman, but what if he was talking about Hurricane Katrina?"

Wade jumped up and headed for his laptop. "So how does that fit in with the whole revenge scenario?"

Nola frowned. "It makes no sense. Why would he want to kill survivors?"

"Without knowing who he is, we can't really answer that," Tate said.

Silence followed, each of them lost in thoughts of what was driving the killer.

"Do we have dessert?" Cameron asked to break the mood.

"If Wade didn't eat all the cookies, yes. If Wade ate all the cookies, no."

Tate eyed his partner and smiled. "I'd say the answer is no."

"We'll bring back some ice cream," Wade said. "What's your poison, Nola?"

"She likes rocky road," Tate said.

Nola rolled her eyes. "He asked *me,* not *you.* My tastes could have changed."

"Well, did they?" he asked.

"No, but—"

He grinned. "Then I rest my case."

"I'll clean up. You guys go do your thing before it gets too late. Places don't stay open here as late as they do in the city."

When Nola began carrying plates to the sink, Tate stopped her, took her by the shoulders and aimed her at the living room.

"You cooked. I clean. Put your feet up and enjoy."

She didn't argue, and within minutes Winger and Luckett were gone and Tate was doing dishes.

She watched him working, remembering how focused he'd always been at everything he did. She guessed it was what made him good at his job, being able to focus on details and the characteristics of the criminals they were trying to catch. He'd always been so faithful. If she hadn't been so young back when they parted, she would have realized something terrible had happened to him to make him feel the need to escape from Queens Crossing and that she needed to give him the benefit of the doubt. If only she'd trusted her heart and not her head, none of this would be happening.

The truth was that she wanted to make love with him. Not many people got a second chance at happiness with the love of their life, and she had come too close to dying to waste hers. As soon as the last dish went in the dishwasher, she stood up.

"Tate?"

He turned. "Yeah?"

"How do you really feel about me?"

In three steps she was in his arms. Without saying a word, he began feathering kisses all over her face, on her ear, on her brow, on the tip of her nose and her chin, at the nape of her neck. Everywhere but her lips.

"That's how I feel about you, like I will never get enough. Finding you again is like winning the lottery, but better."

"What happens to me when you leave here?"

Breath caught in the back of his throat. If he said the wrong thing, would he lose her again?

"What do you want to happen?"

"I don't want to live the rest of my life without you," she said.

"Then we're good, because I feel the same way, only this is now, not back then. I have an investment in a career I like that demands a good deal of travel."

"I have a job that demands very little travel and a good deal of my time."

He cupped her face with both hands. "That sounds like a perfect match."

She sighed. "Do you want to pick a fight and have make-up sex, or should we just skip to the chase and make love? I don't know about you, but I'm eight years and counting since this has happened."

"Are you serious?"

"About what, the making love part, or the eight-year dry spell?"

Tate laughed. This was the way it used to be between them. No hesitancy. No playing around. Just honest-to-God love wild enough to rock a man's soul. He picked her up in his arms and headed down the hall. Once inside her bedroom, he set her down, locked the door and turned around.

"I have had this dream so many times, but it always ends when you start taking off your clothes."

Nola unsnapped her jeans.

"It's not going to end this time," she said, then hesitated, suddenly a little shy. "This used to be easy between us."

"It will be again. Let me help."

But it wasn't really help. It was more like laying claim. He stripped her so fast she didn't have time to be embarrassed. All of a sudden she was naked and Tate was coming out of his own clothes.

He slid onto the bed beside her, then cupped her breast and rolled her nipple between his thumb and finger, just enough to make her ache.

"I left a pretty girl and came back to a magnificent woman. You take my breath away."

She combed her fingers through his hair the way she used to, loving the springy feel of it beneath her palms.

"Make love to me, Tate. I've learned the hard way

that nothing lasts forever. I don't want to die never knowing this again."

His eyes narrowed sharply. "Don't say that! You won't die. I won't let him hurt you."

She shook her head. He couldn't promise that, and anyway, she didn't want to think about tomorrow.

"Just love me now. I won't ask for more."

So he did—smothering her with kisses, turning her on with his hands and his mouth until she was out of her mind.

Ignoring the pull of her healing stitches, she reached for him, encircling his erection with her fingers, feeling the surge of blood beneath the surface as it pulsed between her hands.

"Be with me…love me," she whispered.

He rose up and then over her, parted her legs with a knee and then slid inside. She was hot and wet, and he came close to losing control before they even began.

Nola locked her legs around his waist as he braced himself above her, and when he began to move, she began to cry.

"Don't," he whispered, kissing the tears running down the sides of her face.

"Don't talk," she said, and kissed him long and hard until he forgot about words.

Nola closed her eyes, and just like that, the eight years without him were gone. She remembered it all: the catch in his breath, the beat of his heart, the play of muscles across his back. The blood rush in her body was almost frightening in its intensity. Making love with Tate meant relinquishing control, and she'd done it. With every thrust of his body, he took her closer to the edge. It felt good to play with fire when he was the one fanning the flames.

Tate had long since lost his ability to focus. He was just riding out the madness that was dragging him ever closer to the little death. When the climax hit him, she was already coming. All he could do was hold her, because he was beyond thought.

Nola moaned as the last ripples of her climax rolled through her.

"Oh, sweet Lord," she whispered.

Tate kissed her chin, then her lips.

"I missed you, baby."

"I missed you, too," she said.

"I can't move."

She sighed. "And I don't want to."

Just as Tate closed his eyes, his cell phone began to ring.

"Oh, man," he groaned, then rolled over and got the phone out of a pocket in his jeans.

"Is the television on?" Cameron asked.

"No, why?"

"Turn it on…pick a channel…any channel. Nola is front-page news."

"Damn it," Tate muttered, and grabbed his jeans as he headed for the living room.

Nola flew out of bed, dressing quickly as she followed him up the hall. She was still trying to wrestle her sore arm into her shirtsleeve when she heard her name on TV.

"What the hell?"

Tate upped the volume as they stared at the picture on the screen and listened to the newsreader.

"This is a still shot of well-known regional artist Nola Landry coming out of the doctor's office. Miss Landry has just been identified as the only witness to the serial killer known as the Stormchaser. Although she says she was never close enough to see his face, she did witness the cold-blooded murder of three people who were stranded on the roof of their house just outside Queens Crossing, Louisiana. Landry herself was clinging to the branches of a tree she had climbed to escape the water's wrath, hanging on for her life when the murders happened. Hours later she was rescued by members of the Louisiana National Guard in one of their choppers. Just two days ago the Stormchaser, in an effort to silence his only witness, made an attempt on her life at a local Red Cross shelter, where she, along with dozens of other locals, had taken refuge after losing their homes. She has since been moved to an unknown location. Federal agents are on the scene, following the killer's trail, but as yet have been unable to name a suspect. Landry has garnered a reputation as a talented painter, and people in the art world are praying for

her safety. These are examples of some of her work hanging in a gallery in Savannah, Georgia."

Nola dropped onto the sofa, her eyes wide with disbelief.

"Oh. My. God. They pretty much told everything about me but my current address and dress size."

Tate sighed. "We knew this would happen when they got the pictures, remember?"

She shook her head. "I don't know what I thought would happen, but it wasn't this."

"Your paintings are amazing."

She shoved a shaky hand through her hair. "Thank you for pointing out the silver lining in the storm cloud."

He grinned. "You're welcome."

She climbed into his lap and wrapped her arm around his neck.

"Well, I always wanted to be famous. When I was little, I used to pray to God to make me famous. Obviously I wasn't specific enough. I should have added that I wanted to be famous for my paintings, not for surviving a serial killer's attack."

He kissed her chin and pulled her close.

"Nola Jean Landry, I sincerely love you to the depths of my soul," he said, laughing. "Here I was, fearing you were going to go off the deep end, and instead you're complaining about the price of fame."

She kissed the side of his cheek and then his

mouth, lingering long enough that she made him groan before she pulled back.

"I love you, too, Special Agent Man, and I am putting my life in your hands, because I don't know beans about dodging the bad guys."

All of a sudden things were serious again. Just the thought of being responsible for her life made him sick to his stomach, because the only thing they knew for sure about their killer was how deadly he was.

Hershel was feeling much better and was in the bathroom shaving. He didn't like whiskers. They made his face itch. He would go to work tomorrow and ease himself back into the routine while he watched the Feds' movements and established an escape route before he made his move to snatch the Landry woman. He needed to find out exactly where she'd witnessed him in the act and take her back there. To undo a wrong, he had to go back to the beginning to make it right.

You can't make anything right if you keep doing everything wrong. You're crazy, Hershel. You're certifiably crazy.

"Hush, Louise. I told you I wasn't the man you married. The sooner you accept that, the happier we'll both be."

He rinsed off the shaving cream, eyeing himself in the mirror. In his youth, Louise used to say he looked like a young version of Marlon Brando. Now he looked more like Dick Cheney. Satisfied with his clean, smooth shave, he began drying off. As soon as he was dressed, he moved up front to watch a little TV before going to bed.

He had just turned it on and was channel surfing when a picture of Nola Landry flashed on the screen. He gasped, then raised the volume, listening to the newscaster's coverage of the story.

Just hearing the media say there was a witness made him crazy. Now they would be laughing at him—saying he'd made a mistake. He had to fix it so the laughing would stop. The only positive out of the entire broadcast was that he now knew the kill site. There was only one location that had three people waiting for rescue, and he knew exactly where he'd been. He closed his eyes, thinking back to how the area had looked, and vividly remembered going past a stand of partially submerged trees. So that was where she'd been—up one of those trees. Now that was where he would take her, back to the place where the mistake was made. That was how you made mistakes go away.

Hershel Inman, I will never speak to you again if you hurt that poor girl. Do you hear me, Hershel? I mean it!

"I hear you, Louise, now you need to hear me. I will do it, and there's nothing you can say to stop me. You died and left me alone here, and now I'm doing what has to be done."

Nola was showered and in her sweats watching TV when Wade and Cameron came back. She heard a knock at the door, and then Wade calling out.

"It's just us," he said as the key turned in the door.

They both came in carrying grocery sacks.

She shut and locked the door behind them as they dumped everything on the island.

"Did you bring ice cream?" she asked.

Wade dug through a bag and pulled out a pint of rocky road ice cream. He took off the lid, stuck a spoon in the container and handed it to her.

"Knock yourself out, honey. That one is all yours."

She didn't argue. Instead, she wrapped a paper towel around the carton and headed for the living room with her prize.

"Where's Tate?" Wade asked.

"In the shower. Oh, wow, this is good. Thank you!"

"We figured it was the least we could do after your television debut."

She rolled her eyes.

"I'm not talking about that," she muttered, and scooped up another bite and poked it in her mouth.

"Here he comes. We got your favorite, buddy," Wade said, and tossed Tate a honey bun.

"Thanks. Did you bring any Pepsi?"

Wade pointed to a twelve-pack on the counter.

Tate poured one in a cup, added some ice and then sat down beside Nola.

"Trade you a bite," he said.

"Deal," she said as he tore off a piece of honey bun and fed it to her. Then she scooped up a big bite of ice cream and spooned it into his mouth.

Cameron elbowed Wade, who grinned and nod-ded.

"We leave and look what happens," Cameron said.

Tate heard them but ignored them, and Nola no longer cared.

She'd lost her home.

Someone wanted her dead.

The only man she'd ever loved was back in her life.

Some would say that only one out of three wasn't optimum odds, but life didn't come with guarantees and she wasn't wasting a minute of it with what-ifs.

The morning had dawned clear and cool. It was a good day for early September. The flowers in Don Benton's flower beds in front of the house were still blooming. Asters and chrysanthemums. Julia had called them hardy flowers when she'd planted them. Even though she was long gone from the house, he'd kept everything just as it had been. It was his way of pretending nothing in his life that mattered had really changed.

But it had. Seeing Tate again had rattled him, and

the anger, while not surprising, had been so vicious he would not have been shocked if the two of them had come to blows. He could tell the night he stitched up Nola Landry's arm that their relationship would most likely resume. He didn't care. It was nothing to do with him.

When they'd first left, there had been countless sleepless nights when he'd lain awake, trying to figure out who Tate's father could have been. Finally he'd pushed the jealousy aside and written off his wife and her bastard as a deal gone bad. It didn't matter who she'd had an affair with. They were both out of his life, and now she was no longer of this world. It had been a shock to learn how she had suffered before she died, but as time passed, he decided life had dealt her exactly what she had deserved.

He had some paperwork to catch up on and then was thinking about a short trip to New Orleans. Maybe spend a couple of days there seeing the sights and visiting old friends. The food was amazing and he needed a break.

He was driving down Main Street on his way to the morgue when a car came out of an alley. He caught a glimpse of it from the corner of his eye, and then everything went black.

Nola was sitting at the island in her sock feet eating cereal and watching Tate make toast. Wade was in the shower, and Cameron was on the phone with the director. She could tell by the way Tate's head was tilted that he was listening to everything Cameron was saying. Both men had filed their reports on the copycat incident last night before they'd gone to bed, and she guessed they were waiting to see how their boss reacted.

Tate had just watched Nola take her last bite when his cell phone rang. He noticed it was the hospital and assumed it was probably Beaudry, laid up and bored and wanting an update.

"This is Benton," he said.

"Tate, this is Doctor Tuttle. Your father was in an accident. Someone came out of an alley down on Main and T-boned his car on the driver's side. He has some internal injuries and is losing a lot of blood."

Shock sent Tate back to his childhood, to the man who was his hero, then flashed forward to the night that same man had punched him in the face and sent him tumbling down the stairs. Finally he made himself focus.

"What do you need me to do?" he asked.

"I know this is a long shot, but your dad has a rare blood type and with everything going on, we don't have any on hand. By any chance are you O negative?"

"Yes. Where do I go?"

"Fantastic! Come to the E.R. I'll have them set up and waiting for you. And, Tate…time is of the essence."

"I'll be right there," he said, then glanced at Nola as he hung up.

"What's up?" Cameron said.

"Dad was in a wreck, and they don't have any O negative on hand. I'm going down to donate."

"Do you want me to go with you?" Nola asked.

"I want you to, but you can't. Sorry."

Her shoulders slumped. "Okay, I know you're right. I hope he's okay."

Tate nodded. "I won't be long," he said, then grabbed his wallet and gun and was out the door.

"If the old bastard survives, I hope he'll realize what a mistake he made," Cameron said.

Just then Wade walked into the kitchen to check on breakfast and noticed they were one short.

"Where's Tate?"

When Cameron filled him in, his reaction was the same.

"That's one cold-blooded man. I still can't wrap my head around what he did to Tate. It's just crazy." Then he looked at Nola. "It's part of what broke you guys up, right?"

She nodded. "Only I didn't know it until he told me the same day he told you."

"But you're both okay now?"

She smiled. "We're very okay."

They both gave her a thumbs-up.

"So…what's on the schedule?" Wade asked.

"You mean besides babysitting me?" she said.

Cameron frowned. "Hey. It's not babysitting. It's called protecting a material witness."

"Which we're happy to do, because we usually have to order in when that happens. Your cooking skills are a bonus," Wade said.

She grinned. "Changing the subject now, but has either one of you heard if the river has crested yet?"

"No. That last rain added to the runoff. I heard them predicting it for sometime tomorrow evening, *if* it doesn't rain again anytime soon."

"Thanks," she said, and then took her bowl to the dishwasher as Wade walked into the kitchen behind her.

"Who made toast?" he asked, pointing to the two slices in the toaster.

"Tate."

"Don't want to let them go to waste," he said, and grabbed a plate.

"Are you ever full?" Nola asked.

Wade shrugged. "It's a metabolism thing."

She grinned. "Is that guy talk to get around the fact that you're a walking garbage disposal?"

"I don't know what you're talking about," he said, and stuffed a half slice of toast in his mouth.

Thirteen

Tate sped through town, taking back alleys to keep from hitting stop signs and red lights. He made it to the hospital in just under eight minutes. He entered the E.R. on the run, and was met by a lab tech and a nurse.

He recognized the nurse but couldn't remember her name. She, however, knew him.

"This way, Tate," she said, and led him into an unoccupied bay. "Lie down here and push up your sleeve."

He did as she asked without saying a word. Within moments they had the needle in a vein and the blood began to flow. He glanced over at the tube, watching the bright red blood running down into the bag and thought about the power contained in the dynamics of a family. Did blood prove you belonged? If you didn't, did they care? Did belonging isolate you or insulate you? Some families drew closer when tragedy struck and others splintered. He knew where his fell in that scenario.

The nurse was standing beside him, waiting to rush the blood into the O.R. Without knowing the dynamics of his family, she assumed Tate would be concerned about his father's welfare.

"He's a tough man, Tate. They're doing all they can."

"I'm sure they are. Who was in the other car?"

She grimaced. "Mrs. Coffee. She didn't make it."

"Oh, my God," Tate said, and closed his eyes.

He remembered the little librarian from his high school days and was sad that such a sweet woman's life would end this way.

"Not much longer," the tech said.

He glanced at the bag. It was almost full. If this was what saved Don Benton's life, his dad was going to be pissed.

"That'll do it," the tech said, and stopped the flow, pulled the needle and quickly taped it off. "Here you go," he said, and handed the blood off to the nurse.

"God bless you, Tate," she said, and left the room at a run.

When Tate started to get up, the tech stopped him and handed him a juice box.

"You need to lie here for about ten minutes. I snagged you a fresh doughnut to have with this juice."

Tate thanked him and sat up just enough so that he could swallow.

He ate and drank without thought, taking the food like medicine, and wondered how Beaudry was doing. Since he was already there, he decided go by and check on the chief before he left.

Hershel showed up for work with a snap in his step. Word had leaked out, and like everyone else in town he'd heard all about Leon Mooney being a copycat killer. He considered it a compliment. Too bad his intended victims weren't dead. It would have added to the Stormchaser's cachet, having a successful copycat following in his footsteps.

"Hey, you! Good to see you up and around," Laura Doyle said. "Did you drive here?"

"Yes, ma'am."

"Then I need you to haul some of our supplies over to the First Baptist Church. Take this list and fill it from the storeroom. Do you know where the church is located?"

Hershel took the list, scanning it quickly. "I think so. Isn't it the one a block south of Eats?"

"That's it. Get some of the guys out back to help you load, and take someone with you. Doesn't matter who. As soon as you're through, come back here."

"Will do," he said, and went back out to drive his truck up to the back of the gym.

* * *

When they told Tate he could leave, he went to see Beaudry. The door was ajar, and even before he went in, he could hear the man griping, which had to mean he was on the mend. He knocked once then walked in.

Beaudry looked up and waved him over.

"Good. It's you. I can't see shit without my glasses, and I'm trying to find Channel 10 on this TV. Help me out, will you?"

"Sure thing," Tate said, and got it on the right station for him, then hit Mute. "You're set. All you'll have to do is hit Mute again to get your sound back."

"Thanks. What brings you to the Louisiana Hilton?"

Tate chuckled. "You. How are you doing?"

"I'm okay. It hurts, but it's healing. I'm just grateful to be alive."

"I hear you," Tate said. "That was some crazy stuff."

Beaudry shook his head. "I will never understand the mentality of a copycat killer. How can you fixate on someone who's wreaking havoc in the world and want to be like him?"

"All kinds of things play into it, but lack of self-esteem, feeling like you're invisible, wanting to be famous, hating the establishment, holding a grudge against society...then mix that with just plain mean, or maybe some type of mental illness, and you've got the setup for that kind of hero worship."

Beaudry shook his head. "At any rate, I'm sure grateful you stopped him before he could hurt Jeff's mother. She's a real nice lady. And speaking of nice ladies, how's yours?"

"She's getting better. Frustrated by the imposed isolation. Angry with the situation."

"Any new leads on your killer?"

Tate thought of his last text and grimaced. "Other than the fact that he's right-handed but shoots his victims with his left, no."

"Really? How does this help you find him?"

"It doesn't, actually," Tate said. "It's just a clue for a profiler."

"Do you think Nola is still a target?"

"I know she is," Tate said. "And, speaking of her, I better get back. When do they let you out?"

"'Soon' is all they'll say. The bullet didn't hit anything important, so it's just a matter of flesh and muscle healing. I'll be on desk duty for a while, which sucks, but I'll take it rather than be stuck at home with Elsie. I love my wife, but I do not want to be home 24/7. She never stops talking."

Tate laughed. "Do you ever answer her?"

Beaudry blinked. "Not sure I really do, now that you mention it."

"You might try it. If she got a little cooperation

with the conversation, she might not feel the need to handle it all herself."

Beaudry grinned. "I think I might just give that a try. You're pretty sharp for a local boy."

Tate shook his head. "Not really. Just a student of human behavior. Take care."

"Thanks for stopping by," Beaudry said.

Tate got all the way down to the lobby before his cell phone rang. It was Doc Tuttle.

"Hello?"

"Tate, this is Doctor Tuttle. I wanted to let you know that your father is out of surgery. Your blood donation made the difference for him. He'll be mighty grateful when he finds out."

"No, he won't," Tate said. "But thank you for the information."

He disconnected before Tuttle could say anything more and headed for the parking lot, only to be caught by the media.

"Agent Benton! Do you have a comment about the copycat killer?"

"He's dead."

He kept walking, ignoring the rest of the questions they threw at him, got in the car and drove away.

Hershel had copped an attitude on the way back to the Red Cross Center. Everyone had been talking about the copycat and not saying a word about him. He needed to make something happen to draw the attention back to him, and he needed to do it fast. He wanted to go downriver and find his next kill site, but he couldn't do it until he broke the jinx.

A new volunteer named Floyd Tully had gone with him to the church, and it was Hershel's personal opinion that Floyd was a pain in the butt. He kept talking about football and the New Orleans Saints like they were something next to God. Except for hunting, Hershel had never been much for sports, and he was sick and tired of listening to Floyd talk about the Saints' current quarterback. When he finally got back to the gym parking lot, the urge to throttle him eased.

"Here we are," Hershel said. "We better check in with Miss Doyle and see what she needs us to do next."

"I don't know," Floyd said. "I told my wife I'd be home for dinner at noon. Don't your wife worry about all this killing?"

"My wife is dead," Hershel said tersely, then got out of the truck and slammed the door behind him, leaving Floyd to get out on his own.

I'm still here, Hershel, and you know it.

"Yeah, but you're also still dead," he muttered.

"I'm sorry, were you talking to me?" Floyd asked.

"No."

"Hey! Y'all tell Miss Doyle I'll be back later, okay?"

Hershel nodded and kept walking. It was nearing

the noon hour, and as he walked in he could see lots of activity back in the kitchen area. He guessed she might be there, and he was right.

"Hey, I'm back," he said. "Floyd went home to eat. Said to tell you he'll be back later."

Laura nodded, and kept spreading mustard on bread then slapping ham and cheese between the slices.

"Is there something else you need me to do?" he asked.

"Not right now," she said. "Oh, wait. You're staying out at that trailer park, aren't you?"

"Yes, ma'am."

"We found a bag with some of Nola Landry's things under the cot that she used."

Hershel smiled. "She and the Feds are staying in a rental trailer just a few lots up from mine. I see them coming and going. Want me to drop it off?"

"That would be great. It's on my desk up in the office. Tell her I said hello."

"Yes, ma'am. I'll grab a bite to eat and then be back in time to carry out the garbage, okay?"

Laura smiled wearily. "Yes. You're a lifesaver. Thank you for staying with us."

Hershel smiled. "It's the benefit of being retired. I'm happy to help."

He strode toward the office at a brisk clip, found the sack in the middle of the desk and headed for his truck. He was smiling broadly by the time he got in, and when he drove out of the parking lot he was humming.

He glared at the news crews parked outside the gates to the trailer park as he drove by. News whores. They acted as if the Stormchaser had ceased to exist. Like him, they'd figured out where the witness was being held because the Feds were no longer coming and going in threes. One always stayed behind at the trailer, which they took to mean he was guarding Nola Landry. Hershel was no long enamored of having a copycat. Damn Leon Mooney for stealing his thunder.

He drove to the big trailer on the corner lot and pulled right up into the yard as if he was going to visit. When he grabbed the sack and got out, he was whistling.

Nola was frying hamburger patties when someone knocked at the door. She looked around for the men, but neither one was in the room, so she headed down the hall.

"Hey, guys! Someone is at the door."

They came out of their bedroom armed.

"Stay back!" Wade said, and both men headed for the door.

Wade glanced out the window, recognized the truck and frowned.

"What the hell is he doing here?"

"Open the door and find out," Cameron said. "I've got your back."

When Wade opened the door, he immediately scoped out both the man on the doorstep and the surrounding area.

"Sorry to bother you," Hershel said. "I've been up at the Red Cross station all morning and was leaving to go to lunch when Miss Doyle asked me to drop this off for Miss Landry. She said someone found it under the cot she used."

He smiled, handed over the sack and started to leave, then paused.

"Nearly forgot. Miss Doyle said to tell Nola hello."

"How did you know she was here?" Wade asked.

Hershel pointed. "That's my motor home right down there, see? The one with the green stripe. I've been laid up with a fever and had a lot of time on my hands. Saw you all coming and going over the past couple of days. Besides, everybody knows it. The only reason the press is camped out at the entrance to the park now is in the hopes of getting her picture."

"Thank you," Wade said.

"No problem. I'll be off now. Have a nice day."

Wade watched until the man left, and then went inside and locked the door.

Nola came out of the hallway.

"That's one of the men who works at the Red Cross station," she said. "The cooks think he's cute but too bowlegged."

Wade grinned. "Well, Laura sent him by with this. I guess we missed it when we were gathering up your things. And…according to him, everybody knows you're here." He grinned. "Not that we didn't suspect it, but it's so damn reassuring to hear it from a perfect stranger."

"It's a small town. That's how stuff happens," she said, then took the bag, looked in, recognized the things inside and carried it back to her room.

Cameron was frowning. "That was the guy we interviewed who was so sick, right?"

Wade nodded as Nola returned to the kitchen.

"These are about ready. Has anybody heard from Tate?"

Cameron could see the front yard through the window from where he was standing and watched the SUV turn off the road into the yard.

"He's driving up."

"Just in time. I hope everything is okay," she said.

"Do we have onions?" Wade asked.

"Yes. I sliced some for the burgers. They're on a plate in the refrigerator. Grab them and we'll be ready to eat."

Tate walked in, locking the door behind him.

"Dinner is ready," Nola said.

"Be there as soon as I wash," he said, and disappeared down the hall.

She frowned. He was definitely not happy, but he would talk about it when he was ready.

Tate returned, slid an arm around her waist and gave her a quick hug and a kiss.

"Thank you, honey."

She smiled. "What for?"

"For being you. Something smells good."

"Burgers," Cameron said. "Sit down, Nola. You cooked. We've got the rest of this."

As soon as she sat down, Tate took the chair beside her.

"Doctor Tuttle said Dad came through surgery and that the transfusion probably saved him."

"That's good, isn't it?" she asked.

"I didn't want him dead, if that's what you mean, but I also didn't ever intend to go through that blood relation thing with him again."

"Oh, that."

He nodded. "Yeah, that."

"Here, build your burger and quit worrying about the old fart," Wade said, and slid a plate of burgers and a bag of buns on the table as Cameron added all the fixings that went with them.

"What do you want to drink?" Tate asked her.

"I'll just have water," she said.

He got up and fixed the cups.

She sat back, watching how the men worked in tandem without confusion. It was obvious how bonded they were and that they'd done this kind of thing countless times before.

"We had a visitor," Wade said.

Tate looked startled, then glanced at Nola. "Who?"

"A volunteer from the gym. I worked with him that night I handed out water bottles."

"What the hell was he doing here?" Tate asked.

Wade sighed. "Laura found a sack of stuff under the cot Nola had been sleeping on. I guess we missed it when we picked everything up. I guess she knew the guy was staying out here and sent it with him."

"Do we know him? Did we clear him the night she was attacked? What came up on his background check?" Tate asked.

"He's the one who was sick when we went to interview him. He wasn't faking. Thought he was going to pass out on us just standing there talking. As far as I know, nothing popped on his background check."

"He's not scary, but Leon Mooney was helping out, too, and he sure was. I guess now we know why."

Tate's eyes widened. "Shit. Pardon my French. Mooney said he recognized the Stormchaser when he attacked you, and he obviously knew this guy pretty well if they were working together. Are we damn sure he wasn't there that night?"

"Well, I watched him leave," Cameron said. "Although that doesn't mean he didn't come back. But there you are. He got sick pretty damn fast afterward *if* he *did* come back."

Tate couldn't let go of the connection.

"Everything is a clue and nothing is an accident," he muttered.

"Eat your hamburger now, detect later," Nola urged.

As their meal progressed, the tension eased, and finally Tate was laughing with them, until his phone signaled a text.

The men stopped in midsentence, looking at each other with an expression Nola didn't understand.

"What?" she asked.

Tate's eyes narrowed as he pulled out his phone. He saw the number, then looked up and nodded.

Nola was beginning to get scared. "What, damn it?"

"It's from the Stormchaser," Cameron said.

Shock rolled through her.

"It's part of how he gets his kicks," Tate muttered.

"So what did he say?" Nola asked.

Tate opened the text and felt the skin crawl on the back of his neck.

I am not the fly you swatted. I am the eagle you cannot see. I hunt not for food but for justice and revenge. You do not deserve joy when mine is gone. I will prevail.

Clearly the Stormchaser felt threatened and was trying to reassert himself because Tate had killed the copycat.

Tate shoved the phone across the table to let them read for themselves, then took it back and, within moments, was talking to a tech at Quantico. He gave him both phone numbers, his and the killer's, and ordered a trace.

"Get back to me ASAP."

"We've done this countless times before," Wade said. "We know he's in our area. He's always right under our noses. It won't be any different this time."

Tate was stone-faced. "And I'll keep doing it. Damn me for slacking before. Eventually something has to click." He looked at Nola. She was pale and very quiet. "Nola?"

She looked up with a glint in her eye. "I'm fine. Just find the bastard."

Tate moved back to the murder board and began going over the evidence again out loud as she got up and cleared the table.

"Okay. Even though this has been part of our profile on him, it's the first time he's come out and used the word revenge and if we put Hurricane Katrina into the equation, it leaves us all kinds of possibilities."

Cameron picked up the conversation. "If he and his wife were waiting to be rescued and it didn't happen in time…"

"Who would he blame?" Wade asked. "He'd blame the rescuers. Maybe the government. He'd want them to look bad. He'd want to pay them back."

Tate added. "He uses a lot of biblical references in his texts. He could be angry with God for not saving his wife."

"But why kill people who would most likely have survived?" Nola asked.

Tate began to pace, ticking off the potential reasons one by one. "If he felt let down by God for not saving his loved one, then he could have convinced himself that he's getting back at God for taking people He would have saved. Or maybe he's angry with the government for not responding quickly enough to save whoever he loved and then helping now. He resents other people for surviving when his loved one didn't, or something to that effect. We need to put research on this. They can do it faster and much more thoroughly than we can."

"I'll call it in," Wade said. "So what all do we need? Reports of people who were angry about not being rescued?"

"And coverage on anyone who might have made threats against the authorities in the aftermath of Katrina," Tate added.

"Any particularly tragic stories about couples getting separated, a spouse or child dying, that kind of thing," Cameron added.

"I'm on it," Wade said, and headed back to his bedroom to start the ball rolling.

Tate scooped Nola up in his arms and kissed her soundly. Before now, they'd had nothing but hypotheses as to the reasoning behind the killings, but now they knew for sure that the motive was revenge, and maybe that Hurricane Katrina was involved, as well.

Her lips were still tingling after he'd put her down, and she could tell by the conversation and the phone calls being made that she needed to entertain herself for a while. She grabbed a cookie, traded her water for a cold pop and headed for the living room.

"Will the television bother you?" she asked.

Tate shook his head and went back to working.

Don Benton regained consciousness in complete confusion. The last thing he remembered was looking at the flowers in his front flower bed. And he hurt. To the point that he was one giant ache. Something was beeping. He turned his head, saw the IV in his arm and the heart monitor hookup, and realized he was in a hospital.

But why?

All of a sudden the door to his room opened and a nurse came in.

"You woke up!" she said. "Welcome back, Doctor Benton. You are one very blessed man."

"What hap—" he started to ask, then realized it hurt to talk, too.

"You were in a car accident."

He rubbed a hand over his face, as if trying to wipe away the cobwebs in his memory, but nothing came to mind.

"My fault?"

The nurse's smile disappeared. "No, not your fault. Are you in pain?"

"Yes."

"I'll get you something. Be right back."

"Wait... Who?"

She left without answering, which made him anxious. What in the world had happened?

A few minutes later she came back, accompanied by Aaron Tuttle. She emptied a syringe into his IV port while the doctor began an exam.

"Good afternoon, Don. You've had quite a day. I want to check your incision before we do anything else, so just lie still and I'll do all the work."

Don didn't have to be told to stay still. He hurt too much to move. He watched Tuttle's face, guessing by the man's changing expressions that all was well.

"Looks good," Tuttle said. "The meds she just gave you will work shortly. That should give you some relief."

"What did you repair?" Don asked.

"You had a ruptured spleen, broken ribs, quite a few cuts and contusions, and a concussion. You'd lost a lot of blood by the time we got you into surgery. If it hadn't been for your son, your prognosis would have been a different story."

Don frowned. "What do you mean?"

"Tate donated the blood that saved you."

Don's mouth opened, but no words came. Tuttle

kept talking. "Rare blood types like yours can be an issue in small towns like this, especially during emergencies, although I'm sure you know that. Anyway, crisis averted, thanks to him."

Don's head was spinning. It was extremely unlikely that Tate had the same blood type he did. Julia had said Tate wasn't his. He'd heard it with his own ears. No woman in her right mind would lie about something—

The minute he thought the words, the truth hit him. *In her right mind.* But Julia hadn't been in her right mind, it was just that he'd been in denial. He'd been so shocked by what she'd said that it had never occurred to him that she might have been delusional.

Then he remembered that the nurse hadn't answered his question about the wreck.

"Wreck wasn't my fault?"

Tuttle nodded. "That's correct. It wasn't your fault."

"What happened?"

Doc Tuttle frowned. "Mrs. Coffee broadsided you. God rest her soul."

Don shuddered. "She's dead?"

"On impact."

"Dear God," Don whispered, and closed his eyes. Tuttle patted his knee.

"Get some rest. Barring unforeseen complications, you're going to be fine. I'll be back to check on you when I make rounds in the morning."

Moments later Don was alone, but rest was impossible.

Mrs. Coffee was dead, and he had been party to that, even if it hadn't been his fault. And he had denied his son a thousand times over because of a grandiose ego and a coldhearted refusal to nurture another man's child.

His head hurt.

His body hurt.

His heart hurt.

God help him, but he should have been the one to die.

Fourteen

It began to rain again in the night. Tate heard it first on the roof and then blowing against the windows, and groaned. Dear God, this whole section of the state was going to wash away if it didn't stop. The river had been predicted to crest sometime in the night, and now that prediction no longer held true.

The wind rattling the trailer sounded like rocks in a can. Either that or it was Jonesy's ghosts. Whichever, it still made him antsy, and the agent in him would never be able to go back to sleep until he did a recon of the place, just to be sure.

He picked up his handgun and left his bedroom, using the intermittent flashes of lightning and the night-light in the kitchen to light the way.

Once he reached the living room he stood at the window in the dark, waiting for the flashes to scan the area. The security light at the edge of the street was out. He frowned, certain it had been on every other night, and chalked it up to the lightning shorting out the wiring. After checking the door, the dead bolt and the security chain to make sure they were secure, he rechecked the windows, then the back door.

All was well.

Cameron came out of his bedroom on his way to the bathroom and saw Tate standing in the hall.

"Everything okay?"

Tate nodded. "Just antsy about what this new rainfall will do. In the wake of the copycat, I'm wondering if the killer will take advantage of it to pull the attention back to him. It's crucial for him to establish himself as top dog."

"I know."

Cameron went into the bathroom as Tate headed for the kitchen. He couldn't sleep. Hopefully Quantico would have some new stats for them by morning and they would finally have some facts to work with.

He heard the door shut as Cameron went back to bed and was thinking about getting a snack when the door opened again. He thought it was Cameron and then heard Nola's voice.

He found her standing in the open door to her room, wearing that LSU T-shirt and a pair of panties, and she'd taken down the braid in her hair. It hung around her shoulders and down her back like a dark veil. After thinking about ghosts earlier, her appearance and her silence were slightly eerie.

"Honey, is everything all right?"

She answered, but in a monotone.

"Mama said run."

"Nola?"

"She told me. She said, 'Get up, Nola! Get dressed. Get food. Get water. Run.'"

The hair stood up on the back of his neck. Her eyes were open, but she was walking in her sleep.

"Mama?" she said.

He couldn't believe what he was hearing. Had her mother actually come to her in a dream and saved her life? Damn. This was seriously heavy stuff. He didn't want to scare her, but he knew better than to wake her too abruptly, so he took her by the hand.

"Come with me," he said, and led her back into her room. "It's safe now," he said softly. "You don't have to run anymore. Lie down, baby. It's time to rest."

She crawled back into bed, lay down on her back and pulled the covers up beneath her chin. Her eyes were still open, but she didn't react to the flashes of lightning that were clearly visible through the curtains.

Tate frowned. She was still in sleepwalk mode and fully capable of taking another walk out the door. Rather than worry, he just pulled back the covers and crawled into bed with her.

She let him pull her closer, and when he slid an arm beneath her neck and pillowed her head on his shoulder, she sighed. He watched her face until her breathing eased and her eyes finally closed.

"Poor darling," he whispered, and brushed the tangles of hair away from her face. "Everything and everybody washed away and you watched it happen, didn't you, honey?"

Nola woke up in Tate's arms and thought about waking up that way for the rest of her life. Emotion welled within her, blurring his features. Even in the dark, the strength in his face and his body was evident, and she loved him so damn much it hurt.

She didn't know when he'd crawled into bed with her or why, but she wasn't going to complain. She glanced at the digital clock. 4:45 a.m.—the perfect time for making love.

She shifted to accommodate her stitches, slipped out of her panties and then leaned over his chest to kiss his cheek before kissing her way across his face to his lips.

He woke with a sigh and tightened his grasp.

"If I'm dreaming, don't wake me up," he whispered, and cupped her backside with both hands. He felt the bare skin and rolled over, turning her beneath him. Without a second of foreplay, he slid inside her and began to move, pushing hard and deep.

Nola moaned. She'd been right. It was the perfect time to make love.

The security light outside her window sent a faint

glow into her room, casting shadows of their bodies onto the wall. She watched, fascinated by the image of what she saw combined with the lust of what she felt, then closed her eyes, meeting him thrust for thrust as their lonely years apart fell away.

Time was no longer measured by seconds but by the building waves of rushing blood. One moment she was riding the waves of ecstasy, and then the climax slammed into her so fast she forgot to breathe.

Tate felt it, heard her groan slip out from between her lips and lost control. His body was on autopilot and his mind had already shattered as he rode his climax to the end and then, conscious of her stitches, rolled onto his back, taking her with him and pulling up the covers. The next time they woke, sunlight was spilling into the room and they could smell coffee.

"Good morning, pretty lady," Tate said, and combed the tangles of her hair away from her face.

"What happened?"

He smiled. "You mean besides us making love?"

She nodded.

"You were sleepwalking. I was afraid you'd get out of the trailer and I wouldn't know it."

She frowned. "I used to do that when I was a kid."

He sat up and combed his hands through his hair. He started to get out of bed and then stopped. After what he'd heard her say last night, he had to know.

"You said you'd been sick for days and didn't know about the flood. So when the river got to the house and you woke up in the dark, how did you know to get up?"

"I was dreaming. Mama was running through the house, going from window to window. I could see the frantic look on her face. And then all of a sudden she started yelling at me, telling me to get up and get dressed. She said to get food and water and run, so I did. When I stepped out onto the porch in the dark, I felt water up past my ankles. Even as sick as I was, it scared the hell out of me."

"Lord, Lord, baby. Your mama's spirit saved your life. You know that, don't you?"

She nodded. "Yes. I knew it the moment I saw all that water."

He just shook his head, and handed her the panties and shirt.

"I'll go get dressed. I don't hear the shower, so you can go first if you want."

"What's going to happen today, Tate?"

"What do you mean?"

"The river is still rising, isn't it?"

"It has nowhere else to go but to spread farther."

"Is Queens Crossing in danger?"

"I seriously doubt it. I think it's high enough to keep it dry, but this latest storm is bound to bring in even more people who've been flooded out."

"Will the Stormchaser kill again?"

"Who knows what the crazy bastard will do. We're expecting some data to come in from Quantico. Hopefully it'll give us a new angle on the investigation."

"Okay. I just wanted to know."

"And you *should* know. You're just as involved in this as we are, just for a different reason."

"I'll go shower. I won't be long."

"Hey, Nola."

She paused as she threw back the covers. "What?"

"Love you."

She shivered. They were words she'd thought she would never hear him say again.

"Oh, Tate, I love you, too."

He winked and slipped out of the room, closing the door behind him. Moments later she went into the bathroom with a hairbrush, a hair band and some clean clothes. She paused to look at herself in the mirror. Her lips were slightly swollen and her hair looked like she'd been in an orgy.

She smiled. The look was a good one for her.

Hershel hadn't slept all night. Once the rain began, he'd started pacing. Louise had been on his case nonstop, telling him to lie down and get his rest, but he'd had a meltdown on her like he'd never had before, and now she was silent and it was worse than her harping had ever been.

This was how it had been right after she died, and it had been his guilt and the silence that pushed him over the edge. He needed to regain control, and the only way he knew to do that was to resume his quest. Living witness or not, there would be new people in need of rescue. He was saving the boat for Nola. They would be watching for it and him, by land and probably by air, so he didn't dare use it again more than once.

So how could he make this happen? He didn't know. What he *did* know was that the answer wouldn't come to him in here. He needed to get out among them and the answer would come. It always did.

The first thing he did was select a different disguise. First he packed clothing, then a wig and makeup. He decided to opt for his rifle rather than the pistol today, because he wouldn't be in the boat, which meant he wouldn't be able to get up as close. He listened to the local news reports as he gathered his things, pinpointing the areas along the river that were now in danger. They were announcing more refugee centers being set up farther downstream as well as new ones here in town, but he didn't care. Today he was not a volunteer, he was the Storm-chaser, and he had a need for control.

Louise was still keeping quiet, and it was making him nervous. Everything was off-kilter. As soon as he got the Feds away from Nola, he would rectify his mistake and be on his way.

The day was still overcast, even though the rain had passed, leaving a slight chill in the air. The jacket he had on felt good as he headed out the door. He tossed his duffel bag in the front seat of the truck, checked to make sure his rifle and ammo were still secure behind the seat and got in. He glanced toward the trailer where the Feds were staying. The SUV was still there, and most likely they were, too. He smiled. He was about to scatter them like a covey of quail.

With the news reports in mind, he drove out of Queens Crossing and headed east for ten miles, then cut back south toward the flood zone to scout for prospects. It would be more difficult doing it from land than from water, but it also made his quest that much more interesting.

As soon as he got to a secure location, he changed into his disguise. Black pants and a black leather vest later, he was halfway there. He added a fake tattoo on his arm, some chains hanging from his belt loops into his pockets and more chain bracelets around his wrists, and he looked like a street thug. A shaggy black wig brushed the back of his neck, a handlebar mustache tickled his nose and his baseball cap touted a popular beer. There was nothing he could do about his vehicle, but he changed his license plate to a stolen one from Oklahoma just in case.

The first location he spotted was an older two-story frame house about a quarter of a mile from the road. Even from where he was sitting, he could see two men madly filling sandbags to reinforce the dam they'd build around their house. The water was shallow but had already encircled them. But for their dam, it would already have invaded the house. It was obvious their efforts were futile, and it was a good place to begin. In a way, he was doing them a favor, saving them from pointless labor and a world of grief.

He took the turn down the road, drove as close as he dared and walked along the edge of the woods until he reached the water. They never looked up from their task, and even though he was only a hundred feet from their house, they never saw him.

He stood for a few moments, watching the old man and the younger one work in a well-coordinated routine and scouting the best spot to take his shots. He had no way of knowing if there was a woman inside the house, but he would find out soon enough when the men went down.

The old man moved into position first, but Hershel waited. He needed to take the young one down first. A couple of minutes later he got his opportunity, sighted him through the rifle scope and fired.

The young man dropped without making a sound. A muscle jerked in Hershel's jaw as he waited for the older man to turn. He saw the look of shock on his face. Saw, rather than heard, the cry of dismay, and then took his second shot. He saw blood splatter out behind the old man's head as he went down. Then he stood, waiting to see if anyone came out. Nothing moved except the water. He slipped the rifle into the crook of his arm, pausing long enough to eye the river as it continued to swallow the land, and headed back toward his truck.

By the time she heard the shots and got to the window, her husband and his father were down, and the shooter was staring at the house. She clapped a hand over her mouth to silence her scream and watched as he walked away. As soon as he was out of sight, she ran for her cell phone, sobbing as she went.

Tate was in his bedroom, on the phone with the director, filling him in on the new direction they were exploring. The data they'd requested from Quantico had come through, and the techs who'd sorted it had done an amazingly thorough job, especially given how little they'd had to go on. But because of the devastation of Hurricane Katrina and the length of time it had taken before real help ever arrived, there were literally hundreds of stories to look through.

"Damn," Cameron said as he began scrolling through the online report. "I need this stuff printed out to be able to sort it. I'll print, if one of you guys will separate the copies into three sets, and then we can see if there's anything in there that fits what we already have."

"I'll do it," Wade said.

Nola was doing her part by staying out of the way.

They had every tabletop, as well as the kitchen island, covered in files and papers, and from the sound of their conversation, they were about to make it worse.

She thought about what a hassle Laura must be having at the Red Cross center and wished she could help. It would be a useful way to pass the time, but they'd already gone that route and put a lot of people in danger. It wasn't fair, but while the killer was running free, she was the one in jail.

Tate came back into the room as they were printing out the last pages.

"The director is pleased to learn we have a new angle. He's assigning extra help back at headquarters for us, so we need to sort through this stuff ASAP, eliminating the stories we don't think apply, then give them the names we need further background on and they'll do the rundowns."

"That's fantastic," Wade said. "This would take days otherwise, and that's time we don't have. I'm sorting by date. I'm thinking the earlier disaster stories could be what we need to look at, because later on, after the National Guard and FEMA finally showed up, things changed."

"Agreed," Tate said. "Let's sort by date, then pull any of the stories that have to do with a woman's death, and especially stories where a man and woman were trapped and she didn't make it."

By now it was nearly eleven. Nola was getting hungry, and she knew they would be, too. There was no room to cook with everything going on. It would be sandwiches again. She longed for her old kitchen, and her grandmother's pots and pans. That perfectly cured cast-iron skillet that fried the best chicken in the South, the family silverware that had survived Sherman's march through Georgia and accompanied Great-Granny into Louisiana when she married. It hurt to her very soul to know those links with her family were nothing but memories.

She got up quietly to see what sandwich stuff was left. These three men had gone through in two days what would last her a week or more. Before she could make a decision, Tate changed the plan.

"Hey, honey, don't worry about making something. Call Eats and order some burgers and fries, and one of us will go pick them up."

"Then the question is, how many burgers apiece? I already know Wade wants two *plus* everyone's leftovers."

They all laughed, including Wade.

"Wade, if you ever get married, I hope she can cook," she added.

His smile shifted slightly. "Oh, I've been married, and cooking had nothing to do with why we're no longer together."

"Sorry," she said.

He shrugged. "Life happens. I'll settle for your leftovers and not complain."

She patted him on the back as she left the room to call in the order, and a few minutes later Cameron went to pick it up.

As he did, he passed their neighbor driving back into the trailer park. He waved, but the man didn't seem to notice.

Hershel pulled up in front of his motor home and parked. He got out with the full intention of going inside to change and get back to the gym, but when he turned to glance at the trailer where the Feds were staying, he saw something on their roof, and when he realized what it was and that it was staring back at him, he froze. He kept thinking it would fly away, but it didn't, and he found himself in a stare-down with a vulture.

Nola was at the window when their neighbor drove past their trailer. She watched him stop and get out at his motor home, but instead of going inside, he glanced in their direction, and then didn't look away.

"That's weird," she said.

Tate looked up.

"What's weird?"

She waved him over. "Hurry."

Tate bolted toward the window.

"He's been staring like that ever since he got out of his truck," she said.

His eyes narrowed and before she knew it, he was out the door, standing on the porch. He gave the man a "What the hell's going on?" gesture. The man had a strange look on his face as he pointed up to the roof.

Tate stepped off the porch and backed up to see what was so interesting, then saw the vulture. It was staring straight at the man and the motor home like they were a tasty piece of roadkill.

"What the hell?" he muttered.

The vulture didn't budge, and when Tate turned to look at their neighbor again, he was gone. Tate shrugged, went back inside and shut the door.

"What's the deal?" Nola asked.

"He wasn't looking at us, he was looking at what's sitting on the roof."

Wade looked up. "*What's* on the roof?"

"A vulture. Craziest thing is, it's just sitting there staring at his motor home like it was about to become dinner."

Wade shivered suddenly. "Damn it. We're sleeping in a haunted trailer, and now we've got a vulture using it for a roost. If that doesn't say 'crazy,' I don't know what does."

Nola shook her head. "It's not crazy. My granny would have called that an omen."

Tate frowned. He remembered her granny. She was part Cherokee and lived a lot in the old ways.

"An omen of what, honey?"

She shrugged. "All I'm saying is, if she was here, she'd be saying, 'Somebody's going to die.'"

Tate's phone rang.

"Hello?"

Nola watched his facial expressions, and when his eyes widened, she had a feeling her granny would have been standing there saying, "I told you so."

Moments later, Tate hung up.

"The Stormchaser struck again. Killed a father and son right out in their front yard upriver."

"They weren't stranded?" Wade asked.

"Their house was surrounded by water. They were out in the yard reinforcing the sandbags they'd put around the house. But either he's getting sloppy, or he thinks he's immune to discovery."

"Why?"

"He left another witness. I doubt he knew she was there, just like he didn't know Nola was there, but it's happened twice now. The younger man's wife was upstairs and got a good look at him, although it's probably another disguise. This time he was dressed like a biker. Black pants and leather vest, a bushy mustache, black shaggy hair and wearing a baseball cap. And this time he used a rifle, probably because of the distance," Tate said.

Wade frowned. "A single bullet to the head with a

rifle, from any significant distance, isn't easy. This isn't as simple as driving a boat right up to them and taking them out with a pistol. Our man is either ex-military or a damn good hunter."

Nola slipped into the living room, crawled up into a chair and pulled her knees up beneath her chin. They were talking about murder the way other people talked about going to the store. It was startling and frightening, mostly because her life depended on them finding this particular killer, but also because it really brought home to her that this was Tate's life now.

She heard a car driving up out front and looked out the window.

"Cameron is back."

"Good. As soon as we eat, Wade and I will go out to the site. Cameron can stay here with you."

Wade rolled his eyes. "You'll have to get rid of that vulture before we go, or I swear to God, I'll shoot it off the roof myself."

Tate shook his head. "It may be gone already."

Cameron opened the door.

"You won't believe what's sitting on our roof."

"A vulture," the two men said in unison.

He nodded. "It's pretty creepy, just sitting up there."

"We're sleeping in a haunted trailer with a vulture on the roof," Wade muttered.

"No one is asleep, and it will fly away. Damn, I did not know you were so superstitious," Tate said.

Wade shrugged. "I think hamburgers will cure me."

Laughter followed, and Nola hoped it was enough to chase away lingering ghosts.

Fifteen

Hershel didn't go back to the Red Cross center as he'd promised. In fact, he didn't leave the motor home at all. He was so freaked out about the vulture watching him that even after it finally flew off, he couldn't settle down and turned on the television just to hear someone else's voice. He tuned in right in the middle of breaking news—about him.

He sat down in disbelief. He'd barely gotten back to town and they'd already found the bodies? How the hell did that—

Breath caught in the back of his throat as he heard the commentator.

Another witness? He'd left another witness behind. He jumped up and began to pace. It still didn't matter. Even if she'd seen his face, he'd been in disguise. But now he knew why the vulture had been there staring at him. It was a warning! He was making too many mistakes. Unless he rectified things now, he was going to die.

He sat back down and turned off the TV.

"Louise, I'm sorry I yelled at you. I need you to come back and talk to me. Please? I can't stand being alone. Not like this."

But Louise wasn't talking to him. He had to make something happen, and fast. Surely the Feds would leave now to go out to the kill site. When they did, he had to make his move. He needed to plan what to wear, and how to get Nola out to the boat without getting stopped. That was going to involve getting rid of whichever agent they'd left to guard her, but without killing him. Hershel was fond of the trio. They'd been through a lot together. He didn't want any of them dead. Just out of the way.

Now that he had a plan, he felt better. He made himself a sandwich and ate it standing up, looking out the back window. There was a back door on the Feds' trailer. He could drive right up to the back door and take it from there.

So what if there are two witnesses, not one?

Hershel gasped. "Louise! You came back."

I was never gone. You quit listening.

"No, no, I missed you. I was trying to hear you all this time," he said.

No you weren't, Hershel. You still don't get it, do you?

"Get what? I don't get what?"

You don't need to kill anyone. Neither woman can identify you. Why don't you just pack up and go home? You're only making this worse.

"No, I'm fixing it. They were mistakes. I have to fix the first one, and then the second one will go away."

That doesn't make sense. You're talking crazy.

He threw back his head and laughed.

"That's what they said about me at the hospital when I had my nervous breakdown. 'You're talking crazy, Hershel.' That's what they used to say. I guess I'm showing them now. I'm not crazy. I'm getting even. Thank you for coming back, but I have things to do now, and if you're not going to help me, then you need to back off. I'll talk to you later, okay?"

Silence.

"Louise? I said I'll talk to you later, okay?"

I hear you, Hershel. I just wish you could hear me.

Don Benton was in serious pain, but it wasn't anything that drugs could fix. Mrs. Coffee's daughter had just left his room after coming to make sure he was okay. Even as she was weeping for the loss of her mother, she had been apologizing for his pain and suffering, because she knew her mother had caused the wreck. She'd actually begged for his forgiveness.

He had reassured her that he would heal, convinced her that horrible accidents happen and expressed his regrets and condolences to her for her family's loss. And now she was gone and he was left to deal with what he had done to his son. Don knew that he'd treated dogs better, and he also knew that Tate would never forgive him. What he now had to come to terms with was how to live with himself. It had been much simpler when he'd been the one who had been wronged. He had carried the burden of Julia's betrayal like a shroud, and now the truth of what he'd done would be with him until they buried him in the ground.

He wanted to call Tate, but he had no number to call. What he needed was a go-between, and when he learned the chief was also in the hospital, he found out how to call from one room to another.

They made Beaudry do physical therapy twice a day and had promised to release him in the morning, which couldn't be soon enough for him, because all he wanted was to go home. Even when he finally got comfortable and was able to sleep, someone was always coming in to give him meds, check his IV or ask him if he'd had a bowel movement yet. He'd never felt so invaded in his life, so when his phone rang, he answered it gladly.

"Hello."

"Chief. Don Benton here. Heard about the shootout. How are you feeling?"

Beaudry frowned. Don was an all-right guy but

not the kind for chitchat, and the last person he would ever have expected to call.

"Oh, you know…sore, ready to go home, but still in lockup. How about you? One of the nurses told me about the accident. Really sorry about that."

"Thanks for the sympathy. But the accident's not why I called. I wanted to call my son, but I don't have his number and wondered if you did."

Beaudry frowned. A father who didn't have his own son's phone number…? He knew they had been at odds for some reason, but it said a lot about their relationship that they were so completely estranged.

"Yes, actually, I do. Give me a sec. I have to put this phone down to reach my cell."

Don sighed with relief. "No problem. Happy to wait."

Beaudry scooted himself around until he could reach his cell, pulled up the number then got back on the phone.

"Do you want me to read it out, or do you need to get a pen and paper first?"

"Just read it. I have a perfect memory. I always remember what I see and hear."

"Must be handy," Beaudry said.

Don thought about Julia's false confession and sighed.

"Not always. It seems I have a good memory but no discernment when it comes to the truth."

Beaudry gave him the number, and Don repeated it back, then thanked him and hung up without prolonging the conversation. He needed to get this over with. He got an outside line and made the call.

Tate and Cameron were getting ready to go out to the site where the latest killings had taken place when Tate's cell phone rang. He saw it was from the hospital and hesitated. It could only be two people. If it was Beaudry, he needed to take it. If it was his father, he didn't want to hear it. But without a way to tell, he was given no choice.

"Hello."

"Tate, it's me. Don't hang up."

Tate closed his eyes and then pinched the bridge of his nose in frustration.

"What do you want? I'm busy."

Don was unaccustomed to feeling inadequate, but he was getting a hard lesson in it right now.

"I wanted to thank you for donating blood."

"You're welcome. I hope you heal. Thanks for calling."

"Wait!" Don cried. "I didn't know. I honestly thought your mother was telling the truth."

Tate sighed. "Do you hear yourself? You still don't get it. You were ready to forgive *her* but not *me,* and I was the only innocent one in the picture you thought you saw."

"You don't understand. Look at it from my point of view. It was a horrible shock."

Sarcasm was thick in Tate's voice. "Not half as big a shock as having your own father punch you in the face, and throw you and everything you owned out of your own home."

Don frowned. "I know. All I can say is I'm sorry."

"Well, you should be. However, it's past repairing. Forget it. I know I have."

"I don't want to forget it, but I do want you to forgive me."

"Mom always said, 'Son, you don't always get what you want in life. Be happy with what you have.' Well, you threw me away. It's over. Deal with it."

Don wasn't happy, and yet it was nothing more than what he'd expected. "When did you know the truth?" he asked.

"Almost from the start I suspected it. Six months after you kicked us out, I found your hairbrush in some of Mom's stuff and ran a DNA test."

"Why didn't you say something?"

"Because *I* didn't want *you* anymore. My bloodline shouldn't have mattered. You were the only father I knew, and you threw me away. It's good that you're healing, but I do not want, nor will I resume, a relationship with you. You revealed your true self eight years ago, and you no longer matter to me."

The line went dead in Don's ear. He put down the phone. His hands were trembling, and the walls had begun to blur.

Tate dropped his cell phone in his pocket and then turned around. Nola was standing behind him. He shrugged.

"The call was inevitable. It's over."

"Are you okay?" she asked.

"I will *always* be okay with you in my life." He scooped her up in his arms and kissed her soundly. "We had hopes of viewing the kill site but found out it's already under water. However, the witness is talking to the Tidewater police at the moment, so we're going to go talk to her, too. Cameron will be here with you, okay?"

"Of course."

"There's a big Walmart in Tidewater. I think you're due a sketch pad and some supplies, yes?"

Nola's eyes lit up. "Oh, thank you, Tate, thank you. At last I'll get a piece of my life back."

"And we'll bring back some food for supper, too, so don't think about cooking for everybody. You're not the maid."

"I didn't mind, but I'll gladly pass on the job. Wade is never full."

He grinned. "We know. So, see you later, honey. I don't have to tell you to be careful, because I know you will."

"I trust no one, right?"

"Right."

A few minutes later he and Wade were gone, and she and Cameron were on their own.

"I'm going to take a nap," she said, "so you don't need to worry about babysitting, okay? Do your work or whatever you want. I'll be fine."

"Okay, but I won't be farther than the living room, so yell if you need anything."

"Will do," she said, and then stopped in the bathroom to get a hair band so she could braid her hair. It wasn't the best job she'd ever done, but at least her hair wouldn't be a tangled mess when she woke up.

She pulled back the covers and crawled into bed, then stretched out and closed her eyes.

The vulture was back, sitting on the roof of the Feds' trailer and still looking in Hershel's direction, which reinforced his need to remove what he considered his jinx. He'd watched two of the Feds leaving and knew which one was still there. His name was Winger. A big guy with a steady gaze. It wouldn't be easy to put him out of commission without killing him, but that option was off the table.

The trick would be choosing a disguise that Winger wouldn't see through. He'd already done the cop here, but that would still be the best way to take the Fed off guard. He'd be thinking Hershel was one of his own when he opened the door. Satisfied with his decision, Hershel began pulling out gear and running through the little monologue he would use to get himself inside.

Tate and Wade got into Tidewater just after 1:00 p.m. and went straight to the police station. They'd been there once before, the day when they'd gone to the hospital to talk to Nola, and recognized the sergeant on duty. When he looked up, it was apparent he recognized them, too.

"What are you boys after now?" he asked.

"We would like to talk to the woman who saw the man who shot her husband and father-in-law," Tate said

"That would be Patricia Fremont. She's gone to her parents' house here in town, but I need to call and make sure she's up to it. I heard she's had a breakdown."

Tate frowned. "Tell her that we won't intrude any longer than we have to, but that it's vital that we speak to her."

"Hang on," the sergeant said, and picked up the phone.

Tate stepped away from the desk while the cop made the call.

"What do you think? Will she talk?" Wade asked.

Tate shrugged. "She has to."

A few moments later the sergeant waved Tate over.

"She'll talk to you. This is the address. Go down

the street to the first stoplight and take a right. The street you want is ten blocks down. Take a left. House number is over the garage."

"Thanks for the help," Tate said.

"Just catch the crazy bastard," the sergeant said.

They left the police station, both of them thinking about how hard this interview was going to be. When this woman had woken up this morning, she'd had a husband and a father-in-law, and before noon they'd both been dead.

"She's going to be pretty fragile, probably still in shock," Tate said.

"Do you think the killer will focus on her like he has on Nola?"

"I can't say for sure, but I'd say not right away. He's going to blame any later mistakes on Nola, because she broke his perfect record, and he's going to want to deal with her first, even though she's even less likely than Mrs. Fremont to be able to ID him."

"He's crazy," Wade said.

Tate nodded. "Quite possibly literally. Hey, give Cameron a call and tell him to look for any stories of Katrina survivors who were hospitalized for mental problems after losing someone they loved."

"Will do," Wade said, and made the call.

The phone rang a couple of times, and then Cameron picked up.

"Hey, Wade."

"Hey yourself. Tate wants you to set aside any stories you find of people who had mental breakdowns after Katrina, too."

"Yeah, I figured that out and I've already started separating them out. How's it going?"

"Well, we're here and on the way to interview the latest witness. She's gone to her parents' house. Everything okay there with you two?"

"Yeah, all except that vulture is back on the roof. I heard the damn thing land."

Wade frowned. "Are you serious?"

"Unfortunately, yes. Otherwise, Nola's taking a nap and I'm on the job. See you when you get here."

"We'll call you when we get ready to head back that way and take orders for supper."

"Good. Talk to you later."

"Yeah, later," Wade said.

Tate began slowing down, looking for house numbers.

"There it is," Wade said. "The white frame house with the blue trim."

Tate pulled into the drive. "I'm not looking forward to this, so let's get it over with."

Wade patted his pocket to make sure he had a notebook, and then got out and followed Tate to the front door. It opened before he had time to knock, and a large man stepped into the doorway.

Tate took out his badge. "I'm Special Agent Benton from the FBI, and this is my partner Special

Agent Luckett. We appreciate the opportunity to speak to your daughter."

"Larry Conway. My daughter is in the living room. The doctor's done been here and gave her something to calm her down, so she's a little sleepy, but she wants to talk to you. Follow me."

They walked into the foyer and took a right into the living room. Several people were there, including a twentysomething woman wrapped in a quilt and holding a cup of coffee in her hands as if it was the Holy Grail. Even though the weather outside was sunny and calm, and the temperature was comfortable inside, she was shaking.

"That there's my daughter, Rebecca Fremont. Y'all take a seat on the sofa next to her. Becky, these are the agents from the FBI."

"Thank you," Tate said, and he and Wade nodded to the others in the room and took their seats.

The young woman looked at them blankly and then seemed to pull herself together.

"Is it true you've been looking at this killer for a while?" she asked.

"Yes, ma'am, it's true," Tate said. "May we ask you some questions?"

But she had one of her own first. "Why haven't you been able to stop him?"

Tate sighed. "Because we don't know what he looks like."

"I saw him!" she cried, and then sat up a little straighter. "I saw him plain as day."

"How was he dressed this time?" Tate asked.

"This time?" she echoed.

"We've learned that he most likely uses a different disguise every time he goes out."

"Oh, my God, oh, my God. This is crazy. He was crazy." She started to weep.

Tate waited for her to gather her emotions. When she'd calmed down, he urged her to continue.

"Just tell us exactly what you heard and saw. Don't leave out anything, no matter how small."

"We'd been sandbagging for two days, hoping to hold the water back. I wanted to come in off the farm, but J.R., that was my husband, wouldn't leave his daddy out there alone, and Jacob wouldn't leave. So we stayed. I was carrying the family keepsakes to the second floor, and they were filling bags and patching up the little levee we'd built. I heard a pop, and then another one." She began to rock back and forth, clutching the tissues. "I looked out, and saw J.R. and Jacob on the ground. Blood was running out beneath their heads, and a man was walking out of the trees."

Then she put her head down onto her knees and broke into sobs.

"I'm so sorry," Tate said. "I realize this is painful, but it's also the best time for us to talk to you.

It's when you remember everything most acutely. Do you understand?"

She moaned, then pulled herself upright, wiped her eyes and blew her nose.

"I'm sorry."

"No, ma'am, we're sorry," Tate said.

"If you can, think of this as something you are doing for your loved ones that they can't do for themselves," Wade added.

She nodded. "Yes, I understand."

"You said the man walked out of the trees. What did he do?" Tate asked.

She leaned forward. "He just stood there, like he was admiring the view. He didn't see me. I know that. But I saw him. He was middle-aged for sure, in black pants and a black leather vest with a lot of those biker chains for decoration. His hair was black and shaggy, and he had a big, bushy mustache. He was wearing a baseball cap and carrying a rifle with a scope."

Wade glanced at Tate. That explained the clean shots.

"Did you see him fire the weapon?" Tate asked.

"No."

"Can you remember how he was carrying it?"

She closed her eyes, picturing it and him in her mind, then looked up.

"It was in his left hand, and then he put it in the crook of his arm and walked away."

Strike one, Tate thought. "Did you happen to get a look at what he was driving?"

"Yes. It was a late model, short-bed Dodge Ram pickup. Couldn't tell whether it was black or dark blue. If I had to pick a color, I'd say dark blue."

Tate's heart skipped a beat. Strike two. The man in the motor home near the trailer drove a truck like that.

"Is there anything else you can think of?" he asked.

"He was bowlegged."

Strike three, and he saw from Wade's eyes that they were on the same wavelength. Tate stood abruptly.

"This is my card. If you think of anything else, please give me a call, and again, we are so sorry for your loss." He turned to her father. "Mr. Conway, thank you for allowing us into your home."

Her father got up and walked them to the door.

"Feel free to put a bullet through the bastard's head for me when you finally run him down," he said.

Tate headed for their SUV on the run, with Wade right behind him.

"Call Cameron," Tate said, the moment they got inside.

Wade grabbed his phone and hit speed dial, then waited for the call to be answered.

"Do you think it's actually him?" Wade asked.

"The fact that it *could* be is concern enough.

Using the left hand to carry the rifle, drives the same color and model truck, and has the same damn legs. That's too many similarities to ignore."

The call rang five times, then went to voice mail.

"He's not answering," Wade said. He left a quick "call me" message, then turned to Tate.

"Call the police and have them send a car to the trailer to check it out. In the meantime, we're going back."

Tate pressed harder on the gas pedal, his lips compressed into a thin line. He wouldn't let himself think about what this might mean, or that they'd gotten too cocky about keeping Nola safe.

Sixteen

Hershel was working under time constraints. Without knowing how soon the other two agents would come back, he had to consider his window of opportunity a narrow one. Because he needed to break the jinx, he had to replicate everything from that day, including what he'd been wearing. So he'd packed the same cap and uniform, the wig and mustache, and headed out the door carrying his bag and a baseball bat.

The vulture was still on the roof.

It's an omen, Hershel. You shouldn't do this.

"It's not an omen, it's just a big ugly bird," he snapped, and tossed his things in the front seat of the truck.

But instead of driving out of the trailer park, he drove all the way to the back lot and pulled in behind the bushes around an abandoned trailer falling to pieces on its lot. He dressed quickly, put on the wig, affixed the mustache to his upper lip and then added bushy brown eyebrows over his own gray ones and got back in the truck.

This time, as he drove back toward the entrance, he was coming up on the Feds' trailer from the back.

He parked his truck out in the street so it would not be immediately visible from the front or the back door, then grabbed the bat, slipped his Taser into the holster on his belt, went to the back door and knocked.

When Cameron heard the first knock, he thought for a moment Nola must have awakened and was thumping around in the back bathroom. But then he realized someone was actually knocking on the back door, which made him immediately wary.

He pulled his weapon as he got up, and then slipped down the hallway and looked out a window. When he saw a Queens Crossing officer standing on the steps holding a baseball bat, he frowned.

"What the hell?" he muttered, and with his gun still in his hand, opened the door.

Hershel was all business, as he knew an officer would be.

"Sorry to bother you, sir, but we've had a report of a missing kid who lives out here, and we're checking every residence." He held up the bat. "I saw this laying in the grass and need to check and see if it belongs to any of your kids."

"No, no kids here," Cameron said.

"Be on the lookout, okay? He's ten years old, slight build, shaggy blond hair and blue eyes."

Cameron was disarmed by the question. "Yeah, sure," he said, and looked up and out across the backyard, which was exactly what Hershel was waiting for. He swung the bat, caught the agent on the side of the head and knocked him cold.

"Sorry about that," Hershel said, and dragged him off the steps where he'd fallen. He laid the agent down in the grass beside the trailer skirt, then pulled his truck up to the back door.

He didn't have any way of knowing where Nola Landry would be, but he had to look fast. He moved to the front of the house and realized it was empty, then started down the hall to the bedrooms. The two closest ones were empty, which left the master bedroom.

He turned the doorknob and peeked in, then couldn't believe his luck. She was in bed asleep. He hurried toward the bed and shook her.

"Wake up," he said.

"Huh? What?"

When she began to roll over, he shot her with the Taser, rendering her immediately immobile.

"It's time, Nola Landry. I said I'd come for you, and I have."

The terror on her face was balm to his soul. This was what had been missing. They had to respect his authority.

He threw her over his shoulder and carried her down the hall and out the door, and out to the pickup.

Nola couldn't believe this was happening. The pain she was experiencing from the Taser was nothing compared to not being able to speak or move. Her whole body was seizing, and when she saw Cameron lying in the grass as the killer carried her out the back door, she wanted to scream, but her muscles had been rendered useless. Despite every promise Tate had made, she was going to die.

"Upsy daisy," Hershel said as he dumped her onto the floorboard of his truck, so she was sitting with her back against the seat. He rolled her over like a rag doll, tied her hands and ankles, and then gagged her so she couldn't scream. Only then did he roll her onto her back and pull off the electrodes. The electrical charge was gone, but her heart was hammering so hard it felt as if it would explode, and the muscles in her body were still seizing.

Hershel drove out the front gate, right past two kids on bicycles and a lone news van. As he was turning onto the highway, he met a police cruiser running with lights flashing. When he saw the car take the turn into the trailer park, he panicked. It might be nothing, or it might mean that Winger had already been discovered. Either way, he wasn't staying around to find out. He glanced at Nola, then hit the gas.

If their vehicle had wings, it would have been airborne. Tate was taking the curves on two wheels.

His gut feeling was that the new kills had been done specifically to draw them away, making it easier for the killer to take Nola when just one man was standing guard.

The silence inside the vehicle was brutal as they waited to hear back from the Queens Crossing P.D. When Wade's phone finally rang, they both jumped, and Tate's fingers curled tighter around the steering wheel.

"This is Luckett. Yes. Oh, damn, is he alive? Any witnesses? Thanks." Wade disconnected. "They found Cameron unconscious by the back door with a head injury, and Nola is gone. A news van saw a late model, dark blue Dodge pickup driving out, but they didn't see a passenger. They said the driver was a cop."

Tate was sick. They'd been played, and unless a miracle occurred, Nola was going to pay for it.

"We need a boat," he said. "Get on the phone and find us a boat. We'll be in Queens Crossing in about five minutes, so tell them to have one waiting down at the public boat launch."

Wade made the call to the P.D., who started scrambling to find one. Then he thought of the refugees who had been taken in by the Red Cross. Some of them had actually come into the city by boat, so he made a call to Laura Doyle. It rang so many times he was afraid it was going to voice mail, and then she finally answered.

"Hello, this is Laura."

"Laura, Agent Luckett here. We need help. Did any of your refugees come into town in a motorboat? The killer has Nola, and we're pretty sure he's taking her to the river."

Laura gasped. "Oh, dear God. Wait. I don't know, but I'll ask. Don't hang up. I'm taking the phone with me."

Wade could hear the frantic tone in her voice as she ran out into the gym and explained what she needed. He could hear other voices, all talking at once, and groaned. They needed help, not a debate. And then she was back on the phone.

"There are two men here who brought their families in to Queens Crossing in motor boats. They both have high-powered outboard motors and have volunteered to take you. They know the dangers, but they both know Nola and want to do it."

"We need the fastest boat," he said.

"He'll be at the public dock waiting for you."

"Thank you," Wade said, and hung up. "Get to the dock. We've got a boat."

The scenery was a blur, and when Tate hit the city limits he turned on the lights and siren, then drove all the way through town with lights flashing. When they reached the river, he slid to a stop at the dock. He and Wade got out on the run, heading toward a big fiberglass boat with a large outboard motor. The motor was already running, and the man at the wheel was grim-faced and waiting.

Tate recognized the man as Justin Beaudine, one of their classmates, as they jumped in the boat.

"Justin! Do you think you can find the Landry place in this flood?"

"I've run the river all my life. I know I can, Tate. Hang on."

"Hurry, man. Run it wide-open. The Stormchaser has her, and he's ahead of us."

The motor roared as the boat sped away from the dock, its wake awash in foam and debris.

Hershel was high on adrenaline. Everything was finally falling into place. He would put this woman down and be home in time to help take out the garbage at the gym. He took the turn in the road at a steady speed, not wanting to call attention to himself needlessly, but time was not on his side. The cove where he'd hidden the boat was less than a mile up ahead. He hadn't been there since the last rain, and he hoped to God it had not floated away from its mooring. That was how he'd lucked onto it in the first place, and it could happen again.

As he topped a hill, he saw an old black pickup coming toward him, driving in the middle of the road. He honked the horn, which made the driver suddenly swerve. Hershel cursed as the man finally pulled back into the proper lane and sped past. That

was all he needed—to get in a wreck with a hostage
on the floorboard. He glanced down at her. She was
starting to come around. He hadn't recharged the
Taser, but she wouldn't know that. He picked it up
and pointed it at her.

"Be still, missy, or I'll shoot you again."

*Shame on you, Hershel! Shame, shame! Just look
at her. She's a beautiful, innocent young woman who
deserves a chance to grow old. You let her go this
instant!*

"Hush up, Louise. I'm not letting her go, and that's
the end of that."

Nola moaned as her eyes filled with tears. Now
he was hearing voices—voices that were telling him
to let her go—and he was arguing with them, which
at least must mean he was torn about what he was
doing. She couldn't talk for the gag in her mouth, but
she damn sure wasn't quitting. She wanted him to
think she was, though, so she nodded, but the minute he looked back at the road she began trying to
work her hands free of the ties around her wrists.

As he took a curve in the road, he swerved a little
too close to the shoulder. The right front tire went
off the blacktop with a thump. The pickup lurched,
which threw her against the door. For a few moments
she was cheek down on the floorboard and looking
under the seat at a filet knife.

Her heart began to race, and without hesitation,
she made a big show of trying to roll over and pick

herself up. As she did, she dragged the knife behind her and began sawing at the cord he'd tied around her wrists.

"What the hell are you doing, girl?"

She froze and shook her head, trying to convince him she wasn't doing anything.

Again he picked up the Taser and pointed it at her. She squeezed her eyes shut and buried her face against her knees. She couldn't believe she'd survived so much, only to wind up back in the river. Her mama would never have awakened her and warned her to run if she was meant to die. She had no hope whatsoever that Tate would find out what had happened to her in time to save her, so she had to save herself.

All of a sudden the truck began slowing down, and when it did, her heartbeat accelerated. Was this it? Would this be where she died?

She panicked, but when he got out and circled the truck, she had a few moments more with the knife. She angled it down toward her ankles, sawing frantically at the cord in an effort to weaken the cotton strands.

Then she heard the click of the door latch and quickly shoved the knife back under the seat. The cord was fraying, and looser than it had been. When he grabbed her by the arms to pull her out, he inadvertently gripped the stitches. She threw her head back, groaning in sudden pain, swallowing the scream beneath the gag.

"Oooh, hey…got a handful of the stitches, didn't I? My bad."

He grabbed her under the arms, dragged her out of the truck and then tossed her down like a sack of feed. She landed shoulder first, then rammed her chin into the mud and the dirt, and felt blood spurt inside her mouth. But she was on the ground, which gave her friction to work on the gag. She rubbed her face against the dirt until she managed to work the gag out of her mouth. It fell down around her neck like a dirty necklace, but it was a weight symbolically lifted.

She could hear him banging and splashing in the water behind her, and rolled over to check his location. When she saw the words *Gator Bait* on the side of the boat, her heart sank. It was just as Tate had predicted. The killer was taking her back out on the river to undo his mistake.

She began struggling even harder to pull her hands and ankles free. Each time she tried, the cotton cords stretched just a little bit more.

The sun was in her eyes when she heard footsteps, and she knew he was coming. She blinked, looked up and caught sight of a small squirrel watching silently from the branches above her. Something crawled out of her hair and down across her forehead. Normally that would have freaked her out, but it was nothing in comparison to the man coming toward her.

"Well, I see you've managed to remove your gag. That's okay. There's no one for miles in any direction to hear you, so scream to your heart's content."

She wanted to, but she wouldn't give him the satisfaction. She was trying to remember everything she'd heard Tate say about the killer's mental state. She knew he thought of her as a mistake to be rectified, so she had to play off that fact to her advantage.

"You're the one who'll be screaming when the FBI finally catches you—and they will. If not now, then later," she snapped.

Hershel didn't like it that she wasn't crying. Louise had cried on that roof. She had begged for her insulin, but he couldn't get to it.

"They know nothing about me," he said. "And you can shut up."

"Then I'll talk to Louise," Nola said. "She's the only one around here with any sense."

Hershel frowned. Louise didn't talk to anyone but him.

She's right, Hershel. I'm the voice of reason. You better heed me. I'm telling you now to let her go.

"I'm not letting her go, and that's the end of that, Louise."

"See, she told you to let me go. I told you she's the voice of reason."

"She's dead, so her opinion no longer matters," he said.

"Well *I* didn't kill her, and what you're doing to me makes no sense, so I guess that makes you crazy," Nola said, then waited for rage to follow.

Instead, his eyes narrowed and then he burst out laughing.

"That's what they told me at the hospital. 'You're crazy, Hershel.' That's what they said."

Her heart skipped a beat. "I thought your name was Bill Carter. So you're not only crazy, but you're also a liar? Well, that's just perfect."

Hershel yanked her to her feet, then slapped her.

"Shut the hell up," he snapped, then threw her over his shoulder and carried her to the boat. He dropped her unceremoniously into the standing water that had collected in the hull.

She screamed as something slithered beside her arm.

He glanced down at her and frowned.

"There's a snake in here. Get me out! Get me out or you can't make it right!" she screamed.

Hershel panicked, and before he realized it, he was following her orders. He dragged her out of the boat, then used an oar to find and flip the snake out into the river.

"You better make sure there aren't any more in there or you'll die out here, too," she said.

Hershel stirred the paddle through the water several times, and then went back to the truck and began digging around in the junk in the truck bed for a bucket. As he did, he realized there was a bag of garbage from the Red Cross center still in there that he'd missed dumping in the bins. All of a sudden the sudden appearance of the vulture made sense. It had smelled the rotting food. He laughed again, relieved to have deciphered the mystery, and threw the trash out into the woods.

"You were wrong, Louise! That vulture wasn't an omen. It just wanted the garbage in the back of my truck."

He found the bucket, then went back to the boat and began bailing out the water until he was certain there was nothing else in it. Then he tossed the bucket into the boat and Nola after it.

She was lying in several inches of water, which was stretching the cotton even more, and pulling as hard as she could as Hershel crawled into the boat. He took the oar and pushed them out into the current, then started the engine. The moment it roared to life, Nola could feel her life grow shorter.

She could see very little from where she was lying other than birds, blue sky and the occasional jet trail. With no way to judge where they were, she didn't know how much longer she had left to try to get free. Besides, she realized, even if she'd been sitting up in the boat, whatever landmarks she might have recognized were either washed away or under water.

The outboard motor was a roar in her ears, blocking out all other sounds, and the floor of the boat was vibrating against her back as it sped through the water. She glanced at his face, trying to judge his demeanor. He didn't appear panicked or particularly deadly. If it wasn't for the pistol on his hip and the Taser beside him, she might have thought they were simply out for a leisurely ride.

Knowing she might never see Tate again was heartbreaking. They'd lost precious years of their past because of his father, and now they were going to lose their future because of a madman.

Although she couldn't hear him, when she realized the man was talking to himself again, her panic increased. Despite the raw and bleeding flesh around her wrists, she continued to struggle with the cords, pushing and pulling, pushing and pulling, repeating the process over and over until all of a sudden one hand slipped free. Relief was physical, but brief. Now if she could only get her ankles free, she would have a fighting chance.

When he began to slow down, she panicked. They must be getting close. If she was going to make a move, it was now or never. She began working her ankles as hard as she had her wrists.

He saw her moving around in the boat and yelled at her, but she couldn't hear what he said. To hide what all her movement was about, she raised herself up to a sitting position and screamed a curse at him.

He laughed and pointed the Taser at her again, and when he did, she finally noticed it wasn't ready to fire. Seconds later she felt the cords beginning to give around her ankles. It wouldn't take much more than a kick or two and her legs would be free, as well, so she stopped, waiting for the right moment to make her break.

Hershel eased off on the gas and began scanning the area, looking for landmarks. He remembered what the water had looked like before, but everything had changed. After the second round of storms that had fed into already flooded areas, even trees that had been there before were gone. He remembered coming around a bend and seeing the three people on the roof of a house, and then about a hundred yards or so farther down there had been a stand of trees, which was where Nola Landry had taken refuge, and where she'd witnessed what he'd done.

"They're gone," he muttered. "Everything is gone."

It's a sign, Hershel. It's a sign from God that you need to stop. You have to turn back and let her go.

"Louise, can't you see I'm busy? I'll talk to you later, after I'm done with her."

I'm telling you, stop! Stop now!

Hershel began hitting his fist against the side of

his head, trying to pound the sound of her voice out of his ears. "Shut up! Quit yelling!"

Nola could see he was freaking out. If Louise was yelling at him, then it was now or never. She kicked the cords loose from around her ankles and jumped up.

Hershel was so shocked to see her untied and upright that he froze, and when he did, she leaped at him, grabbing for the gun around his waist. All of a sudden the boat was rocking from side to side, and he was struggling to keep from falling out.

She grabbed the gun out of the holster at the same time as he grabbed her hand. Now they were wrestling for control of the pistol. She kicked at his ankle, knocking him sideways against the outboard motor. The boat was still rocking back and forth as it began to turn in a circle, with both of them fighting for control of the gun.

Nola's hand was on the trigger as Hershel pushed the pistol up into the air. The first shot went off so close to his ear that he thought he'd been shot. He screamed in rage, but she didn't turn loose, and her grip never wavered. As their boat swung back around again, he saw another boat bearing down on them with the other two Feds inside.

This was where a man had to know when to cut and run. He doubled up his fist and hit her on the jaw, then threw her over the side. He palmed the pistol, and opened the throttle as wide as it would go, leaving a rooster-tail of water flying up behind him as he fired off one shot after another at the boat behind him.

Seventeen

Tate thought the river smelled like death. Whatever had flooded and floated away was mixed up into a dark, muddy stew as they raced up-river from Queens Landing.

Wind tore through his hair, burning his eyes and blurring his vision, but his gaze didn't waver as he searched the roiling water ahead for signs or sounds of another boat.

Wade was sitting behind him, watching the riverbanks in case the killer might be moored, while Justin ran the motor at full throttle, keeping an eye out for submerged logs and gators.

They passed a flock of egrets roosting in a tree, and then an old rusted school bus that had become caught on something below the water. There was a gator on the far shore sunning itself, and another partially submerged nearby.

Tate wanted to go faster, but they were already

pushing the engine to the max. Every mile they put behind them put them closer to the Landry homestead, but anything he might have used as a landmark was gone.

Come on, you bastard. Show yourself. Where the hell are you? At the same time he was cursing the killer, he was willing Nola to fight. *Stay alive, baby, stay alive until we can find you.*

They had been on the water for almost ten minutes and were coming around a bend in the river when Tate suddenly shouted and began pointing at a boat circling in the water. Two people were standing up and fighting, and the only thought going through his head was that they'd found them and Nola was still alive.

No sooner had he thought that than the killer swung a fist and hit Nola on the jaw. When the killer tossed her body over the side, Tate screamed and began firing as the killer gunned the engine and headed upstream.

Tate shouted at Justin and pointed in the direction they needed to go.

"She's there! Get me closer!"

Justin swerved, and the boat skimmed across the water toward her body.

"Wade! Aim for the engine!" Tate yelled, because his own focus was on Nola.

She was still afloat, but barely. He could see her beginning to sink, and he began tearing off his jacket and kicking off his boots. He stood up and went over the side after her just as Justin cut the engine. By the time he came up, she was already gone. Only her long dark hair was still floating on the surface, and even that was going down fast. He lunged for it, frantically wrapping it around his wrist as he began to pull. She popped out of the water like a cork on the end of a fishing line, limp and lifeless. Her head lolled against her shoulder as he lifted her out of the water, and then he began to shake her, treading water as he waited for the boat to circle back.

"Damn it, Nola! Don't you die. Don't you dare die!"

Wade was shooting at the killer, but the boat was moving out of range. All of a sudden Justin shouted, "Use this!" and tossed a rifle at Wade.

He caught it and spun, took aim at the big engine on the back of the boat and fired, then fired again.

The explosion sent birds into flight. Gators were sliding into the water as flames shot skyward. The river was on fire.

Justin was already circling the boat. He pulled up beside Tate as Wade leaned over the side and pulled Nola's lifeless body out of Tate's arms. Moments later Tate was in the boat with them and Wade was on his knees performing CPR.

"Let me! Let me!" Tate yelled, and took over breathing for her as Wade did chest compressions.

They worked silently and in perfect unison while

time seemed to stop. One minute passed into another and another, and when she finally gasped and then choked and coughed and began spitting up water, Tate rolled her onto her side.

"Thank you, Jesus," he mumbled, and then rocked back on his heels and kept thumping her back, helping her cough up the water she had swallowed.

"She's gonna make it!" Justin yelled, and then let out a whoop.

Wade was still on his knees and considered it a proper position for a moment of silent thanks.

She coughed again and again, until at last she drew breath without a struggle. When she finally opened her eyes, Tate took his own first easy breath.

"Tate?"

"I'm here, baby."

"…saved me," she mumbled.

Tate began checking her body for gunshot wounds or broken bones, but he found nothing. Her danger was going to be infection and pneumonia. The river was toxic, and she'd had a big drink.

"The boat blew up," Wade said.

"Did you see the body?" Tate asked.

"No, but I saw the gators."

Tate looked up at Justin.

"Take us past the wreckage for a look, then get us back to Queens Crossing as fast as you can."

"Is she gonna be okay?" Justin asked.

"God, I hope so," Tate said as he picked her up

and settled her into his lap, then put his jacket around her and held her close.

Nola was cognizant of two things: Tate had found her, and she was safe. Beyond that, she asked for nothing. The stench of burning fuel was in her nose as they cruised past the site of the explosion, but she wouldn't look. She didn't need to. He was dead, and that was all that mattered.

Tate scanned the surface of the water and the shoreline with a steady eye. If there was even a piece of the killer left, he wanted it. It would be physical proof this bloody chase was over.

Wade pointed to a piece of the boat as it floated past them. *Gator Bait.* The boat had been aptly named.

A gator swam away as they passed. It appeared the man had died in the explosion and the gators had gotten what was left.

"Justin! Take it back!" Tate yelled.

Justin waved an okay, circled the boat and headed home.

Nola couldn't quit shaking, but she was holding on to Tate's shirt with both hands. When the wind began to tear through her hair, she turned her face to his chest and closed her eyes.

Hershel never knew how he got there, but when he came to he was on the shore, lying half in and half out of the water. He was in more pain than he'd ever felt in his life. When he touched a hand to his cheek and came away with pieces of skin stuck to his fingers, he gagged. The stench of burning fuel and scorched flesh was in his nose, and his eyes burned almost as much as his face. As he rolled over, he saw the fire out in the water and another boat a hundred yards downstream, and just like that, memory surfaced.

"Oh, my God, oh, my God," he mumbled, and began crawling on his belly out of the water, up into the grass and into the woods.

He didn't move so much as a muscle until the sound of the outboard motor had completely disappeared. Added to that, his head was throbbing and he couldn't blink without wanting to throw up.

You have a concussion, Hershel. It's a miracle you're even alive. You've got to get back to your truck and run. They know who you are. You waited too long. I told you. I told you to stop, but you wouldn't listen.

"God in heaven, Louise, stop talking. Just shut the hell up. I don't even know where the truck is from here."

You have to go upriver to find the truck, because you were coming downriver in the boat.

Hershel shuddered. For once Louise was actually making sense. He tried to stand up, but when he did, everything went black.

* * *

The next time he came to, the sun was only a couple of hours from setting. He dragged himself upright, and began the long and painful journey back to where he'd left the truck. Every step he took was in pain, every breath he drew an agony and what was left of the right side of his face was in shreds. At least he was on the right side of the river.

He couldn't go back to the motor home, and once they began looking into his life, they would know everything, but he couldn't let that matter. What he needed now was time, and a place to heal.

Wade made a call from the river, requesting an ambulance at the dock, and when they arrived there were several news crews with it. Once again Nola Landry had made the news. As they were loading her up on a gurney, the reporters descended.

"What about the Stormchaser? Did you kill him? Did he get away again?"

"This is yours," Tate said to Wade. "I'm going in the ambulance with Nola. Come get me later."

They loaded up and left the scene as Wade began fielding the reporters' questions.

"What happened to the Stormchaser?" someone yelled out.

He went into agent mode and answered as briefly as possible without giving anything away.

"The boat he was in blew up as he was making his escape."

"How did that happen?"

"He was shooting at us. We returned fire."

"Did you recover the body? Do you know his identity?"

"We did not recover the body and at this point have not made a positive identification, although that will come in time."

"Why didn't you look for the body?"

Wade frowned. "We did look, but there were alligators in the water around the wreck, and we had Miss Landry's welfare to consider. She was unconscious and had stopped breathing when we pulled her out of the water. She was resuscitated on scene and transported here."

"Who's the man with you?"

They were pointing at Justin Beaudine.

"He's the real hero of the moment," Wade said. "He's the man you need to be talking to. If it wasn't for his help, we would never have been able to catch up to the killer or save Miss Landry."

When the crews began focusing their attention on Justin, Wade waved and grinned. Justin looked a little nervous but willingly answered their questions.

Everybody deserves their fifteen minutes of fame, Wade thought, and headed to the hospital.

Nola came to again in the ambulance and mistook the siren for the roar of the outboard motor and the straps holding her onto the gurney as the cords she'd been bound with, and began fighting to get free.

A paramedic was trying to calm her as Tate quickly grabbed her hands.

"Nola! You're okay. You're on the way to the hospital, baby."

She heard his voice but couldn't see him.

"Tate?"

"I'm here," he said, and leaned over from behind her so she could see his face.

"Is he dead?"

"We think so."

She moaned. "But you don't know?"

Like her, he longed for proof.

"Not yet. The boat he was in blew up. There was fire, and gators all over the place. I don't see how anyone could live through it."

"He was crazy like you said. He was intending to take me back to where he made a mistake by leaving me alive. He kept talking to someone named Louise, like he could hear her voice and was having an argument with her. His name is Hershel, but he said he was Billy Carter at the gym."

"Nola, honey, that's great. We'll find out all the details soon enough, but right now, you're the one I'm worried about."

When the ambulance took a sharp turn to the left, she moaned as the gurney shifted with it.

"My chest hurts…hard to breathe."

"We did CPR."

Her eyes widened as his meaning sank in.

"Was I dead? I didn't see any light. I didn't see Mama anywhere."

"That's because it wasn't your time to go. Just relax, Nola. Listen, the siren's winding down. We must be there."

When the ambulance stopped and the doors flew open, they rolled her out so fast Tate had to run to catch up.

Doctor Tuttle was on duty when they came in, and he was visibly shaken to see that the patient was Nola. The paramedics briefed the staff and then left her to them.

"Tate! What on earth! They just said drowning patient," the doctor said as Tate followed them into the examining room.

"It's a long story, Doc, but she was in the river, and when we pulled her out, she wasn't breathing."

"Nola, can you hear me? Can you tell me where you hurt?" Tuttle asked.

She opened her eyes. "Arm hurts. Chest hurts. Hurts to breathe."

"Those stitches will have to be redone," Tuttle said as he eyed the ripped flesh of her arm, and then he began issuing orders to the staff. "Clean up this wound, and be thorough. She was in the floodwater. Prepare for stitches. I want a picture of her lungs. Get a portable x-ray here, STAT."

Nola closed her eyes. There was too much going on to deal with, and all she wanted to do was sleep. But the moment she closed her eyes, they popped open again.

"Tate? Where's Tate?"

"I'm here," he said, and patted her foot beneath the sheet. "Just lie still. You're going to be fine."

Someone was swabbing her arm, bringing fresh tears to her eyes, and her voice was thready when she asked, "Will you be here when I wake up?"

"Always."

She was beginning to shake. "I'm cold," she mumbled.

Doc Tuttle brushed a hand across her forehead.

"She's going into shock. Start an IV."

It was the last thing she heard as she realized Tate was there. It was safe to give up control.

Hershel found the truck after dark just by walking along the shore until he saw the dark hood gleaming in the moonlight.

The pain was his only companion, because Louise had been silent ever since she'd told him how to find the truck, and he was wondering if it was possible for her to die twice. She never had been as strong as he was, but he'd stayed with her through their ordeal, right to the bitter end and beyond. The only reason he could think of to explain why she would abandon him in his hour of need was if she had died again.

When he finally crawled into the cab and reached for the key, his heart nearly stopped. It wasn't in the ignition. Then he remembered putting it in his pocket and wondered if, by some miracle, it was still there. He patted his pocket, and when he felt the bulge of keys beneath his fingers, he started sobbing with relief.

The truck started, but at first he didn't hear it. It was only after he felt the vibration and put it in gear that he knew it was running. He didn't know whether it was a temporary thing from the explosion, or if he'd truly lost his hearing, but it scared him. He turned the radio up as loud as it would go just to reassure himself he wasn't deaf, and drove out of the cove and back onto the old blacktop, then headed east, putting as much distance between him and Queens Crossing as he could manage.

When he saw a highway sign indicating a road that would take him in to Jackson, Mississippi, he took it. His whole body was shaking, and he couldn't focus on one thing long enough to have a complete thought. His only plan was to drive until he found a city, then a hospital. They took in indigents without IDs and good sense. He knew how to blend in. He'd been crazy after Louise died, but he knew how to act. He knew what they looked for.

Twice during the night he had to pull over and throw up. The second time he stripped out of his uniform and into the oldest clothes he had in the truck, pulled out all of his identification papers, fake ones and real, and set the whole lot on fire on the side of the road.

The mere sight of more flames made him weak in the knees, and he was sobbing uncontrollably from the pain in his body.

Once that was done, he removed the license tag from his truck, flung it into a nearby field and put the stolen one back on. Satisfied he'd done all he could to protect himself, he locked himself inside the truck and went to sleep. If he died, then so much the better. If he woke up, then he would keep driving. It wasn't much of a plan, but it was all he had.

A couple of hours later a truck driver honked loud and long as he passed Hershel's pickup parked on the side of the highway. Hershel woke abruptly, his heart pounding, and realized he'd just pissed in his pants.

"Oh, Lord, Lord, just let me die," he moaned.

He began digging through the glove box and the console, looking for painkillers, and when he finally found some, he took a handful and chewed them up like candy. The taste was horrible, and he'd taken at least twice the recommended dosage, but he was past caution. Once he got them swallowed, he started the truck and pulled back out onto the highway.

When he crossed the city limits of Jackson, Mississippi, it was just before 5:00 a.m. The traffic was just beginning to build, with early morning workers heading to their jobs. He followed the signs to the nearest hospital and parked in the back of the lot.

"Oh, my God," had become his mantra, and he kept saying it over and over to keep from screaming as he emptied his pockets, leaving what money he had on him in the console and the keys in the ignition. Having it stolen was the fastest way to remove the last trace of where he'd gone.

When he got out and started walking toward the Emergency Room entrance, he began to stumble and stagger. He made it just inside the doors before stumbling again, and this time he went down, unconscious.

He woke up screaming some time later, as the doctors and nurses were cleaning the burns on his face and arm.

"Stop…oh, my God, stop!" he cried, begging and grabbing at their hands. Then he heard a voice.

"My name is Doctor Hudson. You're in a hospital. Can you tell me your name? Do you know what happened to you?"

Hershel could only see clearly from one eye, and he turned his head toward the man's voice.

"My name is Phil. I think something started a fire. Maybe a crack pipe. I can't remember."

"Do you do drugs, Phil?"

The side of his face suddenly felt as if it was on fire. He screamed again.

"I'm sorry, Phil. We have to remove the dead skin off your face before it can begin to heal properly."

"Can't you give me something for the pain?" he begged.

"Do you take drugs, Phil?"

"No, no, never."

"But you said a crack pipe."

Even in the midst of the pain, he was already playing into his new persona.

"Not mine," he said, and then moaned. "The guy in the alley beside me."

"Where do you live?" the doctor asked as they continued to work.

"Nowhere. I have no home."

"You're homeless?"

"Homeless," Hershel muttered.

"Phil! What's your last name," the doctor asked. Hershel closed his eyes and didn't answer.

"Doctor, I think he passed out," a nurse said.

"It's just as well, poor bastard. This is going to leave one hell of a scar."

Don Benton was being released from the hospital. He was packing his things when he overheard a conversation between two nurses about Tate's heroic rescue of Nola Landry. It was yet another reminder that the son he'd rejected had grown into a man of integrity and courage.

He hailed one of the nurses who quickly came

running. Being a doctor, as well as a patient, in the local hospital had its perks.

"Which room is Nola Landry in?" he asked.

"She's down the hall in 217."

"How is she doing? Is she up to visitors?"

"I'm sorry, Doctor Benton, but I don't know her status. I can find out for you."

"Never mind. I'll check in on her myself before I leave. Thank you for the information."

"You're welcome. When you're ready to leave, call the nurses' station and we'll take you down."

He felt a little unsteady on his feet as he headed down the hall, and he was nervous about seeing her, because he was going to ask a favor. He wanted her to intercede with Tate on his behalf. When he reached the door he didn't bother to knock, then realized that he should have.

When Tate looked up and saw his father coming in the door, he frowned. The bastard never did know when to quit. Without saying a word, he got up and pushed his father back out into the hall, and then closed the door behind them. Nola was asleep, and he intended to leave her that way.

Don wasn't happy. He'd hoped to see Nola alone, but he should have realized that might not be easy. Tate met his father's gaze unflinchingly.

"What?"

His son's lack of emotion was unsettling. Don didn't quite know how to begin.

"Uh, I heard about what happened and wanted to see how she was doing."

"She's alive."

"And the killer is dead?" Don asked.

"I don't know that."

"Really? I thought…"

Unwilling for the whole floor to hear their argument, Tate lowered his voice to just above a whisper.

"You don't give a shit about anything but yourself, and we both know it, so what the fuck are you doing here?"

Don shrugged. "Honestly? I was hoping she might intercede with you on my behalf."

"With me?"

Don nodded. "I'm sorry if you aren't prepared to talk to me, but—"

Tate wanted to shake him and had to remember he had recently been in a wreck.

"Remember the night you wouldn't talk to me?" Tate snapped.

Don sighed. "Yes."

"Well, so do I, and that is never going to change. You are nothing to me. You were dead to me the night you threw me out of the only home I'd ever known like some stray off the street. Go away. You will never be a part of my life."

"But if you and Nola marry, what about my grandchildren?"

"Nothing of mine will ever be yours. Go home. If

you want someone to talk to in your waning years, talk to God. You have a lot of explaining to do."

"But—"

Tate went back inside and shut the door, leaving Don alone in the hall. It was beginning to dawn on him that in working with the dead, he'd lost his ability to communicate with the living, and that was his burden to carry. He put a hand on the door, then turned and walked away.

Inside, Tate resumed his seat at Nola's side, exhausted by the continual pressure from his father. The man was such an egomaniac. He'd rejected him once for a lack of proper lineage, and now that he had proof his precious DNA had been reproduced, he was ready to lay claim to his son again. The sooner they left Queens Crossing the better, and as soon as the entire team was healed at the same time, they would be gone.

Cameron still had at least a couple of days before he would be released for travel, and Nola's welfare was up in the air. They were all holding their breath that she didn't develop pneumonia or some kind of infection. The original wound in her arm had just begun to heal before this happened. She was a long way from out of the woods, and he wasn't leaving without her.

As for the killer's fate, there was a knot in the pit of his stomach that wouldn't go away. Until he had physical proof that the man was dead, Tate would not rest easy. He wanted to go back to the site of the explosion and search the shore on both sides of the river. As soon as the guards he'd sent for arrived to stay with Nola, he and Wade were going, if for no other reason than to complete their final report.

Nola moved restlessly beneath the sheets, which led him to believe she was in pain. A deep frown creased her forehead as she reached for the bandages on her arm.

"No, baby, leave it alone," he said softly.

She reached out again, but this time grabbing his hand and then holding on.

"I'm here," he said. "Rest easy."

"Love you," she whispered, then drifted back into a semiconscious state again.

"Love you, too," he said, remembering the fear that had swept through him when he'd seen her fighting the man they'd been chasing for so long.

She'd had her hands on the killer, which was a hell of a lot more than they could say. She'd fought him for her life and defeated him twice. It couldn't happen again.

The two bodyguards Tate had hired arrived before daylight. He got a text from Wade saying they were at the trailer and would be at the hospital by 7:00 a.m. He sent a text back to acknowledge the message and remind Wade to bring the duffel bag from his bed-room when he came to pick him up.

Nola was dreaming. She was standing on one side of the flooded river, and the killer was standing on the other side. Even from that vast distance she could tell he was laughing.

An ambulance siren suddenly sounded beneath the window of her room and woke her up just as Tate was finishing a call. She saw him drop the phone in his pocket and called his name.

"Tate?"

"I'm right here."

"I had a dream. I dreamed he wasn't dead."

He brushed the hair away from her forehead and then kissed the side of her cheek.

"Dreams are just dreams, honey. Are you in pain? Want me to get a nurse?"

She nodded.

He buzzed for the nurse and then helped her sit up. "Are you dizzy?"

"I don't think so. Just weak."

He took her hair band out and smoothed her hair back down with his hands, then refastened the band.

"Where's a hairbrush when you need one, right?" he said.

She leaned forward and laid her face against his chest.

"I thought I was never going to see you again."

"I was pretty scared about the same thing my-self," he said.

"Ask me to go with you," she whispered.

He wrapped his arms around her.

"When we leave here, will you come with me?"

"Yes."

The love she felt was on her face, and he saw it.

"No matter where my job takes me, I'll always come back to you. Is that okay?" he asked.

"Yes, yes."

"I have a nice apartment in D.C., but we can get a house with a great room for your studio."

Tears rolled down her cheeks.

"I don't care where I live, as long as it's with you."

"Well, *I* care, and you won't regret it. I promise," he said.

"The only regret I've ever had was losing you be-fore. I won't let that happen again," she said.

The door opened, and the nurse came in carry-ing a syringe. After a quick check of Nola's IV and bandages, she injected the pain meds into the port.

"Is there anything else you need, honey? Do you need to go to the bathroom?"

"I can take her if she needs to go," Tate said.

The nurse nodded and left the room.

"So, do you want to go before you lie back down?"

"I guess."

They had to roll the IV stand with her, and as soon as he got her to the bathroom, he stepped out to wait, and in that moment, standing in the dark in the hospital room, he felt his mother's spirit so strongly that he nearly dropped to his knees. His eyes filled with tears, but he wiped them away.

"I miss you, Mom. Go with God. We're fine," he whispered, and just like that, the feeling passed.

When Nola came out, Tate rolled the stand beside her as she walked, then got her settled into bed.

"I have something to tell you," he said.

A frown immediately crossed her face.

"Is it bad?"

"No, but it's business and has to be done. In just a little while Wade and I have to go back out to the site of the explosion. We can't finalize the investigation until both sides of the shore have been thoroughly searched. It's just protocol."

Her eyes widened. "I don't think he's dead," she whispered.

"That was just your dream, remember? We won't know anything until we look. You know that, right?"

She nodded.

"So, what I want you to know is that two bodyguards will be here to watch over you, standing outside the door. When anyone comes inside, one will come with them. I've known these men since my days in the academy. They're both ex-Navy SEALs and good friends. I trust them with my life, and I trust them with you. Are you okay with this?"

"Of course I'm okay. Just do your job, Tate. I'll be here when you get back."

Eighteen

The sun was a faded version of its normal self, which was all the warning they were going to get that the weather was likely to change. Tate didn't care what it did, as long as it didn't rain.

Cameron was unhappy about being left out of the search and as anxious as Nola to find out if the sorry bastard was still alive. It was an embarrassment to admit he'd been tricked, and nothing anyone said made it better. The only positive thing about his situation was that Laura Doyle was visiting regularly.

Tate had changed into the sturdier clothes and hiking boots from his duffel bag and was downing his last bite of doughnut as he drove out of town.

"What do you think we're going to find?" Wade asked.

"I would be happy with a body part."

Wade had worked with Tate Benton for nearly six

years now and considered him more like a brother than just a partner.

"Why do I feel like there's a 'but' in that statement?"

Tate shrugged. "Because I don't think he's dead."

Wade was shocked.

"Why are you so sure of that? You saw the explosion, the fire, the boat in pieces and the gators."

"I don't know. It just doesn't feel over."

"Well, I hope to hell you're wrong," Wade said.

"So do I."

"We're on land, so how do you know how to get to the right part of the shore? There aren't any roads, and all the normal landmarks are under water."

"I grew up here. I'll know," Tate said.

About thirty minutes later, after driving down a lot of rural roads, and winding through a couple of pastures, Tate stopped.

"This is as far as we'll be able to drive. We'll have to walk it from here."

As he got out, he checked to make sure his weapon was loaded, then used the compass on his watch to align with true south and started walking.

The land was spongy and waterlogged, which made walking slower than usual, and the footing was even worse the closer they got to the floodwater. As they entered the woods, their presence was duly noted by the local four-footed denizens, who either fled or took cover. A small alligator slithered out from beneath some leaves and headed for the water, reminding them that far larger ones could be anywhere.

"We're almost there," Tate said. "Keep an eye out for signs of the boat—or a body."

Wade nodded, and a few minutes later they walked out of the woods and stopped just short of the water. Tate looked out across the flood, aligning where they were standing with what he could see of the shore on the opposite side.

"If he got out on this side, it would have been somewhere in this area. If we don't find anything for a mile in either direction, then we'll have to drive down to Tidewater to cross and check the other shore."

"I'll go downriver," Wade said.

"And I'll go up. Call me if you find anything, and watch out for gators. They could be up here sunning."

"Dandy," Wade muttered.

They parted at the water's edge and started moving slowly in opposite directions.

Tate was about two hundred yards up from where he'd started when he stopped, staring in disbelief at what was in front of him. The drag marks here could have been a gator dragging itself out of the water to sun, except for the human handprints on either side. A dozen feet from the water, he saw footprints. His heart sank.

"Son of a bitch."

He grabbed his cell phone and made the call, waiting for Wade to answer.

"Yeah?"

"I found tracks."

"On my way."

Tate disconnected, then switched to camera mode and began taking pictures all the way into the trees.

"In here!" he yelled, when he saw Wade approaching.

His partner came running.

"You're right. Someone crawled out of the water here. The likelihood of it being anyone but our killer is slim to none," Wade said as he stared at the tracks.

Tate pointed. "They lead off in this direction. If we're lucky, we'll find his body."

Wade didn't bother commenting on what would happen if they didn't.

"He has to be hurt," Wade said.

Tate pointed down at the ground. "You can see by these tracks that his steps are all over the place, and dragging." He stopped to take some more pictures. "If we don't find a body, we'll notify hospitals in the area. It's just after 9:00 a.m., so let's go."

They walked for almost an hour before they came up on a little clearing. There was a mooring rope still tied around a tree and tire tracks less than fifty feet away. Once again, Tate felt blindsided.

"This can't be happening," he muttered, and then shoved his hands through his hair in utter frustration.

"Nola had a dream that he wasn't dead. Damn it! I can't believe he not only lived through that explosion *and* the gators, he actually got away."

"It must have thrown him clear," Wade said. "It's the only explanation."

For the first time since he'd joined the FBI, Tate actually felt defeated.

"I do not want to file this report."

"Let's head back. There's a lot we have to do," Wade said.

"We need to get some more pictures. I need some of the tire tracks and of the mooring rope before we leave."

"I'll call Queens Crossing P.D. and have them begin notifying hospitals in the area to be on the lookout for a burn victim."

"Tell them to put a guard on the motor home, too. I don't think he'd have the balls to come back, but I'm not taking chances."

"Will do," Wade said as Tate began taking pictures.

As soon as he finished, he sent everything to his laptop and to Quantico, and then they began the long walk back.

"You do know that he could have driven off and died somewhere on his own," Wade said as they retraced their steps.

Tate shrugged. Anything was possible. They'd just been slapped with that fact.

The trip back into Queens Crossing was all but silent. Finally it was Tate who broke the silence.

"Nola said the man's real name was Hershel. We need to go through that motor home and see if we can figure out what started him killing. Maybe it will lead us to where he would go to heal."

"Are we going to do it here?"

"Initial search here I think. Then have it towed to Quantico. If there's anything in there that might help us run him down, they'll find it."

By the time they got back, the usual small-town grapevine had already heard the news. The Storm-chaser hadn't died in the explosion, and the FBI was no closer to arresting him now than they had been two months ago. It was not their finest hour. The only positive in the entire day was that the news crews had left town, abandoning them for a hot new story.

They stopped by the trailer to shower and change, then Tate grabbed his laptop to file the reports and pocketed a couple of candy bars, and they were out the door.

Wade dropped him off at the hospital and headed back. He was going to do the initial search of the motor home and hope for a break. They were due one.

Nola was sitting up in bed when Tate walked in.

"I heard," she said. "What happens next?"

He put his laptop on the chair and then headed for the bed.

"You are my hero," he said, and wrapped her in his arms. "I screwed up."

"You blew him up and he's still alive. How is that your fault? Stop beating yourself up and kiss me."

He groaned and kissed her until good sense made him stop.

She patted the side of the bed for him to sit down, so he did.

"What did you do with Tweedle Dum and Tweedle Dee?" she asked.

He grinned. "I sent them back to the trailer for the night."

"Do you have to stay here to continue your investigation?"

"We're checking area hospitals for burn or accident victims. If nothing turns up there, and we don't get any leads from the stuff in his motor home, then we go back to D.C. and wait. Either he'll go to ground and call it quits, or something will trigger the urge and he'll start all over again."

She rolled her eyes. "Does this happen often?"

"No, but it happens."

"Does it make you crazy?"

He smiled. "*You* make me crazy."

"When all my bruises fade, I will marry you."

The smile slid off his face. "It feels wrong to be

grateful that a serial killer brought me back to you, but that's pretty much a fact of our life."

"All I can say is that we're not naming our first-born Hershel."

His smile was back. "Uh, Nola Jean?"

"What?"

"When your bruises fade, will you marry me?"

"Yes, thank you."

"You're going to like Washington," he said.

"I know. We're going to find a house with a room for my studio, and you'll chase bad guys and I'll paint pictures, and we'll live happy ever after."

"That sounds like a deal."

She started to laugh and then coughed.

He frowned.

"Lie back down. You're not well."

"But I will be," she said. "You wait and see."

Hershel had little to no memory of how he'd gotten to Jackson. The race to escape through the night had become lost in the haze of drugs and pain that ruled his life for the past week. The burns on his face were beginning to granulize, and the healing was taking place. It was a slow process, but he wasn't going anywhere. The first time he was allowed to get up and walk, the first thing he'd done was get to a window overlooking the parking lot to see if his truck was still there, but it was gone.

He tried to smile, but his facial muscles wouldn't

let him. It was comforting to know his fellow man had done him a favor by stealing it.

Either way, Phil the homeless guy who'd gotten burned by an exploding crack pipe had nothing to do with Hershel Inman or Bill Carter. And he had most of his money stashed in a bank in Virginia under another name, so when he was ready to leave, he had money to help him disappear.

What you need to do is go hide and thank God you weren't caught. This burn on your face is your penance for murder. Go live out the rest of your life in peace.

"So, Louise, you decided to come back just to tell me what to do again? Then explain to me how I would have peace when they keep winning," Hershel muttered.

She was silent. He snorted.

"I thought so."

A nurse came into his room pushing a wheelchair. She had a big smile on her face, which meant they were going to take him to physical therapy. They always grinned like the Cheshire cat when something painful was about to happen.

"Hop in, Phil. It's time to go work those fingers and facial muscles some more."

"I don't need to smile," he said.

"Don't be silly! Everyone needs to smile," she countered, and pushed him out of the room with him griping all the way.

"When can I get out of here? I want out," he asked.

She patted his shoulder as she pushed him down the hall.

"Why do you want to get out? You told me you were homeless. Why would you want to go back to the streets? It's clean and comfortable in here, and you get three great meals a day."

"A man just needs to be able to call his own shots in life, you know?"

She smiled. "I know, Phil. I was just teasing you. You're doing great. You'll be gone before you know it."

It wasn't what he wanted to hear, but it was what he was going to have to work with, so he leaned back and rode in style.

Cameron had been released four days ago, and Nola was being released this morning. She couldn't wait to get back to the trailer, pack up what personal belongings she had and leave this nightmare behind.

She'd been on the phone with the galleries where her work was hanging to inform them of her upcoming move, and for the first time in weeks she felt as if she was finally gaining some control of her life.

Tate had bought her a new outfit to go home in: a white T-shirt, a blue zip-up sweatshirt to wear as a jacket and matching blue sweatpants. They were her favorite colors and felt soft against her healing wounds, which had been his intent.

She had them on and was braiding her hair when he walked into the room. As soon as he saw her, he smiled, and she thought what a blessed woman she was to have a second chance at love.

"You look so pretty," he said as he leaned down and gave her a quick kiss, then pulled at her braid, just like he'd done for all the years they were growing up.

She grinned. "Thanks to you. So, when do we leave?"

"Cameron and Wade are driving us to Jackson, Mississippi, to catch a plane, and then they're driving the SUV back."

"I don't have any identification to travel," she said.

"And that's why we're heading to the DMV first to get you a new driver's license. We'll worry about the marriage license when we get to D.C."

She tied off the braid and looked up.

"I'm not worried about a marriage license. I would willingly live in sin with you for the rest of my life if that's what it took to not lose you again."

He laughed out loud. "And your mama's ghost would haunt *my* ass for the rest of *my* life if I let that happen."

She smiled. "On a different subject, what about the Stormchaser?"

"What about him?"

"Anything new that we should be concerned about?"

Tate shook his head.

"No. If God was fair, although we both know life isn't about being fair, the man would be lying dead in a ditch somewhere. But we did get confirmation that a man named Hershel Inman had a nervous breakdown after his wife died during Hurricane Katrina, and there were plenty of things with Hershel Inman's name on them inside the motor home, along with a lot of disguises. We also found out that he and his wife had no children and had been active in their local theater group, which is probably why he was so good at costumes and disguises."

Nola shuddered. "Lots of people died. Why was he the one who snapped?"

"He claimed while they were stranded on the roof of their home in the Ninth Ward waiting to be rescued, choppers were flying over taking pictures but no one came for them. His wife was a diabetic. She needed insulin, and it was in the flooded house below. She died in his arms while waiting for help, and in the night he fell asleep and her body floated away. When he woke up, help was there and she was gone. He went crazy, and I guess he hasn't come back."

"So he's killing survivors because she wasn't rescued?"

"One of the doctors at the hospital where he was being treated said he was distraught because God saved some but He didn't save Louise. He said he

was mad at God and someone should kill the ones
God meant to save."

"Oh, Lord, your profile of him was so on target.
I can almost feel sorry for him, except for the horrible things he's done. I wonder why they let him go?"

"I don't feel sorry for him. Lots of people lose
loved ones in tragic ways, and they don't turn on
society. As for his hospital stay, he hadn't been
declared insane, just kept for observation because he
pretty much broke down after his wife's death. Ac-
cording to their records, one day he just got dressed
and walked out. They didn't know it until he was already gone. They had tape of him leaving the hospital, but at the time all they had in his file were the
ramblings of a man who'd had a nervous breakdown.
He posed no threat to society and they let it pass, because everything he'd said fell under doctor-patient
confidentiality."

She slipped off the side of the bed and wrapped
her arms around his waist. He leaned in for a kiss as
she closed her eyes. When he finally pulled back, she
reached for him again, pulling him close.

He took a deep breath and gave her another bit of
news he was afraid might upset her.

"We took a boat out on the river yesterday. The
water has gone down enough to see that your house
is completely gone. I guess it washed off the foundation."

"I gave it up in my heart that night in the tree,

and I've learned the hard way that things are never as important as the ones you love. Take me home, Tate. I need roots and a place to fall asleep in your arms at night."

He put his arms around her.

"Then we've got a plane to catch and a life together to start."

She looked up at him with her heart in her eyes.

"Whither thou goest…"

He took her hand.

"…I will go."

Epilogue

The first thing Tate did when he got back to D.C. was pick up his mother's ashes, something he needed to do by himself.

So he found himself standing outside the funeral home, wrestling with the conversation he was about to have, and then made himself walk inside.

A middle-aged woman dressed in a gray suit got up from her desk and went to meet him.

"Welcome to Fielding's Mortuary. My name is Emma. May I help you?"

"My name is Tate Benton. I'm here to pick up my mother's ashes. Her name was Julia Marie Benton. She passed a few weeks ago."

She checked their records, then paused. "Will you be needing a memorial urn?"

Tate took a slow breath. "No, ma'am. They will be scattered at her request."

"Yes, of course. I'll be right back," she said, and left him alone in the office.

He sat down, then stared at the toes of his shoes because he couldn't look up without revealing the fact that he was crying.

When the lady returned carrying a small black box, he couldn't speak. How did a woman as beautiful and vital as his mother had been become condensed to the point of fitting inside a container the size of a box of tissues?

"There are no outstanding costs associated with this account, so if you'll sign here..." the woman said, pointing to a line on the release statement.

One thing his father had managed to do right was pay to put her to rest.

He signed his name.

"I am sorry for your loss," the lady said, and handed him the box.

"Thank you," he said, and held it close to his chest as he walked away.

Once inside his car, he tucked the box close against him and drove out of town, heading for the Virginia mountains. There was a spot overlooking a small valley that she'd loved to go when the leaves were beginning to turn. She'd always said it must be where God lived, because it was so beautiful there.

He thought of Nola as he drove, and realized what

a gift she had given him—this time alone with his mother—because he had not been able to be with her at the end. He began to talk to his mother as he drove, knowing it would be the last time he would have any kind of contact with what was left of her physical body.

"So, Mom, I'm sure you know all about Nola and me. I consider myself blessed to have this second chance, and don't worry, I won't mess it up. As you know, I finally had it out with Dad. I just want you to know that I'm not sad. I don't think I ever really knew him."

He glanced at his GPS and then down at the box.

"We're almost there. You would have loved this trip."

His chest felt tight, and there was a knot in his belly that wouldn't go away. The urge to weep was strong as he reached the scenic overlook, pulled over and stopped.

He took the box with him to the rim, and then stopped to admire the deep rich greens and the ribbon of blue water in the valley below.

"Hey, Mom, just look at all this. You're going to love it here."

His hands were shaking as he took off the lid. He couldn't look at what was in it without remembering his childhood and the nights she'd comforted him after he'd had bad dreams, the cookies she'd made, and the cups of cocoa they'd shared on cold winter nights.

This isn't me.

He heard the soft voice as clearly as he felt the wind on his face. And just like that, the agony of what he was about to do was gone.

"Love you, Mom," he said softly, then tilted the box and let the ashes spill out into the updraft coming up from the floor of the valley.

He caught his breath as, for a few seconds, it appeared as if they were going down instead of up. Then the wind caught them, and swirled them out and away into space.

Tate dropped the lid and then the box down into the valley, and closed his eyes. He flashed on his mother's face, and then, like the ashes, it was gone.

He got back in the car and headed down the mountain, suddenly anxious to get back to Nola, to the warmth of her smile and the love in her eyes. He'd been a long time hurting. It felt good to be loved.

Nola was fussing with her dress and tugging at her veil. Both were simple, short and white, her homage to a formal wedding. She'd always planned to be married in her mother's gown, but that was no longer an option, and with only two weeks to plan...

Tate knocked, opened the door then stopped and took a deep breath.

"Oh, wow."

She looked up at him in the mirror.

"You're not supposed to see me ahead of time."

"I felt the need to break a rule," he said softly.

She turned around and then clutched her hands against her middle. There were tears in her eyes.

He frowned. "Are you sad?"

"Happy tears for sure. So let's do this."

He laughed, grabbed her hand and headed out the door.

An hour later a priest named Father Michael was pronouncing them husband and wife, and their two witnesses, Wade and Cameron, were waiting for their chance to kiss the bride.

Nola had known moments of joy in her life, but nothing like what she was feeling now. It was as if fate had dragged her through hell backward just so she would appreciate how perfect the rest of her life was going to be.

"You may kiss the bride," Father Michael said.

And Tate did, over and over, until Nola's head was spinning and their witnesses were grousing about it being their turn.

Nola could see her reflection in Tate's eyes when he stopped. She looked as happy as she felt.

"Hello, Mr. Benton."

He smiled.

"And hello to you, too, Mrs. Benton. Are you ready for this life?"

"Am I ever," she said, and threw her arms around his neck.

The new scar on the back of her arm pulled, but she ignored it. Pain belonged to the past.

"My turn," Wade said, and kissed her soundly, then handed her off to Cameron.

"Congratulations," Cameron said, and kissed her, too.

Then they both shook Tate's hand as they teased him, Wade wanting cake and Cameron announcing they should name their first child after him.

For a few seconds Nola stepped back, watching these three men who had become such an important part of her life, and realized that, for better or worse, they were part of her new family.

"There's cake at the house," she announced.

"I am so there," Wade said.

"Like we didn't know that," Tate said.

"Are you going on a honeymoon?" Cameron asked.

"No, we're going house-hunting," Nola said. "One with a room big enough for my studio, so I can paint pictures while you three chase bad guys, and when you come home, I will feed you and love you all."

Tate took her in his arms.

"But you'll love me most."

She smiled. "I will love you most."

It was the following spring when a storm front rolling through Texas spawned one tornado after another, then traveled up into Oklahoma and on into Missouri, leaving dozens dead, hundreds injured and millions and millions of dollars' worth of damage in its wake.

It wasn't until the third nude body was pulled out of the wreckage with Taser marks and dark, ugly bruising around the neck that the local authorities realized they were dealing with a serial killer.

Tate had just been called into headquarters to be briefed about the deaths in Dallas, and they were wondering if there was any connection to their old nemesis the Stormchaser, when his cell phone signaled a text. He opened the message and then felt like he'd been kicked in the gut.

The message was, as usual, from an unfamiliar phone number, but it was obvious that the Stormchaser had surfaced in a very ugly way.

I am not dead, so do not weep. It was not my time, I have vows to keep.

* * * * *